RIVAL SECRETS

LOVE OVER MURDER
BOOK ONE

J. D. CAROTHERS

DREAMLIFIC PUBLISHING

ISBN: 978-1-957997-08-7 (Ebook edition)

ISBN: 978-1-957997-11-7 (Paperback edition)

To my husband and my parents
for their love and unbounded confidence
in me and my dreams

1

CASSIE

She can't be gone.

Holding my phone with a shaky hand, I stare at the image of a crumpled, silver Lexus until my eyes burn. The horrific photo of the crushed frame and twisted metal makes me shudder. I can't see straight. My eyes must be playing tricks on me. The car has to belong to someone else.

My hope fades as I force myself to reread the caption for the third time. To my horror, it still says:

"CELEBRITY CHEF BERNARD KILLED IN CAR CRASH"

I'm dizzy. I can't have lost another person that I care about to a car accident.

Taking a deep breath, I exhale slowly. How could this have happened? Needing answers, I click on the article.

Last evening, Chef Allison Bernard's car swerved off the road and, without braking, ran into the side of a pawn shop. She was pronounced dead at the scene.

Visualizing a car crashing into a building sends chills through me, but I keep reading.

Authorities suspect that the accident may be alcohol-related. Twenty minutes earlier, she left the Grand Athena's press conference, where she was introduced as one of the three judges in the upcoming Guest Chef Competition. Chef Bernard was the well-known owner of the Chez Bernard restaurant here in Las Vegas and the host of *Cooking Without Fear* on the Food, Fun & Travel Channel, also known as the FFT Channel.

The breath I was holding whooshes out as the truth sinks in. She *is* gone. She died a few hours ago in a senseless accident. My thoughts drift to her mother and sister, who were frequent guests on her show. With their fun banter and laughter, they seemed so close. Losing her must be heartbreaking for them.

Loneliness and loss overwhelm me as I wipe a tear from my cheek. Most people learn to cook from a parent, but that wasn't an option. Neither of mine cooked, nor did they support my interest in it, insisting it wasn't worth their time or mine. Instead, they pushed me to pursue what they saw as a more financially rewarding career.

Despite my parents' lack of understanding, my love of cooking didn't die, even when I lost them in an accident at the end of law school. My passion remained a hobby rather than a career, and Chef Bernard unknowingly served as my mentor.

She was my favorite chef on the FFT Channel. On weekend mornings, her energetic image filled my screen as she taught me to take risks and experiment with recipes. According to her, fear of failure has no place in the kitchen.

She was everything I wanted to be. If I'd had my way, I'd be a chef now, not a lawyer. Instead, I've lived my culinary dreams vicariously through Chef Bernard and her success, hoping it would be enough. Now she's *gone*. And I feel more unsettled than ever.

I HEAR MY NAME. THEN IT GROWS LOUDER. "CASSIE, UNMUTE. WE CAN'T hear you."

Shit.

I glanced away from my video meeting when my eyes glazed over from boredom. Whose attention wouldn't waver in meetings with a boss like mine? He regularly turns what should be a fifteen-minute discussion into a waste of two hours.

I can't admit to being distracted. My boss wouldn't understand, so I unmute and say, "My internet connection is unstable today. Could you repeat the question?"

My boss, Jackson, responds, "Cassie, this is the last time I'll remind you to upgrade your internet service. Get it done this week, or you can forget working remotely."

"Will do." I've used that excuse one too many times during these interminable video calls.

Today's meeting is even worse than usual though. It's midnight here, and our old-school boss insisted the entire California team wear business attire so he could trot us in front of the European client for this middle-of-the-night strategy session.

It's past ridiculous. I'm sitting at my kitchen table in a silk shirt, gold necklace, and suit jacket. At least my bare feet are comfortably propped on a chair, and I'm wearing comfy pajama shorts. Honestly, I could be naked from the waist down, and no one would know. Except for the occasional "Will do" or "I'll have that done shortly," we're all just staring at our computer screens, watching the client and our boss debate the current deal for almost two hours. If I were the client, I'd wonder why I'm paying for so many silent faces to stare at me during these meetings.

Under these circumstances, anyone would occasionally glance at their cell phone, right? What's the harm in catching up on news and gossip while we wait our turn to answer our boss with the perfunctory "Will do"? At least, that's what I tell myself.

"Cassie, we were asking when you will finish the memo on the licensing issues."

"I should have that done by close of business on Friday."

"Did you say 'should' or 'will'?"

Ugh. What a jackass. He knows I've never missed a deadline, but he can't pass up the opportunity to crack his verbal whip in front of the client. This time, his show of power is at my expense. Needing this job, I grit my teeth and dutifully respond, "My apologies. I meant to say the memo *will* be ready then."

Jackson snaps back, "Speed it up. We need it by noon Friday to close the deal over the weekend."

He's on one of his power kicks today. He already emailed me a fifty-page contract this morning that he also wants me to review by Friday. That only gives me two days, barely enough time to finish both projects.

Biting my tongue again, I hear myself utter the expected "Will do."

The most frustrating part is that everyone on this call knows this deadline is fake. The deal isn't closing before Monday or Tuesday at the earliest.

I hit mute before accidentally verbalizing my frustrations. Not only do I hate fake deadlines, but I also know there will be hell to pay if I miss one, so I don't. Starting with my first homework assignment in elementary school, my parents taught me the importance of taking responsibility and finishing work on time.

Regardless, I don't know how many more "will dos" I have in me. Jackson's crap is becoming too much. But if I don't suck it up, he'll use it as one more lame reason to delay my promotion. His last excuse was that I needed to increase my billable hours by ten percent. When I did, he demanded another ten percent increase, which isn't humanly possible. There are only so many hours in a week.

I'm barely surviving. I rarely see the few friends I have left. The rest gave up on me long ago because I never had time for them. I'm bone tired. It's a struggle to make it through the week. Forget cooking. I can't remember the last time I ate a proper meal. On a good day, I remember to grab a granola bar or munch on an apple. Unfortunately, more often, it's a bag of potato chips that serves as my meal.

Trying to concentrate on the meeting, I lock my eyes on the computer screen.

It doesn't work. I can't stop thinking about Chef Bernard and the cooking competition. Giving in, I google for more information.

The first headline reads, "Grand Athena's Chef Competition Will Go Forward."

In answer to a question about the status of the Guest Chef Competition, the Athena's representative states, "We will continue to accept applications on our website and announce further details as they become available. At a later date, we'll announce the name of the new judge. Tonight, however, we mourn the loss of a great chef."

Huh. That's unusual. Why are they accepting applications? These shows usually invite famous chefs and celebrities to compete—they don't apply.

This one must be different. I'll bookmark the website and check out the details when I can. Hopefully, they'll stream the competition.

2

EVAN

Born into wealth, power, and royalty on the Mediterranean island of Catalinius, I won the lottery for families. Growing up, my older brother and I took private lessons in etiquette, horse riding, and sailing. When I turned thirteen, my parents sent me to the best boarding school in London. At eighteen, I was off to an Ivy League university in the United States. Now, freedom and money are mine, provided I fulfill my princely duties by representing our family at a few events.

Sounds perfect. It's not.

Endlessly cutting ribbons, dedicating hospital wings, and attending charity dinners is less than fulfilling. Anyone could do those things. Why even be here if not to make a difference?

In my twenties, it didn't matter. I traveled and partied with others like me. We had a plentiful supply of beautiful women, fancy cars, private yachts, and high-end alcohol.

Women would hear my name, or should I say my title, and throw themselves at me. That's still true, but it's not *me* they want—it's the money and the prestige my family brings. So, I keep my interactions with these women casual and short. My relationships, if you can call them that, typically revolve around what they want me to buy for them.

I can't complain. At the outset, those women know what to expect from me: a good time, great sex, no emotions. And they walk away with a smile and a new bauble or two. Everyone wins.

If a woman becomes clingy and envisions something more permanent, we're done even sooner. It's easy to remain emotionally detached because the women rarely attempt to learn anything personal about me. They think they already know me from the stories printed in British tabloids and European gossip magazines. Of course, there's not too much truth to those. I haven't even been at all the parties they photoshop me into, much less as pissed as they portray me. I like my alcohol, but I know my limits so as not to embarrass the family as often as reported. The only thing the tabloids report accurately is my excellent and expensive taste in clothes, food, and wine.

When my friends and I turned thirty, most of my mates had to give up the partying lifestyle to work in their family businesses. It was different for me. While my parents assign me various duties, they could be done by any of my extended family.

These changes make for a lonely life. My friends no longer have time for extended vacations, so we rarely see each other. When we do, they talk about their work and spouses. Some even have young children now. I don't have much in common with them anymore.

It's strange how the tables have turned. When we were younger, my friends saw me as important because of my title and all the attention it garnered. Today, my life seems inconsequential compared to theirs. I'm almost embarrassed that my title comes with more money than I could ever spend, and all I do for it is cut ribbons, dedicate buildings, and show up for photos with the family. I feel like an imposter rather than a successful graduate of one of the best MBA programs in the US.

This sense that my life is meaningless isn't new. It's been lurking in my mind for a while—at least since my best friend, Sean, took over his dad's business two years ago. I've kept my anxiety about my future at bay, knowing that as long as our dad remained king, my brother and I still had time to carve our paths. That's about to change though. My brother will ascend to the throne when Dad steps down later this year. We'll no longer be the two princes. He'll be king, but what's next for me?

I'm thirty-four and not meaningfully contributing to society. How can I earn my worth in the world and make a difference? There must be something more I can do while still working within the boundaries dictated by my family. The problem is I don't have a clue what that *more* is.

My brother and I are close, so if he needs me, I'll be there for him and help represent the family, but that's not enough for me. My restlessness isn't his problem to solve though. It's mine, and for my peace of mind, I need a plan before my brother becomes king. That means time is running out. If I'm going to figure out my future direction, it's time for a short break from my parents and family obligations so I can think.

The question is where to go to find a productive place to work through my dilemma.

My standard vacation spots don't make sense. The last thing I need is a place like Ibiza with its all-night parties. What I really need is to talk with my best friend, Sean. He's one of the few people who know me and understand how much the palace pressures me to follow tradition.

He's always said I'm welcome anytime at his hotel in Las Vegas. It's a party destination, but Sean has a business to run. Once he understands my quandary, he'll be supportive rather than expecting me to be the fun-loving partygoer every night.

I'll text him to see if the timing works.

> Me: Mate, can you spare a room for an old friend?

> Sean: Absolutely. When are you arriving? How long will you be here?

> Me: Arriving in about two weeks. Hoping to stay about a month. Will you be there?

> Sean: Yes, that works. You'll be here in time for the Guest Chef Competition.

> Me: Not sure what that is. Sounds intriguing.

> Sean: Will explain when you're here. How did you manage a last-minute trip?

> Me: Need to sort some shite. We'll chat when I'm there.

> Sean: Text when you have an arrival date. I'll have a suite ready.

> Me: Thanks, mate. Knew I could count on you.

> Sean: Always.

WE BOTH GREW UP IN UNUSUAL CIRCUMSTANCES AND UNDERSTAND THE pressures of money and non-traditional family businesses. He won't judge my feelings about my situation, and we can discuss my options. Hell, Sean can help me figure out what my options are.

It's time to clear my schedule, reassign those blasted ribbon cuttings, and reserve the jet.

3

CASSIE

Around 2 a.m., I crawl into bed with my laptop as my only companion. Like every other night lately, it warms my outstretched legs as I work.

It's a sad commentary on my life. My best friend, Lowri, chastised me when I mentioned bringing my computer to bed. She insisted that I need an attentive man instead, but who has the energy or time for a sex life given the hours I work? If it weren't for occasional sessions with my rechargeable, purple friend, my existence would be unbearable.

Instead, I work as usual. I type, delete, reread, repeat. It's a never-ending cycle.

Eventually, the words blur as my eyelids start to droop. At some point, exhaustion prevails.

***

My alarm jolts me awake a mere four hours later. I'm exhausted from the awful dreams that plagued my sleep. Chef Bernard's gruesome demise played in an endless loop all night.

Ugh.

On top of that horror, I'm sleep-deprived and ache from head to toe. I vaguely remember a time when I'd wake up happy and excited about the day ahead. Those days are long gone, replaced with a debilitating dread permeating my body like a perpetual case of Monday morning blues.

I'm on the fast track to burnout—correction, I'm already there. The only thing that keeps me going is constantly reminding myself that I'm lucky to have a good-paying job. With that thought, I grudgingly roll out of bed.

A couple of years ago, my law firm offered me the opportunity to work from home. Jettisoning the daily commute and not having to dress for the office, I suddenly had two or three hours a day for myself. During those first few weeks, I caught up on chores and slept a little later each morning.

Even better, I had time for my real passion—cooking. Ever since my grandparents sent me to a summer culinary program for my sixteenth birthday, cooking has been my creative outlet. It's also a source of pleasure for my friends. They're quick to sign up as taste testers. Unfortunately, it's been months since I've had anyone over because my work hours are unimaginable.

I miss those evenings. Their positive feedback is a powerful drug. For an only child whose outer confidence masks her occasional loneliness and fear of not fitting in, little compares to the natural euphoria of watching others appreciate my cooking. The concentration that cooking requires also provides an essential escape from tough memories that too often take over my thoughts.

Unfortunately, this improved version of life didn't last. When Jackson realized I had more time available without my commute, he interrupted my evenings and weekends with additional demands. He quickly reclaimed every waking minute by piling on more work. Now, I'm genuinely on call 24/7.

I should have gone to med school. At least when a doctor saves someone, they're appreciative. Instead, Jackson acts like I should thank him for deeming me worthy of working for him. What an asshole.

After a quick shower, I make tea and plop on a chair at the kitchen table. As my laptop powers on, Lowri's name pops up on my phone.

"How's it going?" I ask.

"Good. Do you have a minute?"

I should say no with Jackson's deadline looming, but our friendship deserves better.

"Sure. Jackson piled on again with two deadlines for tomorrow, but there's always time for you."

"I've been super busy too. We just finished a big project, so I'm throwing a party at my place on Saturday night. You have to come. Jerry's bringing his friends."

Ugh. That means she's trying to set me up with one of her brother's buddies. Her track record for picking matches is abysmal, so I hesitate before responding, "I need to work, and I don't have time to date."

"You just said your deadlines are tomorrow, and you *do* have time to go out. You don't have to go down the relationship road. Just go on a couple of dates. When was the last time you even saw a real co..."

I interrupt, "Don't go there. We're not talking about that. I'm not the casual type. You do you. I'll do me."

"Well, someone should be doing you." She laughs.

"Very funny."

"I'm just saying, use it or lose it. So, no excuses. Be at my place Saturday night at seven. Most people are bringing drinks instead of food, so please do your magic in the kitchen and whip up a couple of appetizers. I'm counting on you."

With the projects done tomorrow, Saturday night would be the perfect time to let off steam. And, who knows, her brother's friends may not be so bad.

"Okay. I'll bring lasagna dip and roasted veggies. Will that work?"

"Perfect. I almost forgot to ask. Did you see what happened to Chef Bernard? Didn't she host your favorite cooking show?"

I shudder at the recollection of the tragic images. "Yes. I started watching her show during high school. It's one of the few things I still made time for no matter what work threw at me."

"Based on the photos I saw, no one could have survived that accident."

"I know. They said she crashed full speed into the building. The images gave me nightmares last night."

"I'm glad I didn't see it until this morning, or it would have haunted my dreams too. I wonder who will replace her as a judge for Athena's cooking competition."

"I didn't even know about the competition until yesterday, but I assume they'll pick another Las Vegas chef."

"That would make sense."

"By the way, did you know the competition is open to home cooks? I couldn't help daydreaming about applying. Of course, that's not happening."

"Why not? You're an amazing cook, and in law school, you were comfortable speaking to an audience. You'd be perfect in front of a camera."

Striking up conversations with strangers at parties isn't easy for me, but she's right. Speaking to a group isn't a problem because of all the dance recitals and plays my parents signed me up for as a kid. Whether or not my cooking would be competitive—that's the unanswered question.

"You know I have huge student loans to pay off. I can't afford to take chances on a cooking contest."

"What's the prize?"

"I'm not sure."

"Check out the website."

"Give me a minute ... Here it is. The Athena will select the four finalists based on the applications. In addition to becoming the guest chef for a month at the Trendz restaurant, the winner will receive a $250,000 cash prize."

It would be so incredible to have a chance to compete, but with that much money on the line, the pro chefs will all apply.

"Damn. The cash would pay off your student loans," Lowri says.

"It would. There's more, though. Can you believe this? The winner will appear on an FFT cooking show and be interviewed for an article in *Cooks & Kitchens Magazine*. That's incredible."

I'd give anything to have a shot at being on a cooking show on my favorite network. But who am I kidding? I'm an amateur.

"Cassie, you have to apply. Those are phenomenal opportunities, and you said the competition is open to home cooks. What do you have to lose?"

I laugh. "My job and my parents' approval for starters. Mom and Dad wanted me to follow in their footsteps at a major law firm. I can't count the number of times they reminded me to make the 'right' career choices to ensure my financial security. They always joked that I'd give up my cooking hobby as soon as I could afford a personal chef."

"Your parents were workaholics. Their work was their passion. Stop trying to guess what they would think is right for you now. As sad as it is, they've been gone since your last year of law school. That was almost five years ago. Law firm life was your parents' dream for you, not yours. It's long past time that you start doing what makes you happy."

With tears threatening to spill, my eyes automatically clamp shut as I say, "Deep down, I know you're right. That doesn't mean it's easy to let go, particularly knowing they died on their way to see me. I feel responsible, so I can't let them down."

"It wasn't your fault. They loved you and would want the best for you. Tell me the truth. Are you happy?"

After taking a deep breath, my guilty admission escapes. "No, not if I'm honest with myself. If it weren't for my parents' dreams for me and the student loans, I'd use my law degree to help charities or advocate for children. Or I'd walk away from law altogether and spend my days creating food that makes people close their eyes, smile, and sigh."

"See what I mean? You aren't pursuing your dreams. You're going to regret it if you don't start living life your way before it's too late. Don't let opportunities pass you by." Lowri's voice softens, as she says, "If your parents were here and they knew how unhappy and burned out you are, do you really think they would still want this for you, regardless of financial security? Think about it, okay? I have to go, but promise me you'll consider filling out the application for the competition."

"It would be a waste of time. My only 'formal' training was the summer culinary course as a teenager. I'd embarrass myself in a real competition. You know a professional chef will win."

"You don't know that. They may be looking for new talent. It would be great publicity for them. At least consider applying."

"Okay. I'll think about it. See you Saturday night."

Resting my elbows on the table, I bury my face in my hands, reflecting on my admission and Lowri's advice.

I'm torn about what to do. On the one hand, participating in Athena's competition would be a fantasy come true. But is it realistic? Winning the competition is a long shot for anyone, particularly a home cook competing against professionally trained chefs.

Is a mere chance at a dream enough to risk losing my job and not being able to pay back my six-figure student loans? Keeping my current job means those loans will be paid off in a few more years. Even if my job is off-the-charts stressful most of the time, it's the practical choice from a financial perspective.

If I try to become a professional chef and it doesn't work out, I can't come back to my current job. Large law firms don't give second chances. I've watched colleagues pursue other career options and regret the choice when they couldn't return.

Sure, after leaving my current job, I could find another legal position somewhere. The pay wouldn't be remotely close to my current salary though. Only a fool would walk away for an infinitesimal chance at a new career as a chef, and I'm not a fool. The smart choice is to work on Jackson's contract, keep saying "Will do," and let go of this fanciful notion.

But on the other hand, Lowri's right. I'm not happy. My job is stressful and exhausting. The idea of competing is like a beam of sunshine streaming through my morning window, beckoning me to walk into a new, exciting world, leaving behind the old one.

What is wrong with me? That sounds like a sappy message on a greeting card.

It also makes me question whether I ever plan to live my life for *me*. I'm turning thirty next week. Is now the time to make a change?

With a new resolve, my hands move to the keyboard and start typing. Pulling up the application for the competition, I enter my full name, Cassandra Elizabeth Edwards, and take a step for *me*.

Working my way through the questions, it's two hours later when I finish the application. Now all that's left is to submit it.

I pause. Is this a waste of time? Probably, but after filling out the form, why wouldn't I enter?

I mumble to myself, "Here goes nothing." My fingers tremble as I click "Submit."

Reminding myself this is a long shot, I nibble on my lower lip, holding off the grin threatening to pop up as a twinge of hope rushes through me. Regardless, this is a special moment—I just did something for me for the first time in forever.

The application said that the Athena will announce the four finalists in two weeks. Worst case, I have the thrill of being able to say I applied. That will make for a fun story over drinks as long as Jackson doesn't ruin my Saturday night plans with Lowri.

For now, work awaits my attention. It's going to be a long day and night, but at least for once in a long while, the smile on my face will make it a little easier.

4

EVAN

Sinking into the leather seat on one of my family's private jets, I sigh in relief. I'm finally on my way to Las Vegas. It's been three weeks since I reached out to Sean. At times, I thought I'd never be able to leave because of the obstacles in my way.

The first hurdle was explaining to my parents the need to spend a month visiting Sean. That meant walking a tightrope between being honest about my reasons and not offending them. They wouldn't understand my concerns or my need to mull over plans for my future. To them, my role in the family is dictated by duty, and I should perform my assigned tasks without question.

When I explained that Sean needs my help with a special project, they finally understood and supported my sense of duty and loyalty to my best friend. I'm still not sure what Sean's Guest Chef Competition involves, but whatever it is, I'll be helping him.

The next challenge was to free up my schedule by convincing others to cover my events. That took more effort than expected. After the first few people I asked weren't available, Mom's assistant had the brilliant idea that one of my cousins could fill in for me. When I phoned to request her help, she surprised me by thanking me for the opportunity. I hadn't anticipated her eagerness to represent our family. I can't imagine why she's so excited, but as far as I'm concerned, she's welcome to attend as many events as she'd like.

The final hurdle was ditching my security guards for the trip. When Dad learned I planned to travel without them, he was quick to voice his objections. I explained that if he provided a family jet for my travel, I'd be perfectly safe until we landed in the States. At that point, Sean's outstanding security team would ensure my safety while I'm in Las Vegas. I also pointed out that I'd be more conspicuous surrounded by palace guards than Sean's security people, who are routinely visible at the Athena.

In the end, my reasoning prevailed, and I solved two problems at once. A family jet instantly became available at my father's insistence, and the guards won't be following me around and listening to my conversations with Sean. Win-Win.

I thought everything was finally in place, but unfortunately, the drama wasn't over.

Two nights ago, my older brother, the crown prince of Catalinius, had a meltdown. He barged into my palace apartment, livid about Dad's latest demands. I let him blow off steam and kept the drinks flowing while he vented. As brothers do, we bandied about potential solutions and cursed the ridiculous rules that govern our lives as royals.

When we talked again yesterday, I mentioned my trip to Las Vegas and tried to broach the subject of my own struggles. I'd hoped he might be open to discussing options that would transform my role from unnecessary spare to valuable asset. Unfortunately, he didn't open the door for further conversation.

Of course, he said the proper things, reassuring me that my issues are solvable. But I could hear the unspoken confusion in his voice. He must've been thinking the obvious. I have the perfect life. A title. No pressure. Plenty of money. Abundant women. Trips to Las Vegas on a whim. I'm an ungrateful twat.

I didn't push the subject. I understand his perception of my situation, but he's wrong. If my life is so perfect, he'd want to trade places. He doesn't, and neither do I. The real problem is that our lives are at turning points, and we're both having trouble navigating the changes.

Anyone who thinks I'm ungrateful is mistaken. I know my life is one in a million. What bothers me is that my wealth and privilege should be used to make a real difference in the world, not just for shaking hands, thanking people, and traveling to charity events.

There must be something I can do that won't violate the restrictions imposed by my royal title.

That's why I'd rather talk with Sean than my family. His independent perspective will help me devise a creative solution.

5

CASSIE

Why won't my phone shut up? I'm having the best dream. The most amazing guy I've ever known is worshipping my body inch by inch. His godlike body is so warm, and his mouth and fingers are soooo talented. I don't want to wake up.

The buzzing continues. What possessed me to set such an early alarm?

I fumble to hit snooze on my phone, but the noise doesn't stop. Oh, it's not my alarm. The display shows the infamous *Unknown caller*. It must be another person trying to sell me solar panels for my first floor, rented apartment. Can't they figure out I don't have anywhere to put them?

In my dazed state, I accidentally hit accept instead of decline. A voice is asking for Cassandra. Now I know it's definitely a marketing call. No one calls me Cassandra. I'm about to hit end when the woman says, "This is Cynthia Andino from the Grand Athena. I'm trying to reach Cassandra Edwards." I must be asleep, and my dream is morphing into one about the cooking competition. It's not as satisfying as Mr. Magic Fingers, but it's still a good dream.

"Can you hear me? This is Cynthia from the Grand Athena calling about the Guest Chef Competition. Is this Cassandra Edwards?"

Coming out of my sleepy haze, I manage to say, "Yes, this is Cassie Edwards."

"Great. I have exciting news for you."

Jolting upright, I'm wide awake now. My mind races. Does this mean what I think it means? I can't believe I'm actually one of the finalists. Hesitant to hope, I ask, "Really?"

"Yes, I'm pleased to inform you that you've been chosen as the alternate for the Guest Chef Competition."

Deep breath. Deflate slowly on the exhale. I knew it was too good to be true. So much for that great dream. Everyone who applied is probably an "alternate," and they want to sell us sweatshirts or other stuff to commemorate the event. Be polite. Don't let on how disappointed you are.

"Um, thank you. I'm sorry. I'm just waking up. Could you explain again who you are and what it means to be an alternate?"

"Of course. I'm Cynthia Andino, the Director of F&B—that's Food and Beverage—at the Grand Athena. We've completed our selection process for the Guest Chef Competition. We picked four finalists to compete for the title, along with one alternate. The alternate will compete if something unexpected happens and one of the finalists drops out. You're the alternate. You've won an all-expenses paid trip to the Grand Athena to watch the competition and to be on hand if we need a replacement for one of the finalists. So, congratulations! Pack your bags and be ready to catch a plane to Las Vegas a week from today."

I'm stunned and speechless. Watching the cooking competition in Las Vegas would be incredible. Tossing the covers off and swiveling to sit on the side of the bed, I finally ask, "Are you kidding me?"

"No. I'm serious."

I pull up the calendar on my phone. "How long do I need to be in Las Vegas?"

"The competition will take place over two weeks."

My smile flips to a frown as it hits me that this is not merely a long weekend in Vegas. "Oh. I don't know if I can take that much time off from work."

"In your application, you agreed that if selected, you'd be in Las Vegas during the entire competition. Did we misunderstand?"

I'm not thinking straight. I should've remembered that the competition rules require us to be available for two weeks. I pace around my bedroom, trying to think through possible solutions.

After an awkward silence, I slowly respond, "No. You didn't misunderstand." Pausing, and then continuing before Cynthia speaks, I ask, "Will I be busy all the time, or will there be downtime when I could do work for my job?"

"You'll be expected to be available full time throughout the competition. You may have a little free time each day, but we expect you to be available for all the events, tapings, prep sessions, and press conferences to help promote the competition. That is part of the deal. In exchange, you'll receive favorable publicity from the videos and have the opportunity to experience an excitement-filled, two-week vacation in Las Vegas. All you need to do is say 'yes'."

"I understand. I need to check with my boss about the time off. With no real shot at participating in the competition, I need to make sure I'll have a job to come back to. I hope you understand."

Rubbing my eyes with my free hand, I don't know how this could possibly work out, but I'm determined to try.

"It's your choice, but we need an answer by four today. We had thousands of applicants, and most would jump at the chance to put this on their resume. If you don't want the alternate's slot, then we'll give it to the next person on our list. Call me back on this number. If I don't hear from you this afternoon, then I'm sorry, but we'll move on."

"Please understand that I really want this. It's an amazing honor. I just need a little time to think this through and talk to my boss. I respect your deadline and will call before then. Thank you so much."

"Okay. 4 p.m." The line goes dead.

I hug myself, pinching my arm to ensure this is real. I'm excited, but I'm also disappointed because it's unlikely that Jackson will give me the time off.

What am I going to do?

Part of me is ready to jump on the plane—work be damned. The problem is that I don't remember anyone at work who has taken two weeks off. Hell, I don't know anyone at work who's taken a week off without checking their email every day. I watched my parents live this life, so I knowingly signed up for the job. But it's a messed-up environment.

If I don't go, will I always regret it? Is it worth quitting my job over? That's what I'd have to do if I can't get the time off. How will I get another position? I can hear myself in an interview at a new firm trying to explain that I quit my old job to watch a cooking competition in Las Vegas for two weeks. That sounds flaky.

I need caffeine and sugar to think clearly.

My friends need their coffee fix each morning, but that's not my thing. Instead, I grab the last Coke from the fridge. Relief washes over me as I relish the burn of the first bubbles coating my throat and tingling on the way down. I'm a tad dependent on that sensation, but there are worse things.

Now, it's time to figure out how I can go to Las Vegas and not lose my job.

Unfortunately, I only have one week of vacation and sick leave left. The rest of my allotted time off went to recovery from strep throat, the move to my new apartment, and removal of my wisdom teeth.

Even if they let me use the remaining days for a last-minute vacation, how can I arrange for the second week in Vegas? Would the law firm agree to unpaid time off? I hate to think about the snide remarks they'll lob at me when I explain the reason. Jackson will view it as a sign that I'm not sufficiently committed to the firm. But if I don't explain, social media could bite me in the butt if anyone from work sees me in a post about the competition.

Of course, I could quit. Wait a minute. What am I thinking? That's silly. Why would I quit my job for one extra week of time off? I'm never this reckless, but it's a sign of how much I genuinely want to be at the competition, even if it's just as an alternate.

This isn't the first time I've looked for an excuse to quit. I must really be miserable. The competition may be the compromise I need to recharge and recommit to my law career when I return.

Before I lose my nerve, I compose an email to my boss. I type and delete several times before deciding to keep it simple with no real explanation. That's what the guys on the team would do. They wouldn't overthink it. They wouldn't feel the need to explain or justify their decision. They'd just go for it and not look back. It's my turn to do that too.

Jackson,

I have to take two weeks off work starting a week from today. Unfortunately, I won't be able to work remotely during that time. I have one week of vacation left, so I'll let HR know that the second week will need to be unpaid leave.

I'll complete my current assignments before leaving and confirm that other team members can handle any new assignments during my absence.

Thanks,
Cassie

While it's out of character for me to tell Jackson what I'm doing rather than ask permission, I've watched the guys gain respect from this direct, no-nonsense approach. He sees them as assertive, decisive leaders who go after what they want. Let's hope the same approach works for me.

Unfortunately, subconscious gender bias persists in the corporate sea, and navigating those waters can prove hazardous. My default has been to avoid risks, particularly after hearing Jackson chastise a couple of women in our group for being too ambitious and overly aggressive. But the behavior of those talented women was indistinguishable from that of their male counterparts. That means Jackson may consider my direct email to be presumptuous or something worse rather than simply straightforward and to the point. Regardless, there's no going back now. If Jackson or the law firm doesn't like my plan, I'll be looking for another job. So be it!

After pausing for a couple of deep breaths, second thoughts permeate my mind.

No! Stop overthinking.

Lowri's right. It's okay to pursue my passion even if that means dealing with the guilt that I'll be letting my parents down. It's time to take baby steps toward fulfilling the dreams that first took root as a teenager at summer camp. Even if it's only a one-time culinary excursion, it's a start. If I'm going to keep moving in a more positive direction, my new mantra has to be "Don't look back!"

Subconsciously though, I'm waiting for the shit to hit the fan. Will it be a furious email or a phone call from Jackson? For once, it doesn't matter to me. I'm proud of myself for taking a step in a new direction.

I'm going to Las Vegas!

6

EVAN

After arriving at the Athena's Monarch Suite and messaging my father to confirm my safe arrival, I arranged to meet up with Sean.

Not surprisingly, I arrive at the Olympic Torch Bar ahead of him. He's probably stuck in a meeting.

The host leads me across the dimly lit room. Indistinct murmurs and laughs compete with the music, creating a jovial atmosphere. Flickering lights from the seashell candles softly illuminate faces at the cocktail tables, but don't provide enough light for anyone to pay attention to me as we walk by.

I'm seated at a cocktail table on the open-air balcony that overlooks the Athena's version of the Aegean Sea. The Aegean replica consists of a gigantic pool in front of the hotel. It stretches the entire width of the property and all the way to the street where tourists stand shoulder to shoulder taking photos.

As I enjoy the view, a light evening breeze brushes past. It's a welcome change from the earlier heat of this late spring day. Soon, evening will turn to night as the sun sets, giving way to the famous neon lights of the Strip.

Without my asking, my favorite drink appears in front of me.

With a nod of thanks to the server, I turn my attention to my beeping phone.

Sean's Assistant: Mr. Cartwright will join you in 5 to 10 minutes. He apologizes for the delay.

Me: Thanks.

Waiting for Sean, I stare into the distance and sip the welcome liquid.

Our lives have changed so much.

Sean and I met at a post-game party during our freshman year at university in the U.S. I wouldn't have predicted our long-lasting friendship based on that first encounter. Our team had scored on the last play of the game to beat a bitter rival, so one of my friends invited people to celebrate at his off-campus house. The drinks were flowing, the crowd was chanting, music was blasting, and burgers were charring on the grill.

I was sipping my drink near the backyard bar, noting the differences and similarities to sports celebrations back home in Europe. When Sean walked up to the bar to pour himself a refill, he asked whether my bemused smirk meant that I wasn't into football.

I retorted, "That wasn't football."

"What the hell do you mean? That was football at its best."

The conversation quickly devolved into a fierce debate as to the merits of real football, which he calls soccer, versus the American version.

It turned out we were both majoring in business, so that was the first of many encounters on campus. Eventually, while still disagreeing on football and soccer, we found we had a lot in common. Not many people could relate to the way we grew up. Sean lived in a penthouse apartment in a hotel and casino. My home was a palace, which is just as unusual, so he understood. During that first year, we debated, teased, chastised, partied, and supported each other as if we were brothers by blood.

We shared an apartment from our sophomore year through

graduate school. Along the way, we had quite a few adventures, though perhaps it would be more accurate to call many of them harmless misadventures.

When we finished our MBAs at the age of twenty-four, our escapades became a tad more sophisticated, or at least we thought so. Sean and I traveled around Europe. Thanks to our parents, money wasn't an issue. Memories of yachts, scantily clad women, nights drinking, and days sleeping until noon make me smile.

After a year of traveling, I assumed some duties for my family but wasn't expected to keep a rigid schedule. That's when Sean started spending more time working for his father at the Grand Athena, but until he took over two years ago, he still had time for fun.

While so much has changed for Sean and my other friends, my life is substantially the same as the early days after graduation from university. It's frustrating that my life is stuck in one place while everyone else is moving forward to greater things. Even my brother is starting the next chapter of his life.

I can't believe it's been ten years since we graduated. I made a huge mistake by not addressing my situation much sooner. I've been in denial for far too long, taking false comfort from the fact that my brother didn't share my concerns. But I knew better. As crown prince, he didn't have to worry. He was born with his plan in place— to become king one day.

I'm jolted out of my thoughts when Sean slaps me on the back and sinks into the overstuffed, leather chair across from me. Sporting a bespoke suit on his six-foot frame, he looks like he still finds time for the gym.

"Hey man, it's great to see you. I don't think we've been in the same city since London last year," he says.

"That's right. It's been too long."

Sean takes a long sip of the Macallan that silently appears.

"Is your Boulevardier acceptable? I know you're picky about your favorite drink."

"It's excellent."

"You know me. I keep it simple—glass, ice, and Scotch—no complicated mixing or shaking required."

Our drinks mirror our upbringing. His was one of money and excess set in a fast-paced world—no patience for waiting. Mine was a formal, controlled environment where everything followed a strict protocol. "Hurry up and wait" was a real thing for my family, so I'm willing to allow for the extra time to make my drink of choice.

I laugh. "Your staff is ready to please us both."

"They're well-trained. Sorry I was running late. Did you get my message?"

"Yes, your assistant texted, and the server also relayed the message. Once she knew I was meeting you, she wouldn't take her eyes off me. Are all your employees so attentive to your friends?"

He shrugs. "Hopefully, they're attentive to everyone, but especially my friends. I'm sure my assistant, Emily, told them to look after you, but I'd bet our server just likes the view. You seem to have that effect on women."

"Look who's talking. By the way, the Athena is looking great. You've made updates since I was here last."

"We have. It's a never-ending battle to keep up with our competitors."

"I can only imagine."

"I'd about given up on you taking me up on my invitation to visit. You haven't been here since I took over. But what's with the dark circles under your eyes? Are you still partying like a twenty-something?" He half jokes, but I see the concern in his eyes.

"I couldn't keep up with our university days even if I tried."

"How's the family?"

Turning my swivel chair, I stare into the crowded room, avoiding his worried gaze. After draining my glass, I swivel back. "The family is fine. They're a little more dramatic than normal though. As I mentioned, I needed some time away. It seemed like the perfect time for a visit."

"Are you okay?"

"Don't worry. I'm not ill. It's something else."

"Do you want to talk about it?

"Yes, but first, let's discuss what you need help with."

"Sure. It turns out that the timing of your visit is perfect for me. I could use your advice."

"How can I help?"

After savoring a slow sip of his Scotch, Sean asks, "Have you heard about our Guest Chef Competition?"

"Only what you mentioned in your text."

"Let me give you a quick summary. The executive chef of our Trendz restaurant went back to Europe to help his family, so we decided to temporarily close the restaurant while we look for a new chef. After brainstorming, we came up with the idea to invite both professional and amateur chefs to compete for the title of guest chef for a month."

"That's a clever Idea. I assume you have a marketing plan to promote the competition."

"We do. We'll stream the competition on the Athena's Culinary Video Channel and include behind-the-scenes coverage. That should give the Athena some great press and buy us additional time to find a permanent chef. You see, our former executive chef oversaw much more than just the one restaurant. It's not trivial to replace him. Who knows, we may invite the guest chef to stay on."

"That sounds like a solid plan. What's the problem?"

He leans forward and whispers, "I assume you haven't heard that one of the judges for the competition died in a car crash right before you reached out to me."

"Bloody hell. Who was it?" I ask as I stir the fresh Boulevardier that magically appeared.

"Allison Bernard of Chez Bernard." Sean leans back in his chair and turns his gaze toward the water.

"I remember the restaurant. It was one of your father's favorites. If I recall correctly, we went there the last time I was in town."

Nodding, he turns back to me. "Yes, that's the place. The circumstances of Allison's death are troubling. We invited the media and competition judges for an in-person press conference to pump up publicity for the event and make a last-minute push for applications from potential competitors. Unfortunately, Chef Bernard died in a tragic accident on her way home from that press conference. She swerved off the road and smashed head-on into the side of a brick building." Sean cringes.

"That's horrible. It's also bad press for you."

"She was a friend. It was also a horrendously bad start to the competition. To make matters worse, the news reported that she mumbled something about champagne in her dying breath."

"Why does that make matters worse? Are they accusing the Athena of serving her too much alcohol?"

"According to the police, they didn't find any skid marks at the scene of the accident, so it looks like Allison never braked when she went off the road. The press reported that she was driving drunk after the champagne toast at our press conference, but I know she wasn't drunk. We only saw her have one glass of champagne, so I've been anxiously awaiting the final autopsy report."

"Maybe she fell asleep or had a heart attack?"

Shaking my head, I say, "No. This morning, I got a call from Larry, the police chief. Fortunately, we developed a good rapport when the Athena dealt with a couple of guests who thought they could cheat the system last year. Since then, he's been helpful on a number of similar matters."

"What did he say?"

"He had the toxicology results. Allison had enough prescription opioids in her system to knock out someone twice her size. With the alcohol, it was a deadly combination."

"Was she an addict?"

Sean sets his glass on the table. "No way. I'm tired of the negative assumptions about Allison's character."

"I'm not judging Chef Bernard."

"I didn't mean you. It's the press and the police. Allison and I were good friends, so it's been hard. I knew her well enough to know she was a control freak and an exercise fanatic. I don't think she'd purposefully take opioids. Cynthia mentioned that her assistant, Cameron, heard Allison complain about a sore shoulder from a tennis tournament. A doctor must have prescribed the drugs."

I take a moment to really look at Sean for the first time this evening. In the dim light of the bar, I hadn't noticed that his eyes look as tired as mine, not to mention the tenseness in his jaw and his intense grip on his glass.

"You're really torn up about her death. How close were you?" I ask.

"You may not have known, but for a short time, Allison and I dated."

"Wasn't she older?"

"She was but that wasn't an issue. We were just better as friends than something more, so we parted amicably but remained close. When Emily called to tell me the news, it felt like a stab in the chest, and the stabs kept coming with the negative press. I'm tired of everyone assuming the worst about Allison."

"Cameron sounds like a reliable source, so you have your answer. Allison must have hurt her shoulder and accidentally taken too much of the prescription painkiller. She probably fell asleep at the wheel."

Head tilted down, Sean stares into what remains of the honey-colored liquid in his glass, saying, "It's possible, but I'm not sure. In the past, she wouldn't even take an aspirin. She said it poisoned her system and would screw up her training. Besides, why would she drink the champagne if she was taking a drug like that?"

"People change."

"Rarely. Larry also gave me a heads-up that they're going to interview various people from the press conference. Strangely, the police didn't find any drugs in Allison's car or in her home, which is odd if she was taking them for an injury. The police assume she left her prescription bottle here or got the pills from someone at the press conference. Unfortunately, that's not my only concern."

"What else is going on?"

"It's related to our food and beverage expenses. Someone may be stealing from me."

"You can't be serious. Who would have the nerve to steal from you?"

"I don't know. After Chef Maurizio left, we decided to reorganize F&B to redistribute responsibilities so that the departure of a single chef doesn't have as much impact on the department. As part of analyzing our options, I reviewed the most recent audit report, which we just received. The results surprised me in a bad way."

"What did you find?"

"I took over the Athena two years ago, and everything looked normal in our audit the first year. However, the audit for the second year looks great for all departments except F&B, which is a big one. Digging deeper, I learned that our F&B expenses started going up significantly about six months ago. During that time, we saw an increase of more than twenty percent relative to the previous year."

"That doesn't necessarily mean anything. Were revenue and profits up too?"

"That's exactly what I expected. But while expenses increased significantly, revenue didn't increase noticeably, and one month, revenue went down a little."

"Did the cost of food go up? It's possible your chef thought it was important to buy even higher-quality ingredients and more expensive wines. If he didn't raise your prices to match the cost increases, that would explain the problem."

"Perhaps, but it bothers me that no one fixed the problem or brought it to my attention."

"What happened when you asked the department head about the increase in expenses?"

"Cynthia, our F&B manager, said it was a supply issue. Our prior chef signed off on the orders for all the restaurants and catering. Cynthia said she asked him about it several times before he left. Apparently, he assured her that he had to change some vendors due to availability and quality issues. She said the new vendors didn't give us pricing as favorable as the old ones because we were a new customer. She's convinced the problem will go away as the new vendors gain trust that we'll be a long-term customer."

"Interesting. Could be plausible, I guess. But I would've thought new vendors might give you even larger discounts to entice you to make them a preferred supplier."

"I know. Something just doesn't seem right to me. With Chef Maurizio gone, it may be hard to sort this out completely, but Cynthia promised to follow up with him again."

"Is she good at her job? Do you have faith in her?"

"Yes. She worked for my father before me. He always told me to keep her happy because we're lucky to have her. We'll see what else she can learn from Chef Maurizio, but in the meantime, I want to ask you for a favor."

"Okay. How can I help?"

"I need help with the competition. I had planned to attend as many of its events and tapings as possible to make sure it runs smoothly, and the Athena is shown in a positive light. That became even more important after Allison died. But now I need to focus on the F&B mystery, so I'm hoping you'll cover for me at the competition events."

"Won't they think it's odd that I'm attending in your place?"

"No. It's not unusual for me to send a replacement to events when I'm called away on more pressing matters. We can explain that you're my old college friend who's visiting and acting as my advisor."

"Wouldn't one of your staff members be a more suitable choice?"

"I have staff assigned to the competition, but I want someone else there who'll have my best interests in mind. This is even more personal to me after losing Allison. Besides, you're a foodie, so you'll enjoy the competition. The bottom line is that it starts in a few days, and I'd appreciate your help. Are you on board?"

I nod and relax back into my chair.

"Why not? The events will take my mind off other issues. But you understand that I'm not willing to be on camera, right?"

Sean raises his glass in a salute. "I know. Wear a baseball cap if you don't want to be recognized around the competition."

I laugh. "Fortunately, I'm not recognized as often in the US as I am in Europe, but a baseball cap? I don't think so."

"We can both attend the opening reception and final awards dinner, and I'll handle any interviews. If you can cover the rest, that'll give me time to figure out the F&B problem."

"Do you want to give me a quick overview of the key players? You mentioned Cynthia is head of F&B, and Cameron is her assistant. Do I need to know about any others?"

"I'll hold off about the others for now. I don't want to bias your first impressions. You may notice something that will help with my F&B investigation."

As he finishes, trumpets blare, brightly colored lights flash, and the outdoor stage on the left side of the water lights up, capturing everyone's attention.

The spectacle is amusing.

A spotlight draws all eyes to the top of the outdoor staircase near where we're seated above the Aegean. Smoke wafts our way from the torches held by a man and woman standing at the top of the stairs dressed in short, almost see-through, toga-like costumes.

I follow Sean's lead, standing by the glass wall, as the spotlight tracks the torch carriers' descent to the water level. We watch them run around a concrete path circling the water. Torches light up as they pass. The pair stop when they reach the base of a staircase encircling the cylindrical Olympic Tower at the end of the stage nearest us. As the tower lights up with an orange glow, the pair begin their ascent as music beats in sync with their steps. When they reach the top, their torches light a ginormous concrete bowl, illuminating the night and signifying the start of the Grand Athena's Olympic Games.

We watch archers launch arrows, climbers ascend multi-story ropes, "stones" arc from throwers' hands into the water, and a plethora of other reenactments of Olympic games that mesmerize the cheering crowd. After a few minutes, I turn toward Sean. "That's quite the production."

"It is. We added the stage and show the year before Dad died. You wouldn't believe how many people it takes to pull that off each evening at eight."

"I'm sure it's quite a team."

"Now that you've seen the show, can I interest you in dinner? I managed to skip lunch today, so I'm starving. If we're lucky, we'll meet a couple of entertaining women too."

"Dinner sounds good, but I'm taking a break from dating on this trip."

"Why?" He scrunches his forehead.

"Clearing my head. We'll talk about it later."

As we weave between the closely spaced tables to exit the bar, Sean says, "Sure. Which restaurant would you like to try?"

"You select."

"Even our best Italian and French ones won't impress your European palate. So, how about steak and lobster at Athena's Prime Claw?"

"Who could pass up steak and lobster? Lead the way."

7

CASSIE

I pinch myself. *Ouch!*

Yep, it's true. My adventure is underway as the plane screams down the runway for our short flight from San Diego to Las Vegas.

I keep having to reassure myself though. It felt so odd to wake up this morning and not immediately log in to my computer. I pulled out my phone to reread the email from Jackson approving my leave to make sure I hadn't dreamed all of this.

It's too much to comprehend right now. Between my excitement, anticipation, and sheer glee, it feels like it's my birthday. I have two whole weeks with no deadline, so I can actually breathe. I'd gotten to the point where I cringed when my phone dinged with a text or my laptop chimed with a new email for fear it was Jackson assigning me more work. The thought of a good night's sleep and real meals is more than I can fathom. The icing on the cake will be watching professional chefs in person for the first time in my life.

I've barely finished half of my soft drink when the pilot tells the flight attendants to prepare the cabin for landing. That gives me just enough time to reread Cynthia's instructions and double-check where to go. As I finish, my body jerks with the jolt of the plane's wheels hitting the runway and bouncing twice.

Not the smoothest landing, but who cares? We're here.

Exiting the plane, I take in the bright lights and chiming slot machines in the airport, barely resisting the urge to stop and try my luck. As I walk to baggage claim, enormous signs advertise shows with celebrity performers, magicians, beautiful showgirls, and ripped male strippers from Australia! My mouth waters at the depictions of sizzling steaks, gigantic lobster tails, decadent desserts, and overflowing bottles of champagne. Other displays tempt me with spectacular casinos where visitors can spin a wheel for a chance to win big. I've arrived at an adult amusement park, and I'm ready to have fun.

Stepping off the escalator at baggage claim, I see a guy in a black suit holding an iPad that's displaying my name.

Justin introduces himself and retrieves my bags from the nearby carousel. I follow him out the side doors to a limousine. Yes, a black stretch limousine that's so glossy I can see my reflection.

He opens the back door, and I slide across the buttery, black leather seat into relative darkness. Once my eyes adjust from the bright sunlight to the dim, elegant interior, I take in the burled wood trim and side bars with cut crystal glasses and small bottles of champagne. Soft, but lively, music spills from speakers surrounding me on all sides.

After taking his place behind the wheel, Justin tells me to help myself to the champagne, and we drive toward the Strip. Happily following his instructions, I pour myself a glass of bubbly. Why not, right? I'm not working today or any day for the next two weeks. That puts a smile on my face as the bubbles tickle down my throat.

Justin asks whether I want the fast path or the scenic route down the Strip. For once in my life, I'm not in a hurry. The scenic route it is.

As we approach the Athena, Justin explains that the guestroom towers are named after Greek islands. The main rectangular building in front is called the Mykonos Tower, and a second building on the left is the Santorini Tower. The buildings are breathtaking with bright-white walls, lapis blue trim, and beautiful fuchsia bougainvillea flowers draping over the balcony rails.

As the light changes, we turn left, following the curving road behind a giant water feature to the hidden hotel entrance. Pulling to a stop, Justin hops out and opens my door, saying, "Welcome to the Grand Athena. Enter through the doors to your right, and you can check in. I'll take care of your bags."

Walking into the lobby, I'm stunned by the bright and airy atmosphere. The electric-blue and dazzling, white decor make me think I stepped into a photo of the Greek islands. Fuchsia flowers cascade from high ledges and pillars, and individual, white-washed reception desks dot the far side of the lobby. Huge concrete statues of Greek gods and goddesses stand behind each desk with an even larger statue of Athena in the center, reigning over the others.

Surprisingly, the lobby is an island surrounded by water. Behind the reception desks, a Greek village sits in the distance with shops, cafés, and abundant flowers. Swimming pools fill the area between the back of the lobby and the shops.

Small water taxis transport people between the lobby, the shops, the casino to my right, and what I assume are the Mykonos and Santorini towers with the guest rooms. Walking bridges connect all the areas for guests who don't want to wait for a water taxi.

I've never seen anything like this. Exploring will be so much fun.

After taking in as much as I can, I get in line to check in. The line moves slowly, but eventually, it's my turn. The desk clerk types in my info, and she stares at the computer screen. Her eyes narrow, and she picks up the phone, speaking softly to whomever answered.

Cynthia's instructions said a room would be reserved for me. Hopefully, they haven't lost my reservation.

Ending the call, the clerk welcomes me to the competition. She asks if I want keyless access. If so, they need to scan my palm print. She explains it will save time during my stay, so why not? I put my hand on the pad and wait for the green light. It's like stepping into the future. With the check-in process complete, she explains that my bags will be taken to my room.

As she hands me a packet of materials, a well-dressed, thirtyish man appears, saying, "Ms. Edwards, I'm Christian Laurent, the head concierge. We're pleased to have you at the Athena."

He's younger than his title suggests, but he's handsome and professional with his taper fade haircut and well-tailored suit.

"Thank you. I'm ecstatic to be here."

"The competition begins tomorrow morning with a prep meeting, and the opening reception is tomorrow night. We'd love to give you a tour of the Athena today. It will make it easier for you to find the various events tomorrow."

"That would be wonderful."

"Will five o'clock work?"

"Absolutely."

"Your tour guide will meet you in the VIP Lounge then. It's across the lobby." He points to glazed glass doors to our right.

"Thanks. I'm going to find my room now."

Reaching the bank of elevators, my stomach growls. I never had lunch. All I've had was a soft drink on the plane and a glass of champagne in the limo. I'll find food after I drop off my carry-on bag.

Opening the door, I walk into a designer showplace.

I marvel at the blend of comfort and modern elegance. As an alternate, they told me I didn't get a suite, but this ultra-deluxe room has an oversized king bed draped with a stunning turquoise, royal-blue, and gold overstuffed comforter. There must be a dozen decorative, seashell-shaped pillows piled high against a white-leather headboard that goes all the way to the ceiling. I run my hand across the satiny-soft, cotton sheets where the comforter is turned down. Sinking into the softness tonight will be a treat.

An unexpected gift basket with fruit and nuts sits atop a desk in the far corner of the room. The snacks will do for lunch and give me time to unpack before my tour. But first, I take a closer look at the rest of the room. A blue couch and a chrome and glass coffee table are arranged near the floor-to-ceiling glass doors that open onto a balcony. And don't get me started on the luxurious bathroom with stacks of extra-thick, fluffy towels next to a giant Jacuzzi tub on an elevated platform. While soaking in a warm bubble bath, I'll have a spectacular view of the Strip when everything is lit up tonight.

My smile can't get any bigger. I'm so happy.

While munching on salted cashews and dried fruit, I unpack. Hopefully, I brought the right clothes. Despite Cynthia's guidelines, I still had to guess about a lot of things.

The guidelines suggested bringing a mixture of outfits from shorts to jeans to cocktail dresses. I assumed I would be doing a lot of standing and walking, so I brought sneakers, flats, and wedges. Of course, my cocktail dress screamed for high-heeled stilettos, so I brought them too. If Lowri hadn't helped me, I would never have pared it down to four pairs of shoes and only two suitcases.

At 4:45 p.m., I walk into the VIP Lounge and am met by a familiar face.

"Christian, it's good to see you again. Is my guide here? I'm looking forward to the tour."

"Hello, Ms. Edwards."

"Please call me Cassie."

"Of course. Your tour guide was called away, so it'll be my pleasure to show you around the Grand Athena."

"I'm sure you're too busy for that. I can reschedule for another time."

"No, I insist. Follow me. We're going to start on the conference level, which is where your first meeting will be tomorrow morning. You must be excited to meet the finalists and the host of our competition."

"Absolutely. I keep pinching myself to make sure it's not a dream. This is a complete departure from my normal life. I spend my days in front of a computer poring over contracts."

"If I can do anything to make your visit more enjoyable, please let me know."

"It's already perfect."

We arrive at escalators near the back of the casino, and Christian waves me onto the one heading up.

I step off and glance around the enormous space filled with at least ten different sitting areas where small groups of people are chatting. They are all wearing name tags on lanyards hanging around their necks.

The space is relaxing and cheerful. Rather than the traditional dark wood you find in so many hotels, this conference area has an airiness, as light from a wall of windows splashes against the light-blue walls with white wood trim. As we walk across the space, my feet are cushioned by the island-inspired carpet with off-white, aqua, teal, and cobalt-blue designs. I would sign up for a conference here in a heartbeat.

Christian says, "Meeting rooms of various sizes are accessible from this area, and restrooms are down the corridor on our right. Your first meeting will be in the large boardroom that is down the hall on our left. Let me show you the room so you'll know where to go tomorrow morning."

Enthusiastically, I admit, "I can't wait for tomorrow's meeting even though I don't know what to expect. I've seen cooking competitions on television, secretly dreaming of being part of one, but I've never been to one in person. Watching the chefs up close while they create masterpieces under the pressure of time and cameras will be incredibly inspiring. I know I'll spend the whole time thinking about what I would be creating if I were in their shoes. I can't wait!" Pausing, I realize Christian is staring at me with a big smile as we walk down the hall. I blush, saying, "Sorry, I let my excitement take over."

"You have nothing to apologize for. Your enthusiasm is contagious. You even have me smiling about it, and I don't know the first thing about cooking." Arriving at the boardroom, Christian continues, "This is where you need to be at ten tomorrow morning."

"Great. Thanks for bringing me here. It will save time tomorrow. Where is the next stop on the tour?"

"The pool area, so let's go back downstairs."

Walking off the escalator, we head down a hallway that takes us out of the casino. When we reach doors leading outside, Christian places his hand on a nearby scanner. The doors click open, and we exit onto a beautiful patio area overlooking multiple pools.

Each pool has a small replica of a Greek ruin, such as the Parthenon or ancient columns with waterfalls. On the far side of the pools, my eyes wander over cute shops and people eating at small patio tables. The buildings sport the same blue-and-white theme to match their real Greek island counterparts. They're draped with beautiful hot-pink flowers that create a contrasting punch of vibrant color. That's when I realize we are in the area that I saw behind the lobby when I checked in. The water feature that creates the lobby island extends around the left side of the pool area and curves around in front of the shops and restaurants.

"Christian, this is amazing! How do you get to the shops on the other side of the pools?"

"You can either swim across, or there are walking bridges at the far left and far right of the pool area if you prefer to stay dry. From the lobby, you can also access the shops via the small water taxis."

"I could spend a week just hanging out here. I hope there'll be time for relaxing by the pool. A good book, some sun, and a frozen drink would be perfect."

"I'm sure you'll find a little time to enjoy it, but I know they'll keep you busy with the competition."

"My first priority is the competition, but as you probably know, I'm the alternate. I doubt I'll have much of a role."

"Speaking of the competition, let me show you Trendz, where the finalists will be preparing their food. It's on the other side of the casino overlooking the enormous pool of water out front that we call the Aegean Sea."

We go back inside and walk forever. This place is huge. On our way, Christian points out, "If you take a left here, the path leads you to the shopping area called Aphrodite's Way. It's like having the best shopping from Rodeo Drive, New York City, Milan, and Paris all in one place, along with some high-end restaurants and bars in the area called Restaurant Row."

"That sounds fabulous. I can't wait to walk through and take a look."

We keep walking and eventually reach the front area of the casino where I see the sign for Trendz. Guiding me up a wide marble staircase, Christian says, "This is called the Grand Staircase. Trendz and the Olympic Torch Bar are upstairs, which gives them a beautiful view of the Aegean."

Christian ushers me into Trendz as he explains, "This is where you'll be spending a lot of time over the next two weeks."

It's a welcoming restaurant with dim lighting. Booths separated by privacy drapes line the walls, and tables for small groups fill the center of the space. A gorgeous bar area to the right of the entrance sports a three-story wine and liquor room behind clear glass. I can't even estimate how many bottles are in there.

"Christian, how do they access the bottles that are at the top?"

"Oh, it is quite the show. The servers use the silks you see tied up on the sides. They climb up the silks like you may have seen in various acrobatic shows, grab the bottle, and unwind their way back down."

"That would be fun to watch, particularly if the bottle is near the top."

"Well, that's part of the plan. The more expensive the bottle, the higher it's stored. The goal is to entice customers to pay more to watch the server climb higher."

"Makes sense. That's a smart marketing idea."

"It seems to work. Follow me toward the back. I'll show you the kitchen."

I'm surprised to see the kitchen is almost as large as the restaurant area. There are multiple stations and every high-end commercial appliance you can imagine, including a walk-in refrigerator, walk-in freezer, multiple ovens, gas cooktops, salamander broilers, chillers, and two ice cream machines. With goose bumps covering my arms, I bask in the space.

Christian asks, "What do you think?"

As I stare at the fabulous kitchen, my eyes are a little watery at the thought that I'm only here to watch.

I finally say, "I'm stunned. It's incredible. I've dreamed of cooking in a kitchen like this."

Christian responds with a cheery, "Don't give up your dreams. You never know what's possible. Would you like to return to your room now?"

"I would. Thanks."

Shaking off my momentary disappointment, a smile returns. I'd rather be here than at work, even if it's in a backup role.

8

CASSIE

I'm full of energy this morning, which is surprising given that I stayed out late last night. That hadn't been my plan, but it was exhilarating to explore the Athena free from work deadlines pulling me back to my laptop.

After the tour with Christian, I couldn't resist dinner at the Italian restaurant, Wine & Vine. Then I wandered through the casino and watched people play craps. I never figured out the rules, but the enthusiasm was electric as the crowd cheered the wins. When I heard a group talking about the Omega nightclub, I decided to go in search of it. It sounded like the perfect place to snap a selfie so Lowri would believe I'm having fun.

The plan was to take the photo and leave, but as I was admiring the club and the extravagant clothes, a wave of people pushed me onto the dance floor. I started moving to the beat of the music with a random group. The next thing I knew, it was almost 2 a.m., so I hurried back to my room to get some sleep, expecting to wake up exhausted like usual.

Instead, my excitement this morning had me jumping out of bed with plenty of time to get ready for the ten o'clock prep meeting.

As I walk into the boardroom, a handful of people are standing and chatting as they sip coffee near the long conference table that runs down the center of the room.

I spot a buffet table loaded with drinks, pastries, and freshly sliced fruit. It's calling my name. As I'm preparing a cup of hot tea, a woman wearing a charcoal-gray business suit approaches.

"Hello, I'm Cynthia Andino. You must be Cassie. We spoke on the phone last week."

"It's a pleasure to meet you in person. I'm so excited to be here."

"Welcome. Help yourself to the food and then find your seat. We're almost ready to start."

I'm suddenly a little anxious because others in the room seem to know each other. I don't recognize anyone, and walking up to a group of strangers isn't easy for me.

I opt to fill a small plate with fruit and a pastry to give myself something to do as I scan the room for a welcoming group to join. My smile is met with varying responses. A couple of people smile back. Others size me up with furrowed brows. They must be the finalists and haven't figured out I'm just the spare.

Before I decide which group to approach, Cynthia instructs us to take our seats. Clearly in charge, she moves to the head of the table farthest from the door. Everyone else fills up the two long sides of the table according to name cards at each place.

When we're all seated, Cynthia says, "Welcome to the Grand Athena and our Guest Chef Competition. I'd like to introduce our team. Amy is to my left. She's the competition coordinator and will host the cooking segments. Sebastian is the director and producer." He's wearing a faded blue T-shirt, torn jeans, and a baseball cap. Cynthia also points out the lead videographer and the lead photographer, but she doesn't mention their names.

"Now for our finalists."

This is exciting. I'm finally learning who's competing.

"We have Leon Boucher from France, Trenton James from New York City, Jayden Scott from Dallas, and Kai Kahale from Honolulu. Our alternate is Cassie Edwards from San Diego."

I find myself analyzing the finalists as they had done to me earlier. Looking aloof, Leon has olive skin, large dark eyes, and an average build. Trenton is a large man with a perpetually gruff but confident expression. In contrast, Jayden is skinny with dull-brown hair and a narrow face. He can't stop fidgeting, so nerves must be an issue for him. Kai seems the happiest of the group. He sports the perfect natural tan, an athletic build, straight black hair, and a welcoming smile. I'll soon find out if my first impressions prove to be correct.

I've loathed my time in work meetings lately, but this meeting is different. Despite the competitive environment, there's an electric energy permeating the air. I'm hanging on every word, excited to see what happens next.

Cynthia says, "It's time to go over the competition rules, starting with the basics from the packet of materials you received at check-in. We'll start with what I call the Critical Rules. The first Critical Rule is no cell phones, no tablets, no laptops, no internet access, and no calls home from borrowed cell phones or landlines during the competition. We need your full attention on the competition with no outside influences or help."

That's going to be tough for the finalists.

"You have ten minutes to text or email family members, significant others, and emergency contacts. In the event of an emergency, they can leave a message at the phone number shown on the screen behind me. We will relay the message to you, provided it's an actual emergency."

My heart stings a little as I watch everyone except me furiously texting. They all have someone. With no immediate family or significant other, I sit idly. At the last second, I text the number to Lowri just in case she needs to reach me.

"My assistant, Cameron, will collect your electronic devices."

Cameron reminds me of a shy librarian with her large glasses and hair pulled back into a bun. As she walks around the room, everyone places their phones and tablets into the basket she's carrying.

"Violation of the device rule or internet policy will result in immediate disqualification. If you need access to your tablets for recipes you brought with you, we'll arrange supervised access."

Who knew this was going to be such a strict environment?

When Cameron reaches me, I say, "I'm not competing, so I'm not sure the rule applies to me."

Cynthia chimes in, "It does because there's still a chance you could be called upon to replace one of the other finalists."

Cynthia holds up a device that looks like a chunky black watch, saying, "Each of you will receive one of these communication devices. It's called a TekCuff. You must wear it for the next two weeks. It fastens around the wrist like a watch and will keep you tied into the Grand Athena's communication systems. It also has text and audio messaging, alarms, a clock, and a calendar. We've disabled the phone and email functions for the duration of the competition. However, when the competition is over, the TekCuff is yours to keep, and you can activate those features through a mobile phone carrier."

That's an unexpected and generous gift.

"Now for Critical Rule #2. You are forbidden from interacting with the three judges outside of the competition events. Again, violation equals disqualification. Any questions?"

The room is silent.

With those two Critical Rules covered, Cynthia moves on.

"Cassie won't be competing unless someone drops out or is disqualified. However, she'll be attending all the meetings and events just in case she's needed."

As Cynthia starts to go over the competition schedule, I hear footsteps. Turning my head, my jaw drops when I see Sean Cartwright enter the room. After watching him in videos touting this competition, I'd recognize his thick blond hair laced with whiskey-colored highlights and intense, sparkling, azure eyes anywhere. He's taller and more handsome in person though.

My attention quickly shifts when a tall, dark-haired guy with chiseled features follows Mr. Cartwright through the door. His clothes look like they came straight from Paris despite their casual appearance.

Our eyes lock for a second, and his mouth curves upward, forming a hint of a smile. This unidentified guy looks like the one with the magic fingers from the dream I had the morning Cynthia called me. Well not exactly, but this real version is even sexier, which is saying a lot.

His hair is thick and wavy, invites my fingers to comb through it. His sharp jaw and focused eyes exude confidence and success consistent with the smirk adorning his perfect face. His skin is tan and sun-kissed, standing out against his light-blue shirt and dark-blue dress pants molded to his fit physique. His coffee eyes mesmerize me as his intense, self-assured gaze pulls me in.

Murmurs from around the table fill the air as heads turn toward Mr. Cartwright and his dark-haired guest. Cynthia visibly stiffens and stops mid-sentence to acknowledge Mr. Cartwright. I'm surprised to see her rigid posture in his presence. In her position, she must interact with him all the time, but his entrance has put her on edge. Mr. Cartwright quickly tells Cynthia to ignore them.

Instead, she says, "Everyone, it's my pleasure to introduce the owner of the Grand Athena, Mr. Sean Cartwright. Would you like to say a few words?"

"Welcome. We're excited to host this competition. The winner will be the chef who thinks fast on their feet and tackles unexpected challenges with a smile. They must share our belief that the impossible is possible when it comes to giving our guests the best experience imaginable. Most importantly, we want beautiful, delicious food."

He turns to the gorgeous, dark-haired guy. "I'd like to introduce my college friend Evan. He'll be attending the competition events. We'll be working with Cynthia, Amy, and Sebastian on filming locations, brand management, and issues related to promoting the Grand Athena. That means you'll see both of us at various events throughout the competition. However, we won't play any role in judging or selecting the winner."

He must own a management or consulting company, but I don't recognize him. I'm certain if I'd seen his photo somewhere, I'd remember it because I can't take my eyes off him. The flecks of gold in his captivating brown eyes mesmerize me. As he runs his fingers through his dark chocolate hair, I wish they were my fingers weaving through his thick waves.

Evan says, "Hello everyone. It's a pleasure to be here. Sean shared your applications with me, so I'm certain this will be a stellar competition. I look forward to getting to know you, watching you compete, and sampling your creations along the way. Best of luck to each of you."

His good looks and deep, sexy voice draw me to him like a magnet. His posh accent sounds British to me, but I'm not an expert. Whatever it is has me swooning. Hell, I could listen to him read the dictionary to me all night. On top of that, his eyes gleam with mischief, daring me to take a chance.

The temperature is rising rapidly, and my heart is racing. I've never had such an immediate physical reaction to a guy before, but I'm not the only one. Looking around the room, others are affected too. He's hot as hell.

It must be something in the Vegas air. Looking at him makes me melt, but he's off-limits. I'm part of the competition he's overseeing. It would be a conflict of interest, and I'm not ready for any relationship. I may never be. Losing my parents hurt like hell, and then Ben, my boyfriend for two years, left me too. I'm not willing to risk that level of heartbreak.

Even if I can't have him, I can enjoy the view and remember this feeling when I crawl between the silky soft sheets tonight.

My attention returns to the meeting when Mr. Cartwright says, "Evan and I wanted to say hello, but we can't stay for the rest of this meeting. We look forward to the opportunity to chat with you at the opening reception tonight."

As they're leaving, I can't take my eyes off Evan as I nervously fidget with my pen. As he nears, my fingers fumble, letting the pen fall to the floor. As Evan walks by, he stops. On bended knee, he retrieves the pen and slowly hands it to me. Our fingers touch briefly, igniting sparks that ripple up my arm. Our eyes lock, and my vision tunnels, blocking out the rest of the room. Evan's eyes darken, and his smile grows. I hold my breath, not wanting the moment to end.

Sean says, "You ready, Evan?"

Evan stands and walks out, leaving me stupefied and intrigued. That man bent on his knees in his expensive clothes to retrieve a free hotel pen for me. I'm swooning, and he didn't even speak a single word to me.

The moment is broken when Cynthia picks up where she left off, going over the schedule for the competition. The opening reception is tonight. Tomorrow, the finalists will be giving demonstrations by the swimming pool during an event called the Poolside Dip. Each of the finalists must prepare a dip designed for a pool party.

Cynthia tells us that several food items are off-limits because certain contestants, judges, and staff members have food allergies. She explains that only Cameron knows who is allergic to which items because they are treating all information related to health issues as confidential. Of course, those with allergies are free to share the information if they choose.

Cynthia says that Critical Rule #3 is to strictly avoid using bleu cheese, sesame seeds, and soybeans.

"In preparation for the demonstration tomorrow, please write down the name of the dip you will make, along with the list of ingredients, and pass it to me."

She collects the papers and looks up at me. "Cassie, where's yours? You need to turn one in, just in case."

Apparently, my new nickname is Just-in-Case Cassie, but I dutifully consider what dips I'd make that would withstand the heat by the pool. Then it comes to me. I jot down my favorite Salsa Verde, along with the ingredients, and pass the paper down the table to Cynthia.

Cynthia says, "That's all for now. Please arrive at the opening reception thirty minutes early for photos and short interviews. We'll see you tonight."

9

EVAN

I returned to my suite after Sean, and I stopped by the competition meeting. Since then, I've been racking my brain for ideas to change the trajectory of my future role as prince. There must be a way to make use of my MBA that aligns with my interests.

Ideally, I'll come up with a plan that not only satisfies my need to matter, but also, more importantly, will make a difference to others. While my reputation is one of a playboy with a carefree existence, deep down that's not who I want to be for the rest of my life. My family works with a number of charities, and we help raise money for them. But perhaps I can do more if I know where our current efforts are falling short.

I'm doing a deep dive, researching the various charities and the needs of the people in my country when Sean's name flashes on my phone. I'm shocked to see that it's already 6 p.m.

I answer, and Sean says, "Want to stop by my apartment for a quick drink before we make our entrance at the reception?"

"Good idea. Make sure your security knows I'm on my way. The last time I was here, your dad's guards weren't very welcoming when I arrived. I don't relish the idea of being thrown against a wall and handcuffed again."

"Are you still bent out of shape over that? It was funny as fuck. Besides, he apologized. But don't worry, we've upgraded our systems. A simple palm scan will clear you to my place."

"You're kidding, right?"

"No."

"Sean, should I worry that you have my prints in your computer system."

"Quit complaining. You willingly gave us that information when you checked in. You could have opted for an archaic key card instead or used the Athena App on your cell phone."

"I know, but the more I think about it, the more alarming it is to know you store biometric data for everyone. Aren't you worried about someone hacking your system?"

"Not really. We have the finest security system known. Besides, the guests love technology. It's freeing not to carry around key cards and credit cards when you want to go to the gym or pool."

"Overall, I agree, but delete my data when I leave."

"That's how it works. Now get your ass up here for that drink before the reception."

I smile to myself, knowing that at the event tonight I'll have an opportunity to chat with the intriguing Cassandra Edwards. The finalists and alternate submitted videos with their applications. Sean shared them with me, so I recognized Cassandra this morning. When I originally watched her video, she briefly caught my attention, primarily because I was surprised to see an attorney in a chef's competition. Then, when we crossed paths at the meeting, she made a more lasting impression when our gazes met.

Assisting Sean with the competition started out as a favor for a friend. Now, I'm rather looking forward to it.

After a quick drink in Sean's apartment, we arrive fashionably late at the Trendz restaurant for the competition's opening reception.

Inside the entrance, we stop to survey the already buzzing festivities. Bouncing light causes the thousands of carats of diamonds and colored jewels draped around their collective necks, wrists, and fingers to twinkle like sparklers in the dimly lit room.

A pleased smile lights up Sean's face. "Our celebrity and high-roller guests have taken the reception seriously. They're all here and dressed to impress."

A server presents us with flutes of champagne as I respond, "It's a positive sign when the laughter and chatter drown out the background music. With the champagne flowing, I'd say everything is set for a successful beginning to your competition."

"Hopefully, the press reports will match the excitement level."

"I'm sure they will."

"Time to mingle."

"I'm right behind you."

Passing between the high-top tables, we weave through the crowd, repeatedly stopping to greet the various VIP guests, press, and staff. This is easy for me. I'm accustomed to meet-and-greet events. I don't mind them too much. Interacting with people usually energizes me.

Sean asks, "Do you see Cynthia? We barely saw the finalists this morning. I want a chance to talk with them before the introductions tonight."

"You already know quite a bit about them from their applications and the selection process, right?"

Shaking his head, Sean says, "Only the basics. I didn't watch their videos and only had time for a scan of their applications. I chose not to participate in the selection process because I didn't want my pick to have an automatic advantage. As a result, I don't know much about them yet."

I'm not paying much attention to Sean. Instead, my eyes are fixed on an attractive woman across the room. She's the only one here who seems real. There are plenty of women who could be classified as sculpted and flawless, but Cassandra is a natural, unpretentious beauty. She's standing on the sideline, carefully evaluating the crowd, a longing in her expressive grey eyes. I can't help but want to extinguish the sadness I sense in her.

"I feel a bit sorry for the alternate. Her name is Cassandra, right?" I ask.

"I think she goes by Cassie. Why do you feel sorry for her?"

I take a sip of champagne, considering my answer. "It must be hard knowing you came so close to having a chance at the prize but didn't quite make it."

Waving off my concern, Sean says, "Well, she still received a free trip, a line on her resume, and will likely get some good press during all the events. By the way, I see the four finalists visiting with each other, but where is Cassie?"

Eyes still fixated on the woman across the room, I use my glass to point. "She's by the ice sculpture of Athena. She's the one with the dark-blonde hair wearing the blue dress."

"Now it makes sense. Since you haven't taken your eyes off her, I assume you plan to personally express your *sympathy* for her situation."

"Of course not. I was just concerned that she may feel left out and alone—you know, like being the unnecessary spare."

"It's just a cooking competition, but you can sympathize with her later. First, let's find Cynthia. I want to have a quick chat with each finalist before introducing them."

When we find Cynthia, Sean asks, "How are things going so far?"

She waves her extended arm dramatically across the room. "Just look! It's the event of the year. Everyone who is anyone is here, and as you can see, the room is brimming with enthusiasm."

Cynthia is a bit theatrical. She may have had a little too much to drink.

Sean says, "Yes, it's going well so far. How are the finalists doing?"

As Sean talks with Cynthia, I find Cassie again and watch her. She seems a little out of place as if she doesn't know how she fits in here. I admire the way she holds her head high and focuses on tasting the various appetizers. Less discerning eyes wouldn't notice, but I recognize her actions as attempts to hide her discomfort. It takes grace and experience to bury one's inner dilemmas and struggles from the world.

When Cassie walks out of eyesight, I return my attention to Sean and Cynthia in time to hear her say, "I went over some last-minute logistics with them, so everything is set for the poolside demonstration tomorrow afternoon. We're calling it 'The Poolside Dip.'"

"That's a catchy name for the event," he says

Sean's getting into the spirit of the competition, but I struggle to hold back a snicker as I mutter, "It's a rather corny name."

Ignoring me, he says, "Evan and I would like a chance to chat with the finalists before the toast."

"Okay. Let me round them up and meet you by the stage in ten minutes."

"Where is our alternate?" Sean asks.

"She won't be participating in the competition. Did you want to meet her anyway?"

"Yes. Evan and I want to congratulate the finalists and alternate."

"Understood. I'll take care of it." And with a swirl of her chiffon skirt, Cynthia floats off in search of them.

"You owe me one for arranging an introduction to Cassie."

"I told you—I'm not interested."

"It doesn't matter what you say. Your body language says otherwise."

"It's not what you think. I'm curious how she feels being a backup. Is this an enjoyable experience for her, or is it bittersweet?"

It's mysterious how I'm drawn to Cassandra. She's extremely attractive, but she's not my usual type. Based on her application and my initial impression, she seems more serious than the women I typically date—more like someone I might introduce to my family. Of course, I never do that.

We spend the next ten minutes working our way toward the stage, shaking hands with more people than I can count along the way. Arriving at the stairs by the side of the platform, we join the finalists who are chatting with each other.

Cynthia begins the introductions. "This is our first finalist, Leon Boucher, who has joined us from France."

"It's a pleasure to meet you," Sean says.

"Thank you. I'm pleased to be here and hope this will be the beginning of a new career for me here."

We each shake hands with him. A handshake is like the cover of a book. I know it's wrong to judge someone by it, but it provides an important first impression. Leon's firm shake conveys confidence.

Cynthia continues, "Our next finalist is Trenton James from New York City."

"Mr. James, welcome to Las Vegas. We're pleased to have you in the competition," Sean says.

Trenton responds with a husky voice, "Thank you."

I would've preferred to skip Trenton's bone-crushing shake. He's either overcompensating or showing off. He won't fit in here unless he makes some quick adjustments.

Cynthia says, "Our next competitor is Jayden Scott from Dallas."

"Welcome," Sean says.

In a soft voice with a Southern drawl, Jayden says, "I'm pleased to be here. I hope everyone will enjoy my novel approach to Texas-influenced cuisine."

"I'm sure we will," Sean says.

I nod my greeting and quickly pull my hand away from Jayden's clammy palm. It takes enormous self-control not to wipe my hand on my tux pants. He's clearly petrified. Hopefully, Jayden will pull it together quickly.

Reaching the last finalist, Cynthia explains, "Kai Kahale is our fourth finalist. He combines his French training with his Hawaiian heritage."

Sean smiles and says, "Mr. Kahale, I look forward to sampling your creations. They sound fascinating."

Kai offers a nod and a standard handshake that is welcome after Jayden's sweaty one.

Cynthia acts as if we've met everyone, but Sean turns his head toward the intriguing woman in blue. "Cynthia, please introduce us to our alternate."

"Of course, Mr. Cartwright. This is Cassandra Edwards. She's an accomplished, self-trained home chef who took a break from her career in law to join us for this competition."

That description makes her even more interesting.

Sean says, "Welcome. We hope this will be a truly special experience for you and the finalists."

She shakes hands with Sean, saying, "Thank you, Mr. Cartwright. I'm quite honored to be here. As a self-taught cook, I'm in awe of this group of professional chefs who will be competing."

"I'd also like you to meet my friend, Evan."

I approach, saying, "It's a pleasure to meet you. I look forward to learning more about your interest in cooking."

Cassandra's slim hand slips into mine. Her confident touch infuses warmth into my palm. As our gazes meet, I see curiosity and interest in her eyes, confirmed by the adorable blush of her cheeks. On its own volition, my thumb brushes the smooth skin on her knuckles once, then again.

I wonder where else she's blushing, but that's not for me to know. I'm in Vegas for other reasons, and so is she. I'll just avoid touching her hand again. Any temporary attraction between us will pass.

She looks down at our entwined hands. I quickly let go.

Sean explains, "We're thrilled to have you here, and please, remember to call me Sean. As I mentioned earlier, Evan will be helping with the competition. He's a food afficionado, so he's perfect for this role."

"I'm looking forward to observing your culinary talents," I say.

My gaze lingers on Cassandra for longer than necessary. Her lips turn up in a genuine smile.

Regaining my attention, Cynthia says, "It's time to move onto the stage for the announcements and toast. Cassie, you can wait here."

"No problem," she says.

I quickly offer, "Ms. Edwards, I hope you don't mind keeping me company while Sean and the others are on stage."

I should be keeping my distance from Cassandra, but my heart fell when Cynthia excluded her from the stage. I've been in the situation where people want my brother but not me in a photo with my father. It hurts to be left out. I couldn't bear to leave Cassandra standing alone as if she doesn't belong here.

Smiling, Cassandra says, "I'd enjoy that."

The finalists and Sean join the three judges on stage, and a server rings handheld chimes to get everyone's attention.

As Cassandra and I watch, standing shoulder to shoulder, I catch a whiff of her inviting perfume. It makes me smile. It's a light scent that reminds me of the rose garden back home.

When the crowd quiets, Sean says, "Welcome, everyone. We are so excited to have you with us tonight for the kick-off of our Guest Chef Competition. To begin, I would like to introduce our esteemed panel of judges, standing to my right. Please join me in welcoming Chef Gerard, Chef Holden, and Chef Indigo."

As everyone applauds, I sneak a glance at Cassandra. I'm pleased to see her smiling genuinely. That's a good sign.

When the applause dies, Sean continues, "They have been tasked with the difficult job of selecting the winner of the Guest Chef Competition. Now let me introduce our four finalists."

It's hard to concentrate on the happenings on stage when I'd rather be paying attention to the woman next to me. I'm captivated by the way her dark-blonde curls bounce when she claps and her eyes twinkle with excitement.

After introducing the competitors, Sean holds up his glass. "Please raise your glasses to toast these amazing chefs and join me in wishing them good luck in the competition. In just two weeks, one of these outstanding finalists will be named our guest chef. In the Olympic tradition of the Grand Athena, let the games begin. Cheers!"

I turn to Cassandra, whispering, "And cheers to you as well."

10

EVAN

After the toast, Cynthia ushers Cassandra and the people from the stage out onto the balcony for photos overlooking the Aegean Sea. I follow, needing fresh air and wanting to evaluate the group I'll be interacting with for the next two weeks.

When the photographer finishes taking photos, everyone except Cassandra returns to the reception. She stays behind, turning around to face the deep-blue water that's illuminated by glowing torches. Lingering, I find myself captivated by her beautiful, petite body and the positive energy emanating from her. She doesn't notice my quiet approach, so I gently tap her shoulder, softly saying, "It's quite the spectacle, isn't it?"

As I move my hand from her shoulder to the balcony rail, she laughs and says, "That's an interesting choice of words for your friend's hotel."

"I guess it is, but Las Vegas always strikes me as rather comical with its neon versions of Italy, France, Greece, and New York City all within a few city blocks."

"I know what you mean, but somehow, it's still mesmerizing and glamorous. It's like living in an amusement park where they promise that all your dreams can come true, if only temporarily. Doesn't everyone need that feeling sometimes?"

I turn away from the lights to stare at Cassandra. "Yes, we do. Forgive me if you find my next question too personal, but Cassandra, are you okay being the alternate?"

"You can call me Cassie. Everyone does."

I shake my head. "I'm not everyone. If you don't mind, I'd prefer to call you Cassandra."

Looking amused, she replies, "It's strange. I've never liked the formality of my full name, but you make it sound so elegant. You're welcome to call me Cassandra."

Smiling, I repeat my earlier question. "So how are you doing with the role of alternate? You tensed up when they asked you to wait at the base of the stairs rather than join the finalists for the introductions."

"I'm fine. It's an honor to be here. Besides, I have the easy part—no pressure. I'm watching from the sidelines and taking it all in."

I lightly clap my hands. "Well done. Bravo."

Raising her eyebrows in indignation, Cassandra asks, "Are you mocking me? Did I say something wrong?"

I turn back toward the water and rest my arms on the railing, letting out a sigh. "No, but speaking from experience, your words sounded like a well-rehearsed answer crafted to cover up your real feelings. Don't get me wrong. I know it's an amazing opportunity to be one of the top five selected to be here, but aren't you a lawyer?"

Confused, Cassandra answers, "Yes, but why does that matter?"

"Then you were probably a top student in school and are already successful at work. So, I'd bet that you're not used to being the backup. My guess is that you're accustomed to being in on the action. Therefore, I suspect it's particularly hard for you to be part of all the fanfare but not able to experience the adrenaline rush of the competition itself."

"Wow. I'm not sure what to say."

"Am I right?"

"That's pretty insightful. Everyone else keeps congratulating me, so I've been politely responding that being here is an honor. And I *am* honored. On the one hand, it's exciting to have any role in this competition. On the other, I'm disappointed. At one point tonight, I've even wondered if it would have been easier not to be here at all."

Turning toward her as she gazes over the water, I say, "Let's just say I know what it's like to play the backup role too."

Cassandra has no idea who I am, which is refreshing, but a part of me wants to explain why I understand her situation so well. It's too soon though. I can't share more when I don't know her. Instead, I give her time to process what I've said.

She turns, and our eyes lock, sending a bolt of electricity through me. Her body starts to shiver, making me wonder if she feels it too.

Unsure, I ask, "Are you cold?"

Turning, she puts her back to the balcony, eyes staring at infinity. "Not really. I was just thinking, but we should go inside. I'm sure Cynthia is looking for me by now."

She's right. I should walk away now, but I don't. Instead, I step in front of her, lifting her chin with my fingers. She looks up, and I search her eyes with mine. I'm not sure what I'm looking for as I lean my head closer to hers. Our lips are so close I can feel her warm breath.

"Cassandra, are you still out here? We need you for photos," Cynthia calls out.

As we step apart, there's a confused look on Cassandra's face. She mutters, "We're not supposed to interact with the judges. I don't want to get in trouble or be sent home for being alone with you."

I should thank Cynthia for stopping us from taking this further. I'm here to clear my head and plan my future—not to become entangled with a woman, no matter how much I'm drawn to her.

Nevertheless, she has nothing to feel bad about. In an uncharacteristic move for me, I tuck a lock of her hair behind her ear as I whisper, "You didn't do anything wrong. We were just talking, and I'm not a judge anyway. Take a deep breath, and let's go back inside."

She nods slowly but doesn't look convinced. Her obvious regret bothers me, which is odd. I'm not a bad guy, but it isn't like me to give her reaction a second thought. There are plenty of other women who would be at my side with the snap of my fingers. But for some reason, she's different, and I'm not sure why. Whatever her allure is, I want more of Cassandra Edwards, but I can't let that happen.

Placing my hand on the small of her back, I guide her through the French doors and back into Trendz.

Touching her again was a mistake. She's too enticing. If my break from women is going to last, I bloody well can't let myself do that again even as a polite gesture.

11

EVAN

Sean invited me to dinner with the three judges and him, but I declined. It's easy enough to avoid revealing who I really am in a crowd, but harder at a dinner for five. Instead, I'm happily exploring the Athena on my own. I know Sean has security keeping an eye on me, but I doubt anyone else would notice. It's a rare treat to be able to blend in with a crowd like any other tourist, so I'm taking advantage of the opportunity.

As I walk by the Athena's Restaurant Row, an aroma of chocolate wafts past my nose. I search for its source and see a sign advertising: **The Ultimate Chocolate Bar—Drinks & Desserts.**

Being a chocoholic, a bar dedicated to chocolate grabs my attention, so I step inside for a closer look. It's dimly lit with a golden glow. Soft music plays in the background. Small tables fill the left side while a long cherrywood bar with a black granite top fills the length on the right.

My eyes catch the unusual artwork behind the bar. At first, it looks like a three-dimensional painting, or possibly a sculpture, of chocolate flowing from the ceiling down to the top surface of the back bar. Then I see actual movement. I'm surprised to be looking at an enormous chocolate waterfall. What a unique feature!

It's early for dessert, so the place isn't crowded, but as I scan the long bar, my gaze lands on the back of a woman's head. Her long, wavy blonde hair is familiar. I walk slowly toward her and stop a couple of chairs away to leave a comfortable space between us.

"Cassandra, is that you?"

After the awkwardness on the balcony, I'm not sure if she'll welcome my presence. She turns, and to my relief, smiles even though her eyes hint at confusion.

"Hello, Evan. What are you doing here?"

"The scent of chocolate drew me in. Then I saw you and wanted to say hello. Would you mind if I join you? Sean is busy dealing with the judges, so I'm on my own and would love company."

"Have a seat. It's nice to see a familiar face. I don't know anyone in Vegas except for the people I met today."

I slip onto the bar chair to her right. "Thanks. What are you drinking?"

She slides a cocktail menu toward me. Picking it up, I see that martinis come in a variety of unusual flavors such as mint chocolate, chocolate strawberry, chocolate caramel, and for the purists, Just Chocolate.

Her hand brushes over the back of mine as her index finger points near the bottom of the menu.

"This one," she says.

Her welcome touch distracts me from what she's saying. Fortunately, her finger is still hovering near the Just Chocolate martini, so I ask, "Is it good?"

"I like it. Here, you should try it," she says, pushing her martini glass toward me.

Raising the glass to my lips, I watch her over the rim as I taste the dark concoction. Drinking from her glass, the corners of my mouth turn up, enjoying that my lips are where hers have been.

"That's quite nice. What's in it?" I ask, softly.

"The bartender said it's chocolate liqueur, vodka, and a dash of vanilla. Apparently, most chocolate martinis have cream, but they went for a plainer version to match the Just Chocolate name."

Holding up two fingers, I signal to the bartender for a couple of the chocolatey beverages. Turning back to Cassandra, I ask, "Did you order a dessert?"

"Not yet. I've been trying to decide between the chocolate rum cake with pecans and the chocolate waterfall," she says, flipping the menu over to the dessert side.

I place my arm on the back of her chair and lean closer to see the options. "If you pick the waterfall, do they let you behind the bar to spoon chocolate off the wall?"

She laughs and swats my shoulder, saying, "Of course not, silly. They bring you a miniature, tabletop version of the chocolate water-fall. It sounds like fun, but it's for two people, so it didn't really make sense for me to order it."

"We'll share it. Problem solved."

"You don't mind?" she asks, her eyes sparkling with delight.

"You're welcome to force me to eat chocolate anytime," I chuckle, motioning for the bartender, who appears quickly.

"What can I get for you?" he asks as he puts the two drinks I ordered in front of us.

"We'd like to share the chocolate waterfall," I say.

"Excellent choice. You may each choose two dippers from the list at the bottom of the menu. Miss, what would you like?"

Cassandra says, "Oh, they all sound fabulous. If I can only select two, they would be the candied orange peel and homemade marsh-mallows."

"Pick for me too. I can't decide," I say.

"Let's see. Strawberries and chocolate are a classic combo. Oh, and a savory dipper sounds good. Would the peppered bacon strips be okay with you?"

"Absolutely."

I couldn't care less what she selects as long as she keeps smiling.

"I'm like a child in a candy store. This is such an unexpected place. I've never heard of a chocolate bar before."

"Neither have I, but the world needs more bars like this. We also need more people with your enthusiasm for life."

"I hate to disappoint you, but I'm not usually this exuberant. For the last few years, all I've done is work. This is my first vacation in forever and to have it be part of a cooking competition is a dream. I promised myself that I'd enjoy every minute and not think about work for two entire weeks. It's so freeing. I can't stop smiling."

"It's contagious. You have me smiling too."

"That's a good thing. You said you're a chocoholic. What's your favorite chocolate dessert?" she asks.

"I've yet to encounter one I didn't like. What about you?"

"Same here. It's impossible to go wrong with chocolate. I am curious about something though. Based on your accent, I don't think you grew up here. So, how did you and Sean meet?"

"Uni. I came to the US to study business on the East Coast. We met at a party and then learned we had several classes together. Later, we became roommates and have been best mates ever since."

"That sounds like how I am with my bestie. Lowri and I met in law school and have been there for each other since then. I don't know what I'd do without her."

"Loyal friends are irreplaceable. What about your boyfriend? Is he excited you're here?"

I mentally chastise myself for the rather lame attempt to find out if she's in a relationship.

"No boyfriend. My last one wasn't particularly supportive, so I'm not in a hurry to find another. What about you? Do you have a glamorous model waiting for you at home?"

Maybe she *is* interested.

"There's no one special. I'm at a crossroads of sorts, so it's not a good time to be involved with anyone. I'm concentrating on my friendships for now, so I'm here to help Sean."

"I admire that you're helping your friend while you consider which road to take. I'm a tad burned out at work, so I'm here to reenergize Being at the competition is a fantasy that I'm hoping will give me the strength to deal with the stress of my real job."

A darkness, and if I'm reading it correctly, a sense of dread flashes across her face, but she hides it quickly with a smile that sadly doesn't reach her eyes.

Wanting to take away her worrisome thoughts, I say, "It sounds like we both have some serious rubbish we're dealing with, but let's put it aside for now and enjoy this magnificent chocolate fountain that just appeared."

Chocolate is said to improve one's mood. For Cassandra, it seems that even the sight of chocolate is a powerful drug because her grin goes from ear to ear as she studies the melted version flow down the miniature wall into a small trough.

"For some reason, I have this overwhelming desire to stick my finger into it."

I laugh. "Me too. Let's do it."

We each move our index finger close to the little wall, letting the warm chocolate cover the tips of our fingers. I bring mine to my lips for a quick taste, but to my utter pleasure, she lifts her finger to her mouth and slowly sucks the chocolate off.

Good god! She's killing me, and I don't think it's intentional, which makes it even hotter.

"This chocolate is definitely Swiss. It's spectacular, don't you think?" she asks.

"It is," I say, shifting uneasily on my barstool to readjust.

"What should we dip next? I'm thinking the bacon."

She takes a bite, moaning, "Mmmm. That's heavenly."

"Let me help." Using my thumb, I wipe a drip of chocolate off her chin. "That's better. Now, close your eyes. Let me surprise you with the next combination," I say.

I select a small, square marshmallow because it was one of her first choices. I coat it in chocolate and feed it to her.

She takes the quickly melting combo of fluff and liquid chocolate into her waiting mouth.

Sighing, she says, "That's amazing. Homemade marshmallows are nothing like the rubbery store-bought ones. These are tender and luscious."

All I can think is that it's her chocolate-coated lips that are what would be tender and luscious.

"Whoever thought of the concept for this place should get a raise. It's brilliant," she says.

"I agree. Wait a minute. Did the music change?" I ask.

We both turn our heads to the front of the restaurant. There's a piano hidden in a corner. I didn't notice it when I arrived. Now, a man is seated on the bench, playing a song about chocolate. How appropriate.

"Would you like to dance?" I ask.

"There's no dance floor."

"Who cares? No one will mind."

"Why not?"

I guide Cassandra to an open area and pull her close. She fits against me perfectly—like a warm glove on a cold winter's night. We glide to the soft, slow music, and I whisper in her ear, "You dance very well."

"There aren't many opportunities now, but I've always loved to dance."

I hear a longing in her voice. She may be a successful lawyer, but I'm starting to think her life isn't full of enough pleasure.

For the rest of the song, I silently inhale the soft rose and vanilla scent left by her shampoo and savor the softness of her body where we touch. There's no explanation for the way she makes me feel. We barely know each other, yet I want us to spend more time together. It's confounding. I've never felt this type of attraction or connection before.

The song ends too soon. I don't want to let her go, but tonight, I'm being a gentleman, so I step away. "Thank you for keeping me company this evening."

"It's been wonderful, but I need some sleep if I'm going to be awake during the competition tomorrow. I should head back to my room now."

"I understand. Let me walk you there."

"That's not necessary."

"It is. You're alone here. Someone should make sure you make it safely to your room."

"That's very considerate. Just to be clear though, I'm not inviting you in." She winks.

"As sad as that is, I'm not asking you to."

I escort Cassandra to her room and give her a quick hug good-night, departing quickly before I change my mind about wanting to go inside with her.

Walking away, I remind myself that I'll have to settle for us becoming friends, but I desire something more.

12

EVAN

Yesterday, I researched my new idea for a charity in hopes of sketching out a plan for myself. After hours in front of my laptop trying to find data, I'd taken a few steps forward but almost as many backward because I hit dead ends. Originally, I'd planned to dive back in today, but something is nagging me about the path I'm heading down. I need to step back, clear my head, and then look at the big picture again.

I need to concentrate on something else for a few hours, so I arrive at Sean's office at 7 a.m. to insist on helping him sort out his F&B mess. He initially protests but relents when I remind him that I have an MBA and nothing better to do this morning. We bury our heads in the documentation, each making our own notes while consuming copious amounts of caffeinated liquid—coffee for him, tea for me.

Ring. Ring. Ring.

We both jerk at the interruption.

"Shit, it's my private line," Sean says.

"Hello, this is Sean," he answers on speakerphone.

"It's Larry."

"When the Chief of Police phones at this early hour, it's usually not a social call."

"It's not. We have more information on Chef Bernard's car crash."

"What did you learn?"

"One of your employees mentioned that Chef Bernard was complaining about a sports injury. We checked with the chef's doctors, but none of them prescribed any opioids to her. The coroner also said the chef must have taken the pills before leaving the Athena. Otherwise, they wouldn't have had time to take effect."

"What does this mean?"

"One explanation is that someone at the event gave her the pills, and she took them willingly. However, another possibility is that someone spiked her drink at your reception. I'm not saying that's what happened, but we need to rule it out."

The police chief's theories seem logical to me, but Sean furrows his brows in confusion and disbelief.

"Why would someone do that? It doesn't make any sense," Sean says as he stands and begins pacing.

"We don't know, but I promised to keep you posted, so don't shoot the messenger."

Running his fingers through his hair, Sean says, "I just can't imagine anyone would've wanted to harm Allison."

Clearly, this is weighing heavily on him. The bags under his eyes evidence his lack of sleep.

"At this point, we haven't found any reason for someone to specifically target Ms. Bernard. Would someone want to sabotage the Guest Chef Competition to target you or the Grand Athena's reputation?"

"I highly doubt that. I can think of other more impactful ways to attack the Athena."

"It's more likely that she took the pills intentionally, but give it some thought and watch your back."

"I will. Goodbye."

I'm worried about my friend. He needs my help. His life's more cocked up than mine.

Of course, I almost overcomplicated mine on the balcony last night. Based on what I've seen so far, Cassandra doesn't seem the type for a quick fling. I'm certainly not interested in more, and she doesn't need someone who is struggling with his own issues. We're going to be stuck watching the competition together though, so I'll need to be careful not to go so near the line again.

Wait a minute. Cassandra will be closely monitoring the competition. I have a brilliant idea. If Sean will let me confide in Cassandra, she could be a second set of eyes. As an attorney, she's bound by various ethical obligations, so we can trust her to maintain what we share in confidence. If something strange is going on with expenses or if someone is sabotaging the competition, she may spot something. She'd also be able to ask innocuous questions about how things are run at the Athena without anyone giving her a second thought.

I'm about to ask Sean what he thinks of my idea when he's called away to meet with the casino manager about some problem. I'll have to ask him later.

13

CASSIE

At 10 a.m., everyone meets in the Trendz kitchen for the prep segment of the Poolside Dip event.

My eyes sweep the room, finding Evan standing on the other side, watching. He spots me and nods. I automatically smile but know I have to keep my distance. Sharing chocolate with him last night was the best evening I've spent with a man in years, but that's because there were no expectations or pressure. Any zing I felt was just the martinis talking. Evan and I are just new friends. It can't be more.

Someone bumps into me, letting me know I need to move. Stepping to the side, I watch the staff scurry around. The camera operators ready their equipment, hot lights illuminate the kitchen, and an infectious tension fills the air around the finalists.

My shoulders tense as I watch Trenton repeatedly stretch his arms as if readying for a tough workout. Kai stares at his hands, willing them to stop clenching and unclenching, and Jayden nervously rearranges the cooking utensils at his workstation. Watching a few teardrop-shaped beads of sweat trickle down Jayden's forehead, I wonder if they're from the bright lights or nerves. Even Leon, the calmest of the group, is taking slow, deep breaths.

I secretly consider what it would be like standing at one of the stations readying to prep a dip myself. It gives me goosebumps to know how close I came to that opportunity.

Cynthia and Amy give last-minute instructions, and the finalists receive a ten-minute warning before filming starts. It's strange to stand on the sideline while everyone is getting ready. I walk over to one of the tables that has supplies and dishes to straighten things up, but Amy pulls me back. She explains that the finalists must do all the preparation themselves. I mumble an apology and move behind the camera crew so that I won't be in the way.

Sebastian, the director, shouts, "Action!"

Amy lights up with a smile. She welcomes everyone to the cooking competition and introduces the chefs. A giant timer on the right wall is set to one hour. Amy explains that before time runs out, the finalists must create one finished dip and prepare a second set of ingredients for making the dip at the pool during the demo.

It quickly becomes clear that each finalist has a different style and personality when it comes to their cooking. Trenton, calmer now, organizes his work with each ingredient laid out separately and starts methodically prepping them one at a time. Jayden, on the other hand, is running back and forth to the pantry and haphazardly piling things on his station, not leaving much space to work. Has he never heard the term *mise en place*?

When the timer goes off, everyone stops working. The finalists place their food for the demo on carts and roll them into the walk-in refrigerator.

Amy announces that the demonstrations start at two this after-noon, but we must be there forty-five minutes early to make sure everything is set up properly.

Looking at my TekCuff, I have almost two hours for lunch. I'm dying to try the Athena's Crêpery. Supposedly, it serves savory crêpes that rival those in France. My stomach growls as I hurry toward the exit.

Before I make it out the door, I cross paths with Evan. He reaches toward me, resting his hand gently on my upper arm. When I stop, his hand sadly drops away. He bends down, placing his mouth close to my ear. His breath tickles my skin as he whispers, "Can we meet for lunch? There's something I'd like to discuss with you away from potential eavesdroppers. I'll send directions to your TekCuff."

My temperature rises every time he's near me. While lunch with him would be fun, I need to keep a professional distance, or I'll risk giving into his charm. He may not be a judge, but he's officially overseeing the competition. A repeat of last night's almost kiss wouldn't be smart. If he really has anything important to discuss with me, we can talk at the pool this afternoon.

Determined to follow my plan, I walk down the stairs and around the corner toward the Crêpery. On the way, my TekCuff vibrates. It's a voice message. Evan says, "Take a water taxi to the Santorini Tower. Christian will be waiting to escort you to our lunch destination. He's been instructed to wait until you arrive, so please don't keep him standing there for too long. Ciao."

My whole body tenses. Evan's message essentially orders me to show up at the Santorini Tower. How dare he think he can tell me what to do? But, as an image of his glimmering eyes and devilish smile pops into my head, my tension surprisingly evaporates. I have to admit there's something sexy about Evan's insistent invitation.

Should I follow his instructions? No, I have no desire to be bossed around, at least not outside the bedroom—and even there, only sometimes. Who am I kidding? I haven't let myself get close enough to anyone to share a bed in a while.

A couple of months after my parents died, I took another emotional hit that's had a lasting impact. My boyfriend, Ben, dumped me, saying I wasn't fun anymore. What the hell? I'd just buried my parents. He was an asshole, but it was a good lesson. Relationships aren't worth it because loss follows love, and the loss part is too painful.

Why am I thinking about love, sex, and sad stuff at the same time? I need to focus on the reason I'm here.

It's not like I'm competing. I'm here for the adventure. As Cynthia has made clear, I'm Just-in-Case Cassie, the spare who's "observing." Besides, if I don't show up, Evan made it sound like Christian will be stuck waiting for me for the rest of the day. He can't really mean that, can he?

At a minimum, I should relieve Christian of his duty, so I quicken my steps and find a water taxi. Sure enough, Christian is standing at the elevators for the Santorini Tower, hands clasped in front of him. When he sees me, his face lights up.

"Christian, it's so good to see you. Can you please give Evan a message for me?"

Shaking his head, he turns to summon the elevator and responds, "I'm sorry, but my instructions are to take you to him. Please follow me."

A little louder than intended, I quickly say, "Oh, no! I can't have lunch with him. I just wanted you to thank him for the invitation. Please give him my regrets."

Christian shakes his head again, accompanied by a shoulder shrug and upturned palms. "I'm sorry, but I can't do that. I'm to stay here until you agree to have lunch with him."

Who does Evan think he is? I was on the fence about whether to have lunch with him, but now he's going to see my stubborn streak. With animated arms, I declare, "That's ridiculous. I'm not going to be goaded into anything. As I said, I appreciate the invitation, but I can't join him for lunch. Please let him know."

Clearly, Christian is accustomed to dealing with frustrated guests because my reply doesn't faze his determination. As if sharing a secret between friends, Christian calmly says, "Ms. Edwards, please follow me and give him your message in person. He's Mr. Cartwright's best friend, and I don't want to lose my job."

Squinting with confusion and incredulity, I matter-of-factly state, "If you would lose your job merely because I choose not to have lunch with Mr. Cartwright's best friend, then that doesn't speak very well for either man!"

Panic crosses Christian's face. "Oh, no! That's not what I meant. Mr. Cartwright is a wonderful person and very professional, and his friend is a considerate man."

I fold my arms. "Then why are you worried about losing your job?"

"Please forgive my exaggeration. Mr. Cartwright expects me to take care of our VIPs' requests. I merely meant to be persuasive, but I've given the wrong impression and am ruining what Evan intended to be a lovely surprise. I'd be grateful if you would accompany me to the lunch location. I guarantee that no one will force you to stay, but your host has gone to a lot of trouble. It would be sad to see his efforts go to waste."

Waving his explanation off, I say, "This whole thing is ludicrous, but I'll tell Evan myself. This is not your fault. Please take me to him."

"Thank you. Right this way." Christian places his palm over the hand scanner, and the elevator doors open. Without another word, we're transported to the penthouse level of the Santorini Tower. When the elevator stops, Christian gestures for me to exit.

I step into the foyer of a magnificent, two-story suite overlooking the Las Vegas Strip. Christian says, "Welcome to the Grand Monarch Suite. Lunch is set up on the outdoor balcony. This way, please."

With confident strides, I follow him, ready to say my piece, but I'm the one with butterflies circling inside because every time I'm near Evan, something about him draws me closer. It's a chemistry that's new to me.

Walking onto the balcony, I'm overwhelmed by the fairytale-like setting. Fine white china with silver rims and intricately cut crystal glasses adorn a table for two covered with pale-lilac linens with faint butterflies woven into the fabric. Soft yellow, white, and lavender roses fill the center of the table. It's the epitome of spring.

Evan stands on the other side of the table. He's beyond handsome in his perfectly tailored, khaki linen pants and dark-blue, collared shirt, having lost the tie from earlier and unfastened the top two buttons.

His mischievously sparkling eyes lock on mine and reel me in, causing me to question my plan to leave. When he looks at me like that, all I want to do is kiss him.

Why am I fighting this so hard? We are two adults. What's wrong with a nice lunch on the balcony of the most beautiful suite I've ever seen? Why not see where this goes? I hear Lowri in my ear, saying, "If someone catches your eye, give him a chance." And, damn, he has definitely caught my attention.

I know what's wrong. Sure, I'm annoyed at his insistence that I have lunch with him, but that's not the only problem. I've put up walls to protect myself and worked hard to become a strong, independent woman so I won't ever feel the pain of losing someone I care about or need to rely on someone else for a secure future. That's why none of my more recent attempts at dating have worked out. I pushed the men away before things could become serious.

But something is different with Evan. I'm trying to push him away before we've even had a date. It must be this new adventure that has me on edge. I need to let loose, live a little, and quit over-thinking everything.

I should stay. It's just lunch with a new friend—albeit one who almost melted my panties off with an almost kiss last night. Who knew that could happen?

Christian says, "Sir, Ms. Edwards is here. Can I be of further service?"

"No. That's all. Thank you very much."

I may be staying for lunch, but I need an escape, so I say, "Christian, could you return here at 12:45 to show me the way to the pool for the demos?"

"Of course, Ms. Edwards. Have a wonderful lunch."

Christian leaves as I say, "I'm not sure I should be here."

"Why? Are you afraid to be alone with me? Is that why you wanted Christian to return at a set time?"

I blurt out, "First, I don't appreciate being essentially ordered to be here, and second, it doesn't seem appropriate. I don't know anything about you, and here I am in your hotel room. They took away all my electronic devices, so I can't even google you. And I don't have any friends in Vegas to make sure I'm okay. This has horror movie written all over it. Besides, I'm here for the competition, so I need to focus on it."

Evan frowns. "I apologize. You always have a choice. I only

wanted to ensure that you took my invitation seriously and were safely escorted here. I'll be more careful with my wording next time."

"Thank you."

"And I understand your concerns. I have a little sister. It's unfair, but I know women need to be careful. I can assure you that you have nothing to fear. I'll be on my best behavior during lunch, and Christian will be back to check on you. As for your concerns about my relationship with the competition, please remember that I'm not a judge. You're not a finalist."

"I know, but I need to be professional."

"I understand, but we're both adults, and based on our chat last night, we enjoy each other's company. Let's have lunch and entertain each other with interesting conversation. A chef such as yourself would never want to waste amazing food, right?"

"It *would* be tragic to let good food to go to waste."

"Brilliant. Please have a seat. Just so you know, we aren't actually alone. The suite's private chef, Eduardo, is in the kitchen preparing lunch for us."

Perhaps I overreacted, but I'd rather be safe.

Eduardo appears with two plates and explains, "I'm pleased to serve you a salad composed of spring greens tossed with a light lemon vinaigrette and adorned with a rainbow of radish discs, asparagus tips, multicolor carrot curls, thinly sliced avocado wedges, fresh strawberries, and edible flowers. Please enjoy."

"Evan, this looks like a work of colorful spring art."

"It does. Aren't you glad you didn't skip lunch? Look what you would've missed." He winks, sporting a devilish grin.

"It would have been a great loss," I tease.

"From your application, I learned that you work hard at your law firm, and you love cooking. What else should I know about you?"

"Work fills most of my waking hours, so I'm not sure there's much more to tell."

"What would be your perfect vacation?"

"That's easy. I'd be sitting by the beach with a frozen, fruity drink and a romance or mystery book."

"Does that mean you like to travel?"

"I look forward to the opportunity to travel more. I've always dreamed of taking time off to sample the actual food and wine of Europe rather than just the American version. Tell me about you."

After wiping his mouth with the linen napkin, Evan says, "I'm not that interesting."

"Come on. Turnabout is fair play." I set my fork on my plate with a soft clink and fold my arms on the edge of the table, fixing my full attention on him.

"What do you mean?"

"I shared things about me. You have to do the same." I shrug.

Leaning back, Evan contemplates my question more seriously. "Fair enough. Let's see. Like you, I like to travel and go to beaches. While I'm here, I'll play a few games of blackjack. I work in the family business. Our family is going through some changes soon, so I'm taking a short break before they happen."

"What type of changes?

"My father is about to retire, and my brother is marrying soon."

"Who will take over as head of the business?"

"My older brother."

As I'm about to follow up about what his family's business is, Eduardo presents a beautiful second course consisting of a filet of trout topped with finely crushed pecans and lemon butter served with a side of roasted broccolini with red pepper flakes.

He says, "This oaked Chardonnay should be the perfect complement to the trout. Please enjoy."

"Mmmm. This is delicious," I say.

"I'm glad a chef such as yourself approves." Evan looks amused as he raises his glass for a sip of wine.

I laugh. "Don't be funny. You know I'm not technically a chef. Besides, while I suspect the professional chefs in the competition are snobbier than I am, even they would approve of Eduardo's excellent meal."

"Given you made the top five for this competition, you *are* a real chef."

"Thank you for the compliment, but I don't think being the alternate in this competition magically elevates me to chef status."

"Humor me. Let me think of you that way. And while we're talking about chefs, I'm curious about something. Do chefs have to like all foods?"

"That's an interesting question. I think most chefs are willing to try almost anything. I can't stand mayonnaise, though, and the idea of eating raw fish isn't appealing, so no sushi for me. What about you? Are there foods you avoid?"

"My parents have always expected me to be polite and eat any and everything put before me. But if given the choice, I would never eat aubergine or Brussels sprouts. And to be honest, I'm not a fan of mayonnaise either."

"Really? I've always thought I was the only person in the world who doesn't like mayo. Now I don't feel so alone." I laugh.

"You're definitely not alone."

"Did you say your dad is retiring soon?"

He leans forward as if imparting a secret, his elbows resting on the table. His shirt sleeves are rolled up, exposing beautiful, toned forearms. But rather than share a confidence, he reaches for my face. His thumb gently traces the plump curve of my lower lip.

I quiver from his touch.

"I didn't want to risk the butter dripping onto your shirt," he says, but his husky voice belies his words. I think he just wanted an excuse to touch me, and I'm so glad he found one.

"Thanks," I murmur, reaching for my napkin as he pulls away.

"Yes, my dad is planning to retire soon."

My lips are still warm from Evan's touch, and his eyes hold mine captive, which makes it almost impossible to carry on a conversation, but I manage to ask, "What does he plan to do when he retires?"

"Travel and continue their charity work, I think."

"That sounds great. You mentioned that you have a brother and a sister, right?"

"Yes, I have an older brother, Xander, and younger sister, Bri. Do you have any siblings?"

"No. It's just me."

"Did you want a sibling?"

"Not necessarily. My life was normal to me. Are you and your siblings throwing a retirement party for your father?"

"There will be a celebration. My brother's wedding will be around the same time, so it'll be busy."

Having finished eating, I lean forward, resting my arms on the table. "It sounds like an exciting time for your family."

"To be honest, it'll be overwhelming, but hopefully, all the events will go as planned. It's too bad you won't be there. It would be the perfect opportunity to travel and sample European food and wine," Evan says, chuckling.

"That would be fun. Someday, I'll visit Europe." My heart stutters, wishing Evan were inviting me, but that wouldn't make any sense. We just met.

Gazing directly into my eyes, Evan takes my hand, raising it to his lips. He gives it a soft kiss and caresses it with his thumb, making me tremble as electricity charges through me.

"I'm sure you will visit Europe. Who knows, our paths could cross again when you do."

Without thinking, I nod.

Squeezing my hand, Evan continues, "I'm facing some difficult business choices, so it's been hard for me to relax lately. Lunch with you today has been like a welcome breath of fresh air. You make me smile and think about much more pleasant things."

"I'm glad. This competition is giving me a reprieve from a stressful work situation, so I understand. Let's focus on less stressful topics. Tell me about where you're from."

Evan gently releases my hand and takes a sip of wine. I miss the warmth of his touch.

"My home country is an island just south of France, near Italy. Our food is heavily influenced by their cuisines, and being an island, seafood is commonplace."

"I would be in food heaven there. But I'm curious. If you're so close to France and Italy, how do you explain your accent? I'd assumed you were British."

"That always confuses people. Britain played a significant role in our history, so English is the national language, and the accent remains prevalent. I also went to boarding school in London, which reinforced it."

"Tell me more. What's the landscape like?"

"It's varied. We have citrus orchards, vineyards, and grazing land for cattle and sheep. Our island is also known for its beautiful beaches."

I sigh. "I think I'd love it."

"You said you don't have any siblings. Do you see your parents often?"

My eyes grow weepy. "No, they died in an accident a few years ago. I'm on my own."

"You have my sincere condolences. They must have been proud of you though."

"Yes. I followed in their footsteps. They were both lawyers, dedicated to their work night and day."

"When you speak about your work in law, there's no passion in your voice. But when you talk about food and cooking, your eyes sparkle and your face lights up like a carnival ride. Why is that?"

"My work as a lawyer pays the bills and would make my parents proud. Cooking is a hobby."

"I see. When I invited you to lunch, I had two motives: to get to know you and to ask you about a confidential matter. Sean may need someone who is involved in the competition to help him look into something. I thought of you because, as a lawyer, you would keep requests confidential."

"Confidentiality applies to our clients, and Sean is not a client. Of course, if someone asks me to keep a secret, I will if I legally can. But to give legal advice, our law firm requires that a client formally hire us. I'd love to help Sean if he needs me, but if it involves legal advice, I can't help without the request going through my law firm. Does that make sense?"

"It does. I should have thought of that. Forget I said anything. He'll find another solution."

I admire the loyalty he shows Sean, who apparently needs Evan's help. I'd do the same for Lowri in a heartbeat. Evan is also dealing with something tough at work just as I am. I can't help but wonder if we aren't kindred spirits.

Eduardo reappears with raspberry sorbet and a shot glass of limoncello to pour on top. Is it the alcohol that's making me wish I could take the trip with Evan? It's good I'm not actually competing after wine and limoncello for lunch!

"We have a little time before Christian returns. Let's move to the sitting area and watch the people strolling along the Strip."

He reaches to pull me into a hug, but I stop him, placing my hand gently on his chest. He looks at me with confusion, but I don't want a hug. He's showered me with attention, listened and shown me empathy, and revved me up with every single word he's spoken in his hot-as-hell accent. What I want is his lips on mine. Emboldened by the wine with lunch, I step closer, tentatively kissing his lips— softly and slowly. My heart plummets when he doesn't immediately reciprocate. I pull my mouth away slightly. Just then, his hand dives into my hair, pulling my face flush to his and crashing his mouth against mine. He kisses me with a need and fervor that I've never experienced before.

As I lean into him, he tilts his head and deepens the kiss. Our tongues dance as Evan's other hand runs up and down my arm. Without thinking, I wrap my arm around his neck, holding on for dear life as our kiss intensifies beyond what I thought was possible. His teeth lightly nip my lower lip as his hand slides under my knees, and he carries me to the couch, slowly sitting with me on his lap. My eyes close as his tongue teases my earlobe. It tickles and sends waves of need through me. As I tilt my head back to let Evan taste my neck, I hear footsteps.

Damn. I quickly scoot off Evan's lap, smoothing my hair.

Christian appears a second later, saying, "Pardon me, but it's time for me to escort the two of you to the pool for the demon- strations."

"Christian, you are quite prompt. I *usually* admire that. Please escort Ms. Edwards to the pool. I need to handle a couple of things first. I'll meet you there shortly. Cassandra, let me walk you to the door."

"I'm ready to kill the next person who interrupts us," Evan whispers into my ear.

I laugh. "I think they're protecting me from myself."

"Thanks for having lunch with me. I'm glad you changed your mind."

"Me too."

As I walk away with Christian, I can't stop smiling.

"It seems like you enjoyed lunch, not that it's any of my business."

"Yes, lunch was nice."

Did I just say that? Really? I just called my best date in recent memory "nice." Had I been of a mind to share my true thoughts, I would've said lunch was amazing, delicious, exhilarating, pulse-pounding, and fucking great, but those thoughts are best kept to myself. As the elevator descends, I wish there could be more "nice" lunches in the near future, but I'm not sure that's a good idea.

Evan will be going home to Europe soon, and I'll never see him again. That ending has hurt written all over it.

14

CASSIE

For a sun and beach lover, the Athena's pool area is like walking into heaven on earth. I take a couple of steps and stop to absorb the vibrant, sunny surroundings filled with swimsuit-clad partiers and upbeat music mixed with the hum of poolside conversations.

The crystal-blue pools glimmer like diamonds as the sunlight bounces off the water's surface, and iconic Greek ruins rise from the pools' depths as if they're floating on the water. From my college art history course, I recognize that the rectangular group of columns in the far pool forms a replica of the Parthenon, and the columns atop a curved marble arch in the pool to my right must be the Arch of Hadrian.

Some of the columns have waterfalls flowing from their precipices, drenching couples, who embrace in the pools below. Watching the happy couples kiss makes me wish Christian hadn't interrupted Evan and me.

I felt like a teenager whose parents came home early when Cynthia interrupted our almost kiss last night and again when Christian walked in on us today. Even though Evan isn't a judge and there's no prohibition on us dating, it still makes me nervous. I need to push him away, but it's unnerving that he so easily finds weaknesses in my protective shield. He makes me want to let him in, and that scares me.

My walls are in place for a reason. I need to remember that.

A server in a blue and white, filmy minidress carrying a tray of frozen drinks with bright-blue straws brushes by me. It ends the debate I'm having with myself and reminds me I've been standing here too long. This is not the place for such serious thought.

Letting the party vibe envelop me, I vow to enjoy a beautiful afternoon at the pool. As my eyes linger on the white lounge chairs that look like comfy beds, I want to stretch out on one. Even better, I could sample a frozen, fruity concoction and relax in one of the private cabanas that line one side of the pool area.

Turning my head to the right, I see the film crew moving equipment into place for the demo. The finalists are already working at the tables beneath each of four small pergolas draped with gauzy white fabric. Given the pressure they're under, every second is needed to prepare. I weave my way through the small crowd of curious onlookers. Nearing the chefs, I'm met by aromas of sautéing garlic and fresh, minced herbs—not the usual poolside scents, but nonetheless welcome.

Those thoughts vanish when the music suddenly stops, and my attention is drawn to Amy as she announces the Poolside Dip demos will start at 2 p.m.

I'd love to be standing under one of the pergolas chopping cilantro and squeezing limes to demo my favorite dip. That thought vanishes when I sense someone approaching from behind.

Evan whispers in my ear, "See, aren't you glad you didn't skip lunch with me? You still had plenty of time to make it to the demo." His breath skidding across my ear sends tingling sensations running through my body and soaking my underwear yet again. Damn, I should have packed more.

I turn, whispering, "Stop that."

"Stop what? I merely pointed out the facts. You had nothing to worry about from our moment on the balcony last night or our lovely lunch today," he says, a reserved grin on his face and a twinkle in his eyes.

"You know what I mean. The whispering in my ear."

"I only whispered so no one would hear about your earlier concerns."

"Oh?" Then, without another word, he turns and, with hands casually deposited in his pockets, saunters toward the finalists and crew as if nothing happened.

Damn, he's smooth. I may regret telling him to stop anything.

I've barely regained my composure when Sebastian, Amy, and one of the camera guys approach. Amy wants to interview me. The idea of being on camera is exhilarating and a little frightening at the same time. As the camera guy moves into place, I quickly smooth down my hair and check my required competition attire—black cotton pants and a tucked-in, button-up blouse.

A few jitters suddenly bubble to the surface. I don't want to blow my chance to shine given that my backseat role won't provide me with many opportunities like this one. The words "Don't mess up" start competing with the mantra of "Seize the moment." Unfortunately, my initial confidence and excitement may not be as powerful as the fear of failure.

When the recording begins, Amy says, "Everyone, meet Cassie. She's the alternate chef for the competition. Cassie, are you excited to watch the demonstrations?"

"Absolutely. I'm especially looking forward to the tasting part."

"What's your favorite dip for a poolside event?"

"There are so many possible choices, but I love Roasted Pineapple Tomatillo Salsa because it can be served at room temperature and holds up well under this warm, poolside sun."

"That sounds delicious. What goes into your tomatillo salsa?"

I'm having fun, and my nerves are subsiding as we talk.

"It's easy. Simply combine roasted tomatillos, jalapeños, onion, and pineapple with fresh cilantro, lime juice, and a little salt."

"I'll try that sometime. It sounds like you're ready to step in quickly if one of the finalists bows out."

"Oh, that won't be necessary. They're all here and ready to

compete. At this point, I'm enjoying the opportunity to watch and learn from these masters."

Sebastian yells, "Cut."

Amy turns to me. "Great job. You're a natural. Enjoy the demo."

"I will. Thanks for including me in the interviews." I sigh in relief that it went well.

AT 2 P.M. SHARP, THE DEMONSTRATIONS BEGIN. AMY REMINDS US THAT EACH finalist will have ten minutes to show how to make their dip. Then we can taste their creations.

After the finalists draw chips to determine the order of presentation, the crew shouts instructions and scurries to position the cameras and lights in front of Trenton's table for the first demo. With a clipboard and pen in hand, Cynthia checks off items on her list while Amy touches up her makeup in preparation for hosting the demo. Trenton exudes a serious, no-nonsense attitude with his lips pressed into a straight line, arms crossed, and chef's knife in hand.

When the demo starts, I'm torn between watching it live and watching it on the almost life-size screens set up on raised platforms throughout the pool area. Amy's white-toothed smile and vivacious energy fill the screen, welcoming everyone to the demo as she introduces Trenton and his Roasted Tomato, Kale, and Garlic dip. As the camera moves from Amy to Trenton, I feel a pang of envy, wishing it was me in front of the camera. But that wasn't meant to be.

Over the chop-chop sounds of Trenton's knife rapidly hitting the cutting board, his commanding and noticeably gruff voice explodes from the speakers around the pool as he explains how to mince the garlic and chop the kale for his dip. It's a good thing he isn't auditioning for a television show. It sounds like he's bossing around his kitchen staff rather than teaching a novice audience.

With a swift turn of the wrist, Trenton swirls a couple of tablespoons of olive oil into a pan that sits atop a portable burner. He adds garlic, then kale and red pepper flakes. When the kale wilts, he tosses in roasted cherry tomatoes.

Once the dip is finished, Trenton plunges a pita chip into the tomato and kale mixture and slips the chip between his thick mustache and beard. He concludes with a chef's kiss, declaring the dip "pure perfection."

Trenton may not be the friendliest chef, but based on the demo, he has a strong skill set, and his food looks delicious. I can't wait for a taste.

Jayden is up next. After about fifteen minutes for setup, the cameras roll, and Jayden explains he's making Texas Fondue. The contrast between Trenton and Jayden is dramatic, both in confidence and physical appearance. While Trenton bellowed his instructions, Jayden is talking so softly that Amy keeps interjecting comments intended to encourage him to speak up. And the rising inflection at the end of his sentences makes it sound like he's asking questions rather than instructing. As far as looks go, Trenton and Jayden are opposites. In contrast to Trenton's imposing figure, Jayden has a sparse, scraggly mustache and a thin frame swallowed by his chef's jacket.

As Jayden steps through his demo, I'm confused by his choice of dip. At first, I assume that Texas Fondue is a creative name for an upscale version of a warm, Texas cheese dip, but I'm wrong. He's making a Southern sausage gravy served with toasted biscuits and cornbread cubes for dipping. Who knew gravy qualifies as a dip?

As the demos continue, I learn that filming a show is not the day of glamour I'd always thought it would be. Each "informal" ten-minute segment takes at least thirty minutes to an hour, due to the setup time. Also, the conditions are more challenging than I'd realized. We're at a hot pool in direct sunlight dressed like we're in an indoor, air-conditioned space. The chefs are battling sweat while trying to remember to smile.

By 3:20, it's finally Kai's turn. He brings a calm, self-assured tone as he starts his demonstration of Papaya Tapenade. If I didn't know he was a chef, his laid-back attitude, nicely tanned skin, and athletic physique would suggest that he's a surfer ready to use his muscular arms to paddle out in search of the next wave. But as he explains the steps for his recipe, I find myself immediately connecting with him and trusting his knowledge as a chef.

Kai's never-faltering smile and easy-going personality invite me to join his journey as he conveys a genuine desire to share his work with the audience. He's also creating some interesting flavor combinations. I never would have thought to combine minced olives with finely chopped papaya, red pepper flakes, and minced garlic. But he makes it sound delicious and new, particularly when he explains that he likes to serve it with taro chips and sweet potato chips for a tropical-meets-French fusion.

As Kai points out, his dip is great for a poolside party because it can be served at room temperature. If you ask me, Kai just nailed the presentation with his friendly personality, intriguing combo of flavors, and theme-appropriate dip. I'll definitely be in line to taste it.

Finally, it's Leon's turn. He looks fresh and prepared despite the sizzling Vegas sun and being the last to do his demo. Leon expertly prepares his white bean dip as he explains it has a smoother texture than hummus. He uses canned cannellini beans, so the dip doesn't take long to make. Based on the crowd's reaction, I'm not the only one who finds Leon knowledgeable and his French accent endearing.

We're anxiously waiting for Leon to taste the finished dip, but it looks like he forgot that part. Being a seasoned host, Amy steps in and asks him what he recommends for scooping up the creamy concoction.

Realization flashes across Leon's face. While moving a pre-made bowl of the dip into the center of the table, he explains that any type of chip will work. He's using tortilla chips today. That's a clever choice. Given that the dip reminded me of hummus, I would have expected him to use pita chips. It's a reminder to think outside the box and not always go with the traditional choices.

Leon grabs a tortilla chip and loads it with the bean dip. He stuffs the whole chip into his mouth. Within seconds, he gets a strange look on his face. Oh no, he can't talk with a full mouth. That's another lesson. If they ever ask me to taste something on camera, I'll take a tiny bite so I can immediately comment on the flavors.

I keep watching, but it's making me uncomfortable. He's struggling with his overstuffed mouth. As we wait for Leon to regain his ability to speak, I glance around the pool area to see what else is going on. Evan is standing a couple of feet behind me, watching everything. As our eyes lock, I hear a commotion in the direction of Leon's table. Quickly turning back, I watch in frozen horror as Leon clutches his throat, his eyes bulge, and beads of sweat form on his forehead as he stumbles backward.

He falls into the pool with a hard thud as his head collides with the nearest concrete column, and he slides slowly down, leaving a bright-red trail on the column as his limp body disappears under the water's surface. Screams ring out around the pools as my hands instantly cover my gaping mouth.

A lifeguard on my left abandons his perch and jumps into the pool with an elongated flotation device in tow. Staring at the water, I'm worried that no one has pulled Leon's head up yet. The lifeguard needs to hurry. Everything is moving in slow motion. I feel helpless with so many people between me and the pool. Why didn't someone from the crew jump in to help him? They're closer than the lifeguard.

It seems like an eternity before the lifeguard carries Leon's lifeless body out of the pool and lays him on the deck. After checking for a pulse and leaning down to listen for signs of breathing, the lifeguard starts CPR as another lifeguard quickly joins him to help. A pool of blood forms under Leon's head. A third lifeguard tries to control the bleeding by applying pressure with a towel.

Minutes pass. The crowd watches silently, hoping for any sign of movement from Leon. The pool event turned from a party to a somber state of worry. The music is gone. The big screens are black.

The quiet is broken when security guards rush in. They're followed by EMTs rolling a gurney to the pool area and taking over. They stabilize Leon's neck, load him onto the gurney, and rush him out.

Silent tears are running down my cheeks when Evan appears by my side, his dangling hand brushing across mine. He discreetly hooks his pinkie around mine, squeezing it in support.

I don't say anything. I can't—my emotions are too fragile. I wish he could wrap his strong arms around me right now and let me bury my face in his chest, but I'll settle for the reassurance of his closeness and small point of contact.

We barely know each other, but it's comforting when he checks on me. First, at the reception, he sensed I was feeling left out. Now, he wants to protect me from this horror, and he doesn't even know the awful memories it's making me relive. I've spent so much time shielding myself from hurt and harm, I'm not used to having anyone other than Lowri read my thoughts or make sure I'm okay. I didn't think I wanted that connection with anyone, but Evan's understanding and attention to my well-being are unexpectedly welcome.

I watch in a daze as the camera crew packs up the equipment. The hotel's staff announce that the pool is temporarily closed and encourage the crowd to disperse.

Sean quietly enters the pool area, accompanied by several employees dressed in security uniforms. He walks purposefully toward Cynthia and Amy. We watch them confer.

When Sean steps away, Cynthia says, "Everyone involved in the competition, please move to the largest cabana on the side of the pool. We'll meet with you shortly."

Does this mean they have an update? My mind races through possibilities. I'm not sure whether Leon was breathing when they wheeled him away. The EMT was still doing chest compressions until just before they left.

At that memory, my body shakes as the reality hits that Leon may not survive. Evan's hands give my shoulders a firm squeeze, as he says, "Let's go to the cabana and find a place where you can sit down."

15

CASSIE

As if in a trance, we slowly walk to the cabana. Security personnel now stand guard over the demo table where Leon fell into the pool. They're turning guests away who get too close or try to get back into the pool.

I'm not sure why someone would want to get in the pool now. How will they clean it? Do they have to drain it? Why are my germophobe tendencies surfacing when I should be worrying about Leon? I barely know him, but his enthusiasm was infectious, and his food today was spot on. It would be tragic for one of the leading finalists to be knocked out by such a freak accident.

Sean enters the cabana and stops in front of the assembled group. Cynthia and Amy follow closely and stand nearby. Amy is staring at her shoes, using her index fingers to wipe her eyes as tears and mascara run down her cheeks. She was standing within a foot or two of Leon when he fell into the pool. No wonder she's shaken and distraught. Cynthia, who is at least twenty years her senior, takes on a motherly role with an arm around Amy's shoulder. Cynthia's wrinkled brow gives away her underlying concern.

Running his fingers through his hair, Sean looks worried, but he stands tall and in control as he raises his other hand to silence the group's side conversations.

An eerie quiet descends over everyone.

"Please let me have your attention for a few minutes. The EMTs have taken Leon to the nearest trauma center. I know you're as concerned about him as I am, but unfortunately, it may be several hours before we receive an update on his condition. I ask for your patience during that time."

Everyone starts throwing questions at Sean about whether Leon is going to be okay and what is going to happen with the competition.

Holding up his hand for silence, Sean continues, "Right now, that's all we know. We all hope that the medical staff will stitch up the cut on Leon's head and that he'll be back here very soon. But we don't have any more details at this time. Therefore, we're going to put the competition on hold for a day. Please be sure to wear your TekCuffs at all times. We'll send updates as we have them. We'll meet in the Zeus conference room at 3 p.m. tomorrow."

I'm shaking as my mind replays Leon falling backward and hitting his head on the column while clutching his throat. Unexpectedly, a hand rests on the small of my back, and a strange, tingly warmth eases my trembling. I don't have to look to know it's Evan. I'm starting to like that he knows when to move next to me. His breath skims across my skin as he whispers, "You may not be an alternate much longer. That looked like a nasty head injury."

"As much as I'd love to compete, I want Leon to be okay."

I never thought they would actually need an alternate. Or if they did, I thought it would be because of some less traumatic reason, like someone coming down with the flu or landing another job before the competition started.

"We all want Leon to be okay. I have to do something first but meet me at my suite in an hour. We can have a drink and talk."

"I won't be good company. The image of Leon's accident keeps replaying in my head."

"You shouldn't be alone after this. Don't worry about entertaining me. We don't even have to talk. We can sit quietly and watch people from my balcony if you like."

"How do I get access to your floor?"

"I'll ask Christian to escort you. He'll be at your room in an hour."

The next hour is going to be a long one.

16

CASSIE

Reaching my room, my mind is still spinning. I can't erase the image of Leon slipping under the water.

Hopefully, he'll be okay, but what will happen if Leon can't return to the competition?

A hot shower will clear my head.

As I shampoo my hair, it hits me that I'd be uncomfortable stepping into the competition after the accident today. I doubt it will be an issue though. Either Leon will return, or the Athena won't replace him at this point because one event has already taken place. They'll move on with only three finalists as if they eliminated one—that's a poor choice of words. Regardless, there's nothing for me to worry about. I won't be put in an awkward position.

As I dry my hair and put on clothes, I think positive thoughts for Leon.

I've barely slid into my shoes when the doorbell to my suite rings.

I throw the door open and immediately ask, "Christian, have you heard any news about Leon?"

"Hello, Ms. Edwards. No, I don't have an update about Mr. Boucher. I'm sorry I can't ease your mind. Are you ready to go?"

"Yes, let me just grab my purse."

Without further conversation, he drops me off at the Monarch Suite.

Evan opens the door and wordlessly pulls me in for a hug, sensing that's what I need more than anything else.

He's right—I needed a hug. I've faced the last five years of life without anyone to hold me or ground me in this way. I press my face against his shoulder, steadied by the rhythm of his heartbeat and his now familiar scent.

"I want to make this better for you," he says.

"That means the world to me. I'm still shaken by what we saw, but I'll be okay. It's Leon that I'm worried about. Christian didn't know anything. Do you?"

"No news yet, but he's in good hands at the hospital."

"I know you're right, but he was underwater for a long time."

"It wasn't as long as it seemed, and head cuts bleed. I'm sure he'll be fine, but I doubt we'll hear anything before morning."

With his arm around my shoulders, we walk to the couch as I explain, "I know, but today's events created uncertainty in the competition and dredged up bad memories of another accident. I'm trying not to freak out."

"Well, I ordered snacks, and we can sip wine and relax. How does that sound?"

"Perfect."

"We can't help Leon, so let's focus on something else. What would you like to talk about?"

"Tell me more about what I could do as a tourist if I came to visit Catalinius."

"Let me open a bottle of wine first."

He turns on soft music and hands me a glass as he joins me on the couch in front of floor-to-ceiling windows overlooking the Strip.

"Thanks. This will help."

"Good. You were asking about tourist attractions. We have the most pristine, white-sand beaches with warm, crystal-clear, turquoise water. Our waterfront resorts are spectacular with all the amenities and beach activities you'd expect at five-star destinations, but it's the private coves that are my favorite hideaways. Some are only accessible by boat. My brother and I like to take our friends sailing. We anchor at one of the coves and relax while we swim, sunbathe, and enjoy lunch."

His cultured accent is melodic and soothing like the water he's describing. It's as if I'm there with him on the sailboat, basking in the sun.

"You make the beaches sound perfect. I want to curl my toes in the warm sand and then dive into the water to cool off. What does the rest of the island look like?"

"We have lush rolling hills, and our towns sport Mediterranean-style buildings and homes. It's quite beautiful. There are vineyards with outstanding wines, and I already told you about our food. We're fortunate to have access to so many local ingredients."

What he describes as home is quite the opposite of the cold and lonely city apartment I'll return to after this is over. I don't want to think about that now, so I say, "I'm sold. It's going on my list but wait a minute."

As Evan starts to answer, his phone rings. "It's my brother. Excuse me."

"No problem."

After a few minutes, he returns to sit next to me, putting his arm around my shoulder and pulling me close. "Sorry about that."

I snuggle against his warm chest, gradually letting go of today's events, even if only temporarily. I need to be careful because it's not only comfort I'm feeling, which is a problem. I've also never been one for a casual hookup. Given that Evan and I aren't even from the same country, that's all this can be.

Regardless of what my head is warning, there's a sizzle between us that I've never felt with anyone else.

He bends his head toward me and nibbles on my earlobe. I shiver, and he peppers warm kisses along the side of my neck, moving toward my collarbone. This man is driving me wild.

Not wanting to lead him on, I need to move away. Before I do, he takes my wine glass and sets it on the coffee table in front of us. He places both hands on my face and pulls me toward him. Our lips collide as if there's a magnetic force pulling us together. Soon, our mouths and hands are exploring with fervor. I know there was a reason I should put a stop to this, but I can't remember what it was.

My right hand starts caressing the taut peaks and valleys of his chest as his left hand makes its way down my arm and across my body. My thin shirt and lace bra are doing little to hide my excitement. Evan notices and rolls my nipple between his fingers as I moan. He slides his hand down and massages my thigh as our lips remain locked.

Evan's hand moves higher up my leg and rests at the crease where my thigh joins my body. Pulling his lips away, he looks into my eyes as though asking permission to take the next step. That brief pause brings me back to my senses.

I jerk away.

Panting, I say, "I don't know what comes over me when we're together. This is moving too fast for me. This may be Vegas, but I'm not a one-night-stand type of person—not even a two-night-stand person. I'm sorry if I gave you the wrong impression."

His eyes ablaze with hunger, he runs his fingers through his hair as he takes a deep, controlled breath. "You didn't give me that impression, but it doesn't mean I don't want you. We can slow things down if you prefer. Let's take our food onto the balcony and enjoy the fresh air," he says, his voice growly and raspy.

It's thrilling to know I have the same effect on him that he has on me, but I can't let myself be swept up in this.

"I should leave. I don't want to lead you on."

"Don't leave. Let's keep each other company and talk like we planned. I promise to be a gentleman. I'll walk you back to your room at the end of the evening. Deal?" Evan smiles.

Relief washes over me that he respects my boundaries and still wants to spend time with me. I don't want to be alone right now. Trusting his word, I say, "Deal. Thanks for understanding."

He leans forward and kisses my forehead. "Let's go. I'm starving."

Like toggling a light switch, Evan's open desire for me morphs into a genuine and immediate need for food.

17

EVAN

I arrive at Sean's office in response to an urgent, early-morning text. As I take a seat in one of the guest chairs across from his desk, Emily rushes in.

"What's wrong?" Sean asks.

"There's a police detective at the front desk. He insists on speaking with you immediately. It's related to Leon Boucher. Is Chef Boucher really dead!?"

Bloody hell. That's why Sean summoned me so early. My mind goes to Cassie. This news will devastate her.

Sean says, "Emily, take a deep breath. Then tell me, did the front desk check the detective's ID?"

"Yes, his name is Geoff Fielder, with a G for Geoff. He's with the Las Vegas Police Department's homicide division."

"Okay. Call security and have them send up two officers to stand guard at my door just in case this Detective Fielder isn't who he says he is. Remember the guy who showed up with forged credentials from Scotland Yard last year and insisted he had to inspect our vault?"

"Who could forget him? He was dressed like Sherlock Holmes!"

"Not all imposters are that easily identifiable, so we can't be too careful. After you speak with security, please go downstairs and personally check his ID. If it appears valid, then bring him to my office."

"Yes, sir."

When Emily leaves, I ask, "Is Chef Boucher dead?"

Sean scrunches his brows together.

"Unfortunately, yes, but I don't understand why a homicide detective is here. It was an accident. Give me a minute to make a call."

This competition is a disaster rather than the marketing win that Sean expected, and now he may have a murder to deal with in addition to everything else.

Sean dials a number and puts the call on speaker.

"You've reached the Chief of Police."

"Larry, this is Sean Cartwright at the Athena. How are you today?"

"I'm fine. How can I help you?"

He sounds like an ally. Hopefully, he'll be able to put Sean's mind at ease. The last thing my friend needs is the emotional strain and publicity that a homicide investigation would bring.

"You tell me," Sean says in a stern voice, asserting his power while hiding the concern I see plastered on his face.

"What do you mean?" Larry asks.

"There's a Geoff Fielder downstairs. He claims to be from your homicide division. Do you have a Detective Fielder on your force?"

"Yes, he's one of our rising stars, but I don't know why he's at your place today. I thought they already finished their interviews related to Chef Bernard's car accident."

That's not good. Something must be terribly wrong for the police to send one of their best homicide detectives to investigate. Sean didn't miss that reality either. He's clenching his jaw so tightly that he'll crack a tooth if he's not careful.

Sean says, "Your detective insists on meeting with me about another accident. One of the chefs in our Guest Chef Competition choked on food, fell backward into the pool, and hit his head yesterday. I learned late last night that the chef didn't survive the injury. Why would a homicide detective be here to investigate a fall?"

"That type of accident doesn't usually make it to my desk. My best guess is the coroner found something out of the ordinary. I'm sure Fielder will explain."

That's exactly what I was afraid the detective's appearance meant. Sean's day just got even worse, and I'm not sure what I can do to help him.

"We'll see what he has to say. I just wanted to make sure he was legit. We have too many people making up excuses to gain access to my office. The last one was dressed in full regalia, entourage in tow, claiming he was the pope here to bless me," Sean says.

Larry chuckles. "You do get the crazy ones! Geoff is about thirty-eight and around five foot ten with short, medium-brown hair. He speaks with a slight Southern accent from his days in Louisiana. Between my description and his ID, you should be able to verify that it's him."

"Thanks, Larry."

The call ends, and Sean closes his eyes and rubs his jaw. I'd swear the dark circles under his eyes doubled in size since Emily announced the detective's arrival. It's not surprising that the stress he's dealing with is getting to him.

Trying to add a calming logical perspective, I say, "I witnessed the accident along with tens of other people. I don't see what there could be to investigate. Let's wait to see what this police detective has to say."

"You're right, but you should leave. Your family doesn't need to get wind of this."

"Don't worry about that. You're my best friend. I'm here for you. My parents understand loyalty to those close to us."

"I'm not sure they would understand you being involved in a murder investigation though."

Before we can discuss the situation further, three firm knocks interrupt us.

I won't abandon Sean, but I do need to be careful about publicity. The king and queen won't want to read about this in the tabloids.

"Come in," Sean says.

"Mr. Cartwright, the security office said you needed protection this morning."

"Yes, we have someone claiming to be a police detective on the way up. Given the abundance of fake IDs, I'm being cautious and upping my security, but I have reason to believe this person is legitimate. However, please remain by my door while he's here. If you hear anything out of the ordinary, don't knock. Come in."

"Yes, sir."

As the guard is about to close the door, Emily arrives with a man matching the description provided by the police chief.

"Mr. Cartwright, Detective Fielder is here to see you. Everything appears to be in order," Emily says.

Standing, Sean says, "Detective Fielder, please come in. This is my good friend, Evan Catalinius. Please have a seat and tell us what brings you here."

"I assume you know that a Mr. Leon Boucher died here yesterday."

"Not exactly. My understanding is that he died at the hospital, not at the Athena."

"Were you present at the event with Mr. Boucher?"

"No, I didn't attend the event. When I was notified that an ambulance had been called in conjunction with the competition, I went to the pool area. At that point, emergency personnel were loading Mr. Boucher onto a gurney and taking him to the hospital."

"What do you know about the incident?"

"Evan, you were there. Tell him what you saw."

"Of course. Mr. Boucher choked on food he'd prepared for a demonstration. In his struggle to clear his throat, he tripped and fell backward into the pool, hitting his head. A lifeguard pulled him out and performed CPR until the emergency medical people arrived. It was a simple accident."

"Unfortunately, it's more complicated than it may have appeared. I'm told that Mr. Boucher was participating in a competition. Is that correct?"

"What was the cause of death?" Sean asks.

"We'll get to that, but first, please answer my question. Was the event part of a competition?"

Sean says, "We're mourning the loss of Mr. Boucher. If his death wasn't an accident, I have the right to know what happened. But yes, we're holding a competition to select a guest chef for our Trendz restaurant. Mr. Boucher was one of the finalists."

"Mr. Cartwright, this is an ongoing police investigation. We aren't required to share our findings with you. My understanding is that this is the second death associated with the competition, correct?"

Sean slams his open palm on the desk, and his cheeks turn slightly red as he says, "I will not tolerate being spoken to like that in my own office. How dare you not only twist the facts but also act like I have no right to know what happened to Mr. Boucher? I'll be speaking with Larry about your complete disrespect in the wake of a tragic death. And you are incorrect. There hasn't been any other death during the competition. If you're insinuating that the death of my friend, Allison Bernard, is related to the competition, you're way off base. She died in a horrible car accident. It's true that she was scheduled to be a judge in the competition, but I don't see how her death had anything to do with the Athena."

Bristling, Detective Fielder counters, "First, feel free to contact the chief. I'm just doing my job. As for Ms. Bernard's death, we haven't closed that investigation. In fact, we understand that the cause of her accident was a combination of alcohol and opioids that she apparently consumed at a press conference here at the Athena."

"Mr. Fielder, I don't see why you think that is related to the competition. However, we have been cooperating and will continue to assist with that investigation to the extent we have any information. Now, why is it you think Mr. Boucher died from a cause other than the head injury he sustained when he fell?"

"It's *Detective* Fielder. The doctors treating Mr. Boucher identified a different cause of death. We now need to determine whether it was an accident or murder."

Taken aback at the direction this conversation is going, I ask, "Murder? You must be joking. I watched him prepare the food during the morning prep session. Then he choked on a bite and fell into the pool. No one killed him.'"

Sean follows up. "Exactly. If we're going to help you with your investigation, you need to tell me what you think happened. Whatever you tell us will remain confidential. I don't want more bad publicity."

"Mr. Boucher was highly allergic to sesame seeds. According to the doctors, they found evidence that he consumed hummus during the demonstration. We're waiting for the autopsy to confirm that finding."

Squinting in confusion, Sean asks, "What does that have to do with being allergic to sesame seeds?"

"One of the main ingredients in hummus is tahini. Tahini is sesame seed paste," I explain.

"Sounds like a horribly unfortunate accident," Sean says.

Detective Fielder shakes his head. "We have reason to suspect otherwise. Mr. Boucher wore a medical alert necklace indicating his allergy. He knew to avoid sesame seeds, and as a chef, he would've known that hummus contains a form of them."

I rub my hand over my mouth in my well-practiced move to look like I'm deep in thought while hiding my reaction to news. As a royal, we learn at a young age to be the picture of stoicism. Contrary to my outward appearance, my thoughts run rampant. Is Fielder saying that someone knew of Chef Boucher's allergy and used that information to kill him? Does this mean the other finalists are in danger too? What about Cassandra? Is she in danger if Boucher's death is related to the competition?

"Damn. Why didn't you start off the meeting with that info?" Sean asks.

"I'm not accustomed to sharing details with the people I interview. As long as you're open to assisting us, I'll consider being more forthcoming going forward."

"What do you need from us?" Sean asks.

"We would like to find the containers from the demonstration yesterday. We would also like to interview everyone who was around when the food was prepared and those who were at the demonstration."

"Understood. We're scheduled to meet with the people involved in the competition later this afternoon to give them an update. You can join us there," Sean says.

"I will. In the meantime, we need access to the leftovers from the demonstration and any videotapes you have."

"The videotapes are easy. We can arrange a meeting with the head of our security so you can see the videos. The film crew for the competition will also have videos that could be helpful. However, we had no reason to suspect any issues, so I can't promise that anyone saved the leftover food or containers. But our F&B manager, Cynthia Andino, will know or can find out."

"Thank you."

"My assistant, Emily, will make the arrangements. Let me send her a message now. As for the interviews, I'll be sitting in on the key ones."

"That would be highly irregular."

"I don't care. This is my hotel, and I want to resolve this quickly. These people are much more likely to cooperate if I ask them to, and I'll also be able to provide background information on some of them."

"That may not be a bad idea."

"Second, Evan has been attending all the events to cover for me when I can't participate. He can tell you if anyone isn't telling you the truth about what happened."

There's a knock on the door.

"Come in," Sean says.

"Mr. Cartwright, I have everything arranged. Should I escort Detective Fielder to the Trendz kitchen now? Cynthia will meet us there."

"Yes, please. Then see that he gets to the security office in time to watch the videos before we meet with the competition group this afternoon."

"Of course, Mr. Cartwright."

When they leave, Sean discards his suit jacket, rolls up his sleeves, and begins pacing back and forth as we digest the news.

His expression is flip-flopping between anger and disbelief. He needs to snap out of this cycle. I could slap him on the face or hand him a brandy. Opting for the latter, I walk to his bar and pour him a healthy dose.

"Here, drink this. Then we'll decide what to do next."

He downs the three fingers of brandy, rubbing his throat as the burn flows downward. With a hard thud, he slams the glass onto his desk, sighing heavily.

"Evan, this place is falling apart. The F&B expenses are still skyrocketing despite my recent efforts to determine the reason. I've put spending limits in place this month, but that's only a stop-gap measure. The competition was supposed to be a great marketing event to bring positive attention to the Athena's outstanding culinary options. Instead, we lost Chef Bernard before the contest even started. And now, we've lost a well-known French chef to sesame seeds of all things! These catastrophes seem unrelated, but what if Fielder is right, and they're more than coincidences?"

"One was a car wreck, and the other was a food allergy. I don't see how they could be related. I'm sure someone accidentally switched containers, and Leon ended up with hummus."

"What do you remember from the prep and demonstration?"

I stare at the ceiling, trying to remember as many details as possible.

"Leon was making a white bean dip. It was straightforward. He put all the ingredients into a food processor, blended them, and tasted the dip. At the end of the prep session, he placed his finished dip along with another batch of ingredients onto a rolling cart and wheeled it into the refrigerator. At the demonstration, he repeated the steps for making the dip, and prompted by Amy, he tasted it on a tortilla chip. I remember thinking it looked like hummus. You know the rest."

"Did anyone assist him in prepping the food?"

"Definitely not. Cassandra asked if she could pitch in and help the finalists, but Amy said that was forbidden."

"Cassie didn't go near the food that the finalists were preparing?"

"No, that's what I just explained. She stood by and watched."

"Did she have any opportunity to switch out his prepared bean dip for hummus?" he asks as he returns to his desk chair.

My voice turns to a soft growl, and I work to contain my frustration, as I say, "No. Like I already said, she just watched the competition. Then she left the kitchen immediately after the prep session. We met for lunch about fifteen minutes later. When we finished lunch, Christian escorted her to the pool for the demo. Don't tell me you think she killed him."

"Calm down. I thought you were taking a break from women. It must have been a short one if you're already having lunch with her. Regardless, she had the best motive of anyone."

"That is absolutely ludicrous. She wasn't anywhere near him. The other finalists were in much closer proximity, both when the food was prepped and at the demonstration."

My anger toward Sean is irrational, but I can't control it because my gut is telling me that Cassandra had nothing to do with any of this. He'd understand if he saw how devastated she was. Someone needs to look out for her.

"Calm down. I'm just stating facts. The police are going to watch the security videos and the videos from the pool. Let's join them and see for ourselves."

"Fine."

"You know they're going to want to interview you in more detail."

"Why is that a problem? I already told Fielder what I know."

"Your true identity is going to come out. Even if you give them your alias, they'll figure out who you are."

"It's not an alias. It's a shortened version of my real name to let me fly under the radar when I travel. It makes it easy to avoid recognition in the States. Not many people pay much attention to our small island nation. I don't even think the press noticed me at the opening reception."

"That's true. You have done a good job staying out of the US press. People here don't typically recognize you on the street. Unfortunately, Leon dying under suspicious circumstances threatens your anonymity. Now that the police are conducting a murder investigation, they'll check everyone's background. You'd be wise to tell them who you really are if you want any hope of them being discreet."

"Bollocks. Can we trust them to keep my identity a secret?"

"I hope so. If it were the chief of police, it would be no problem. However, Fielder is a new guy in town who's trying to prove himself."

"He was rather arrogant and liked throwing around his power, at least verbally. So much for my quiet time away. My family will not be happy if the press ties me to a murder investigation. At a minimum, let's try to keep my name out of police reports that are available to the media."

"Agreed. We'll talk with Fielder again privately before the interviews."

Sean stands and grabs his suit jacket from the hook, saying, "I feel terrible about getting you into this mess, but let's go meet Detective Fielder in the security office to watch the videos. If we're lucky, this will be resolved quickly."

I can only hope.

I need to find Cassandra before she hears that Leon didn't make it. She'll be heartbroken over his death and then even more devastated when she learns that she's one of the suspects. I need to be there for her. She doesn't have anyone else to protect her from all this.

18

EVAN

This is my first time in the small auditorium that serves as the control center for the Athena's security. I'm awed by the ultra-modern setup. They could direct a mission to space from here.

The lights are low for easy viewing of the curved floor-to-ceiling displays covering the front wall. The displays provide eyes on the entire Athena hotel, casino, and grounds. Terraced rows of charcoal-gray tables line the room in front of the wall displays. Black-suited security personnel operate the computers on each table.

Supervisors roam the area via the middle and side aisles of stairs leading from the back of the room down to the front displays. Thick, black carpet suppresses their footsteps. With everyone focused on their work, the room is quiet except for the occasional whispers and keystrokes.

"There's Fielder on the far side," I say.

Reaching him, Sean whispers, "Detective Fielder, I see you found our security headquarters."

Respecting the room's quiet, he softly replies, "Yes, sir. They're setting up the videos from the security tapes and the footage shot by the camera crew for our review."

"Excellent," Sean says.

"Good afternoon, Mr. Catalinius. I'll want to talk with you in more detail later, but it's not appropriate for you to be here now."

"Detective Fielder, Evan is staying. This is my hotel. I say who is allowed where and when. Those are my terms if you want to see the videos now. Otherwise, leave and come back when you have a court order. We're all trying to determine what happened. Evan was present at the events, so he may notice things that seem out of place, whereas you and I would discount them as unimportant."

Gritting his teeth, but acquiescing, Detective Fielder says, "Fine. Play the videos of the food prep session. I want to see anything that shows Mr. Boucher, the food he was prepping, or anyone who came near it."

Standing shoulder to shoulder with our eyes glued to the monitors, we watch as the videos play. No one goes near Leon's station while he's prepping his food. He leaves the area a couple of times to retrieve equipment and ingredients, but we don't see anything unusual. As the video continues, we watch Leon fill a serving bowl with his finished dip, taste it, and place the ingredients for the demo into separate containers. He didn't have a reaction to tasting it then.

"Stop the video. Rewind and replay the part where Mr. Boucher is placing his containers onto the cart," Fielder demands.

Rubbing my tired eyes, which are dry from staring so intently at the monitors, I ask, "Detective, did you see anything amiss? What are we looking for?"

"I want to see which containers he used so we can verify the same ones show up in the poolside video."

"I see."

We stare intently, looking for any small thing out of place. After Leon exits the refrigerator, the other three finalists wheel their carts inside, one by one. Hmm. Were any of the other finalists in the fridge long enough to tamper with Leon's food? I don't think so, but it wouldn't take long to make a switch if someone planned ahead.

"Detective Fielder, are they sure he consumed hummus, or was tahini added to his pre-prepared bean dip?" Sean asks.

"Good question. I'll ask the coroner to clarify that point. We need to know whether someone altered his food soon after he prepared it or substituted a new bowl of dip at the pool. It will definitely help to know when the tampering took place and who had the opportunity to do it. It certainly doesn't look like he accidentally put any tahini in the dip while he was preparing it."

This is taking longer than I'd hoped. I assumed that with all the cameras, Sean's security team would have already identified the culprit before we arrived, but that wasn't the case.

"How can I find out who had access to the walk-in refrigerator between the time of the prep and the poolside demonstration?" Fielder asks.

Sean says, "The videos of the kitchen should answer that question. We can also check with Cynthia to see who was working the event and who brought the carts to the pool. Unfortunately, there would have been a few opportunities for someone to add an ingredient or make a substitution, but I assume they would've been caught on video."

"I agree, Mr. Cartwright. It's unfortunate that the scene was not secured after Mr. Boucher consumed the dip."

Sean barks, "Detective, you have no basis to insinuate that the Athena's procedure was improper. We had no way of knowing this was anything other than an accidental fall. Even then, we immediately stationed security officers at the location of the accident. I'm also told you retrieved the unwashed dishes from the Trendz kitchen, so back off."

Ignoring Sean's comments, Fielder says, "As we watch the next videos, please let me know if you recognize anyone who comes near Mr. Boucher's food. Also, look for anyone who appears out of place or unexpected."

"We will," Sean says.

We watch closely, but everything looks just as I remember it.

Suddenly Sean orders, "Stop the video. Go back about fifteen seconds and play it in slow motion."

"What did you notice?" I ask.

"It's strange. The guy who walked by Leon's table is one of my friends. Until recently, he was one of our primary food suppliers.

During my recent review of the F&B department, I learned that we aren't using his company anymore. What would he be doing at the pool?"

"What's his name?" Detective Fielder asks.

"Wes Griffin."

"Why did you stop using him as a supplier?" Fielder asks.

"I don't know yet. I've been investigating some recent anomalies relating to our food expenses. Unfortunately, our head chef, who oversaw the suppliers, no longer works here. He made the changes before he left. I'm trying to collect more info before reaching out to him for answers."

"Would a disgruntled supplier want to sabotage your event?" I ask.

"I can't imagine that. I've known him for years. Besides, how would he know about Leon's food allergy?"

"Good point, but it's still strange that he was there. We'll interview him. Who knew about the food allergy?" Fielder asks.

Sean says, "I'm not sure. My understanding is that anyone involved in the competition who may be tasting food was asked to submit a list of allergies. The finalists were told they couldn't cook with those items during the competition."

"So, everyone was told who was allergic to which items?"

"I certainly hope not. We consider knowledge about allergies to be health data. The law requires us to keep that information confidential. The list of allergies would have been provided without matching them to specific individuals. We can double-check that with Cynthia though. She would have overseen that aspect of the competition."

"Okay. Can we see a wider-angle view? I'd like you to point out the other people you recognize," Fielder says.

"Sure. As you can see, each finalist has his own table. Amy is the one wearing the blue top and white shorts. She's overseeing the competition and is the on-camera host. Cynthia is the one in the suit with the clipboard. She's our F&B manager. That's Evan standing near Cassie. She's the alternate. If the competition proceeds, she'll replace Leon."

"I see. Cassie had the most to gain from Leon's death."

My hands curl into fists wanting to punch Fielder for even thinking that Cassandra could do such a thing, but I bite my tongue, letting Sean answer first.

"That's not clear. She's a home-trained chef. All the other finalists are professional chefs. Even if she competes, we don't know how well she'll do against the pros," Sean says.

Disappointed that Sean didn't say something stronger in her defense, I add, "It seems to me that the other chefs had more to gain by getting rid of a well-respected competitor such as Leon."

"Interesting. Why did you include a home-trained chef in such a high-end competition?"

Sean says, "Optics mostly. The goal of the competition was to garner widespread attention, so we invited everyone, including home cooks, to apply. The idea was to give everyone an opportunity to chase their dream. That's what Las Vegas is about. Anyone can change their life here. In this case, one home cook made it to the top five, which was a little surprising and quite an accomplishment. Even though she didn't make it into the final four, we're including her in some of the interviews and events. It's good press for us and gives her positive publicity as well."

"In other words, she was the token 'real person.' But as an alternate, you didn't risk her actually winning or worse yet, embarrassing the Athena," Fielder says.

"That's harsh and wasn't the intent. I left the selection of the finalists and the alternate to Cynthia, Amy, and Sebastian. He's the producer and director for the Guest Chef Competition. You can ask them how they selected these individuals. I played no part in that process."

"Mr. Catalinius, were you involved in selecting the competitors?"

"No. I wasn't even aware of the competition until shortly before I arrived for my extended vacation. Sean asked if I would attend a few events in his place. It sounded like fun, and I looked forward to sampling the food created by these top chefs. Otherwise, I'm not involved."

"You seemed rather cozy with the alternate in the videos."

"She's not actually competing but is required to attend the events. We've found ourselves standing together in the background. We chat while we watch."

"Detective, it's almost time to meet with the people involved with the competition. I need to inform them of Chef Boucher's death and give them an update on the plans going forward. I can't fathom that any of the finalists would kill someone just to be the guest chef at one of our restaurants for a month. But if you want to interview them, they'll be assembled in a few minutes."

"People kill for much less, so yes, I want to interview them. I also want to interview the alternate."

19

CASSIE

When I arrive at the back of the Zeus ballroom, there's a podium at the front and rows of chairs facing forward. It reminds me of generic setups for conference presentations, but that's not why we're here. A message on my TekCuff summoned me and everyone else involved in the competition.

Scanning the rest of the assembled crowd, I sense an uncomfortable vibe. The air is heavy with confusion and uncertainty. People are whispering. Concern mars their faces as some wring their hands, while others scour the crowd with searching eyes. It's eerie and foreboding.

I overhear opinions as to the likely fate of the competition and whether Leon will return. Even the crew is conjecturing that the Athena is canceling the competition. They're worried about a decrease in pay if their filming assignment is cut short. The uncertainty makes the tension in the room palpable.

Cynthia and Amy stand near the front with their heads tilted toward each other and hands shielding their mouths. Whatever they're saying, they don't want anyone eavesdropping.

I find the finalists collected in a corner and join them. The stress has put them in a talkative mood. Their concerns are deeper than those of the staff and crew because the finalists have more riding on this competition. This could elevate the winner's career significantly.

As each one shares their situation, I listen with empathy.

Trenton explains, "I need to move west because my ex-wife took my young children to California. If I don't find a new job, I can't see my kids as often as I'd like."

Jayden says, "I shouldn't admit it, but I had to leave my job in Dallas over creative differences with the restaurant's owners."

I can't help thinking that the owners weren't impressed with gravy as a dip, but I keep my thoughts to myself.

Kai laments, "It's hard to face stereotypes. I need a venue like Vegas that will allow me greater freedom to fuse French and island cuisines."

I ask, "Do you know why Leon applied to the competition?"

Kai says, "He mentioned wanting to move to the US permanently. He needed a job here before he could get a visa."

"That makes sense," I say.

Of course, they're all also counting on the publicity from the televised competition and possible future shows on the FFT Channel to boost their careers.

Our conversation is interrupted when Cynthia steps to the podium, saying, "Please take a seat. We're almost ready to start." She walks away, and along with Amy, moves to the back of the room.

I look around for an empty chair. Finding one next to the camera crew, I slip into it.

Behind me, someone mutters that this competition is jinxed and should be canceled. I hope the competition continues, but I'll understand if it can't go forward due to Leon's injury.

I'm not ready to go home, but the trip was worth it even if it ends now. Up until Leon's accident, I've had a wonderful adventure and a welcome break from work. I've had a fantastic time watching professional chefs compete, exploring the Athena, and hanging out behind the scenes at a real restaurant. Evan's panty-melting kisses were an unexpected bonus. Yes, I'm almost ready to admit that I want more time with him even if it can't be anything serious.

Fueled by the anxiety surrounding me, I shift nervously in my seat as my brain runs at full speed. Will the competition continue? Is Leon out for the duration? Am I going to compete in his place? Will they move forward with only the other three finalists given that one event has been completed? It was just a demo, though, so it may not count. Do I even want to compete under these circumstances? Is this competition truly jinxed?

My blood pressure is rising with each passing minute. Stop thinking.

When I'm certain my head's going to explode, the room goes quiet. Facing the back entrance, the reason is apparent. Sean and Evan are walking into the room, followed by another man. Sean signals for Cynthia and Amy to remain at the back, which seems strange given that they stood alongside Sean at prior events.

Heads slowly follow the men's trek to the front of the room. The quiet becomes eerie as we wait, and a coldness runs through me as I have a premonition that bad news is coming.

Reaching the podium, in his deep, authoritative voice Sean says, "Thank you for your patience as we waited for more information about Mr. Boucher's condition. It is with great sadness that I must share that he did not make it."

The collective gasp reverberates through the room.

The world around me slows—my eyes blur, my mouth goes dry, and my hands shake. The only thing I can hear is my own pulse pounding in my ears as my mind replays the moment Leon clutched his throat and his eyes bulged with fear as if he knew what was about to happen. I lean forward, hiding my face in my hands as I grapple with the fact that Leon is gone. Yet another tragic loss.

Sean continues, "I'm certain you're just as upset about Leon's death as I am. Therefore, out of respect for Mr. Boucher, we're going to wait another day to determine how to proceed with the competition. I would like to thank you for your patience as we work through this difficult situation and determine the best plan moving forward. In addition, the police must investigate incidents such as this, so they want an opportunity to talk with each of you to understand how Mr. Boucher fell into the pool."

My mind is hazy and has trouble grasping what this all means.

In a cacophony of voices, the audience hurls questions at Mr. Cartwright. He simply holds up one hand and says, "Please hold your questions for now. Let me first introduce Detective Fielder. He can explain more."

"Hello, everyone. My name is Detective Geoff Fielder. I'm handling the investigation of the death of Leon Boucher. We want to understand the events that led up to Mr. Boucher's choking and falling into the pool. Therefore, we would like to have short chats with each of you. This is standard procedure. I'd like to thank you in advance for your cooperation. We don't expect to take much of anyone's time and hope to have this case closed quickly."

Murmuring fills the room. Some seem appalled they're expected to talk with the police, while others seem outright scared. My reaction is different. Detective Fielder's comments don't make sense to me. Something is off. Standard procedure? No way. Determine the events that led to choking? Is the detective kidding? Leon put a whole, dip-covered chip in his mouth, and it blocked his airway. What needs to be investigated? People choke all the time. Fortunately, they don't do it near a concrete column in a swimming pool, but there's nothing mysterious or sinister about choking and hitting your head when you fall.

The detective regains everyone's attention, saying, "Please let us do our investigation. Since everyone is already assembled, we'll conduct the interviews now. Mr. Cartwright will explain where they will take place."

"We'll use two nearby conference rooms and an office so the interviews can proceed in parallel. Emily or another staff member will direct you to the right place when it's your turn. In the meantime, I'll have snacks and drinks brought here to keep you from starving. Thank you for your help. It's greatly appreciated."

Nervous chattering fills the air.

Without knowing it until now, I watched a man die yesterday.

20

EVAN

When Sean and I walked into the Zeus ballroom to inform everyone about Leon, the first thing I did was locate Cassandra. My gut wrenched when I didn't see her sitting with the remaining finalists, but instead, hidden among the crew. In a roomful of people, she might as well have been alone. No one was offering their support. It crushed me that I couldn't go to her.

I repeatedly checked on her during the meeting, watching as she struggled with the news. At one point, she turned ghostly white, and fainting seemed a real possibility. I was seconds from striding to her, lifting her in my arms, and taking her to my suite. The person next to her finally noticed and handed her a bottle of water. Color started returning to her face, but she was truly shaken by Leon's demise.

Near the end of the meeting, Cassandra looked up and caught me watching her. Tears were forming in her beautiful blue-gray eyes. I wanted to leap over the chairs between us and let her curl up in my lap with my arms wrapped around her.

What has come over me? When did I become emotionally attached?

I'm questioning my decision to remain neutral publicly. But

otherwise, Fielder would exclude me from the interviews. It's better for Cassandra if I know what's happening, although I'm sure she's questioning my lack of interaction.

Vowing to myself that I'll find a way to protect her, I follow Sean and the detective out of the conference room.

Sean says, "Let's head to my office. That'll be a more convenient place for us to talk with the key people. I assume you have officers who can interview the crew in the two conference rooms near here."

"Yes, my officers will do interviews in parallel. Isn't there somewhere closer than your office for my interviews?"

Sean explains, "My office gives us greater privacy, which I prefer. We can take a shortcut through the Maze."

"What's the Maze?"

"It's our underground tunnel system for quickly getting around this place."

"Convenient."

We use the nearest Maze entrance and are in Sean's office within ten minutes.

After motioning for Detective Fielder and me to sit in two of the three chairs in front of his desk, Sean sinks into his high-back, leather desk chair.

Not wanting to waste time, I say, "Detective, I assume you are ready to interview me. But first, I want to share some additional information. You undoubtedly will figure it out anyway, but I'd rather be upfront with you to avoid any perception that we're keeping something from you."

The detective nods.

Sean interjects, "When you met Evan earlier, I introduced him as Evan Catalinius, which is technically accurate. However, he's more formally known as Garret Evan Louis Francesco, Prince of Catalinius."

Doing a double take, Detective Fielder asks, "Did you say prince?"

I interject, "He did. I'm usually referred to as Prince Evan, but my title isn't particularly important in the US. It's my older brother who will eventually take the throne, not me. As the press likes to say, I'm the spare prince. I'm here for a break from my public life, so I'd greatly appreciate it if you would keep my name and my title out of the news. That's why I am traveling as Evan Catalinius."

"I understand. As long as it doesn't impact the investigation, I'll honor your request—for now. How do I address you? Is it Your Highness?"

"If we were going with titles, it would technically be Your Royal Highness. However, for now, please call me Evan or Mr. Catalinius."

"Okay. My apologies, but I don't know where Catalinius is."

I laugh. "That's why I usually can avoid recognition in the States. Not many people are familiar with my home. It's a small island country off the coast of Italy and France."

"I assume you're exercising diplomatic immunity in this matter. Is that correct?"

"Detective, I have no need for any sort of immunity. I had nothing to do with this incident, and I'm happy to share anything I saw if it's helpful. Sean's my best friend, and I want this cleared up for him as soon as possible. I just want my name kept out of it. I don't want to embarrass my parents or my country by having our name connected with a murder investigation in Las Vegas."

"So, where are your bodyguards?" the detective asks with raised eyebrows.

My jaw clenches. "I didn't bring any. As the spare heir, I don't typically face many threats, particularly not in the States. Besides, Sean has an excellent security team here. Please, can we get on with this? What questions do you have for me?"

Detective Fielder opens his pocket-sized, spiral notepad and asks, "Who had access to the food Mr. Boucher ate during the demonstration?"

"That's hard to say. I guess anyone with access to Trendz could have gone into the kitchen after we left. There were also lots of people at the pool who could have had access. Staff, crew, other finalists, and hotel guests were roaming around the demo area."

"Who had the most to gain from his death?"

"I didn't know the man, so I don't have any way of knowing if he had enemies. I assume the other finalists would have seen him as a threat though."

"What about the alternate? Her name is Cassie, correct? You mentioned chatting with her in the kitchen during the prep session and again at the pool."

"I did. Her name is Cassandra Edwards. Some people refer to her as Cassie."

"Wouldn't she have even more to gain than the other finalists?"

"Detective, I highly doubt Cassandra had anything to do with this. She stood on the sidelines. She didn't go near the food."

"Mr. Catalinius, the perpetrator is usually the person who has most to gain. Wouldn't that be the alternate because she doesn't have a chance at the prize unless someone is knocked out of the competition? Given those facts, why are you so certain she wasn't involved?"

"As you said, we've chatted while watching the competition. She presents herself as honest and straightforward," I say in a clipped tone.

I can't explain why I'm so protective of Cassandra or how she wormed her way into my life in such a short time. She's an enigma—an enticing one. I admire her confidence and independence. She's vulnerable and caring, yet at times, she can put on a mask to hide from the world. I can identify with that skill. Nevertheless, my instincts tell me she didn't have anything to do with Leon's death.

"Did you see any suspicious activity during the preparation of the food or during the demonstrations?"

"No. But I wasn't looking for anything. This was supposed to be a fun event."

"If you were here to escape from the public, why were you attending the competition where you risked being recognized?"

"Sean asked me to attend a few events to allow him time to deal with another pressing matter. My assumption was that I could stay in the background without much risk of being identified. If I'm recognized, it wouldn't be the end of the world. However, being linked as a witness who was interviewed as part of a murder investigation is a problem for me."

Detective Fielder jots notes before saying, "Mr. Catalinius, thank you for your cooperation. Do you plan to remain in Las Vegas?"

"I haven't decided yet. I was planning to stay at least another two weeks. Maybe a month."

"If that plan changes, please let me know in case I have any more questions for you. And, if you remember anything else, please contact me. I've left my phone number with Mr. Cartwright's assistant."

"I will."

Turning toward Sean, Detective Fielder says, "Mr. Cartwright, I have a quick question for you before we move to the next interview. What was the pressing matter that required your attention?"

"Detective, I don't want to go into the details of unrelated hotel and casino business."

"Mr. Cartwright, let me be the judge of whether it's unrelated. What was the pressing matter?" he asks more firmly.

"We've had issues with unexplained increases in food and beverage costs over the last few months. I'm trying to track down why. I was also hoping Evan might see something that would help explain the situation while he watches the competition."

Turning back to me, Detective Fielder inquires, "Mr. Catalinius, have you seen anything that explains this issue?"

"Not yet. The competition had barely started when Mr. Boucher died."

"Thank you. Let's bring Ms. Edwards in next. Mr. Cartwright, can you have someone escort her here?"

"Yes." Putting the phone on speaker, Sean asks, "Emily, can you bring Cassie Edwards here?"

"Of course, Mr. Cartwright."

"Emily, please bring her through the Maze," I say.

"Mr. Cartwright will need to approve that option," Emily says.

I implore, "Sean, show her some respect. There's no need to parade her through the main areas when we know how distraught she was yesterday. Besides, walking an upset woman through the Athena can't be good for business."

Detective Fielder's face jerks up from his notepad when he hears my request, but he remains silent and returns to writing.

"I'm not sure that's necessary, but okay. Emily, please bring Cassie up via the Maze. Do the same for all the finalists when it's their turn."

21

CASSIE

While waiting my turn to be interviewed, I should grab a snack, but I'm too nervous. I can't fathom the police would go to this much trouble over a choking accident. There must be something more to it.

What could it be though? How could his death have been anything more sinister? Regardless, I didn't have anything to do with it. Still, the idea of being interviewed by the police is intimidating.

I almost jump out of my seat when Emily surprises me from behind with a tap on my shoulder. "Cassie, it's your turn."

While it felt like I was waiting forever, I'm the first person she's personally come to get. What does that mean?

Trying to mask my anxiety, I smile and say, "Okay. Where do I go?"

Inside, I'm barely holding off a panic attack. It's my nature to worry because in the past, good things have come at an extremely high price. I'm still dealing with emotions from what should have been one of the best weekends of my college life: law school gradua-tion. It turned tragic when the police showed up with the horrifying news that both of my parents were killed on their way to the ceremony. Then, a few weeks later, the boyfriend I'd assumed was "the one" left me.

I was so excited about this cooking competition, but tragedy struck. I wasn't prepared to hear that Leon is dead. Now, I don't know how to prepare for the next blow that my senses tell me is coming.

Emily softly replies, "Just follow me."

I get up, knees weak, and follow her out the door and toward the end of the hall. It's a dead end.

"Emily, where are we going? I thought the interviews were in nearby conference rooms."

"Some are, but others are in Mr. Cartwright's office, which is further away. We're going to take a shortcut through the Maze."

"What's the Maze?"

"A series of underground tunnels. You'll see. The entrances are hidden and require authorization."

"It hadn't occurred to me there would be underground tunnels, but that makes sense. It reminds me of the secret passages described in novels about old castles."

We walk to the end of the hall, and Emily places her hand against the palm of the man in a large painting. The wall pops inward, and we walk through. The hidden door closes almost instantly, and we step down a staircase to a waiting golf cart.

A few minutes later, we're riding an elevator that opens into Sean's office.

Emily says, "Many people may know or suspect that the Athena has an underground tunnel system, but we do our best to keep the locations of the hidden entrances a secret for security reasons. The nondisclosure agreement you signed prevents you from discussing the Maze even with others involved in the competition."

I nod in acknowledgment, but if the Maze is such a secret, why did they let me see it? Are they bringing everyone up to the owner's office this way?

As soon as I enter, Evan walks up to me with an outwardly calm but concerned expression. It looks like his hands are balled into fists inside his pockets. Is that as a reminder not to pull me into an embrace? I hope that's it. In a soft voice, he asks, "Are you okay?"

Whispering back, I say, "I'm not doing great. This whole thing is horrible and confusing. I can't believe Leon is dead, and it makes no sense why they're investigating a choking accident."

"I know. Hang in there. Detective Fielder is going to ask you a few questions. Come have a seat." Turning and extending his right arm, Evan gestures to an empty guest chair by Mr. Cartwright's desk at the far end of the room.

I've never seen an office this big or with so many things vying for my attention. If circumstances were different, I'd enjoy a closer look at the photos of celebrities on the wall to my left, what looks like a Miró painting behind Sean's desk, and the view provided by the forty-foot-wide floor-to-ceiling windows on my right, showcasing the Strip. Even the furniture is unique and modern. I'm not sure if the woven tangle of white acrylic and chrome across from a couch is a table, a chair, or an art sculpture.

Mr. Cartwright extends his hand, saying, "We know yesterday and today have been difficult. However, we need to understand more details about what happened. Your help would be appreciated."

"I'm not sure I know anything useful, Mr. Cartwright, but I'll do my best to answer any questions."

"Thank you. And, please, call me Sean."

Barely having had time to perch on the edge of my seat, which is sandwiched between Evan and Detective Fielder, I'm caught off guard when the detective says, "Your friend, Evan, insisted they bring you up through the Maze. Am I to assume you two are close?"

Common sense tells me to answer the questions without further reaction, so after taking a deep breath, I respond, "Detective, I met Evan through this competition. Because I'm the alternate, I've spent my time standing on the sidelines at the events. Evan has been doing the same, so we've had a couple of opportunities to talk. He's been kind to me."

"I see. Just how kind has he been?"

I tilt my head, and my eyes squint in confusion. "I don't understand your question, but based on your tone, I think I should be offended."

Coming to the rescue, Evan sits up straight and barks, "Detective, you are way out of line. We understood these interviews to be about Leon Boucher's death, not whether I am nice to someone. It's my practice to treat people well."

Not backing down, Detective Fielder admonishes, "I'm letting you and Mr. Cartwright sit in on these interviews against my better judgment, so either stay quiet or leave."

Holding up his hand to silence the detective, Sean says, "Detective, we're cooperating with you, but we expect you to be respectful to our employees and guests. I agree with Evan. You're out of line here. Either investigate the incident or you can leave."

"I *am* investigating. If your best friend is having an affair with a participant in the competition, then that is highly relevant."

How dare he ask such a question. My nerves vaporize almost instantly, replaced with anger. My personal life is none of his effing business.

It's my own fault though. I never should have let my emotions overrule my logic. It went against my judgment to have lunch with Evan, and I certainly never should've kissed him. But who would have thought a social interaction would be used against me as a motive for murder?

Not only that, but the detective's question also is borderline sexist and definitely presumptive. I bet he didn't ask Evan the same thing. Regardless, a few kisses don't equate to an affair. I'm not competing, and Evan's not a judge, so my personal life is none of the detective's concern.

Indignant and disgusted, I interrupt the debate between Sean, Evan, and the detective, saying, "First, I'm an attorney, which means I understand what should and shouldn't be asked during an interview. And detective, your question is wholly inappropriate. But I'll answer it to avoid further waste of our time. I'm not having an affair with Evan. Now, do you have any relevant questions for me?"

Moving on, Detective Fielder instructs, "Please explain to me what you know about the food Mr. Boucher prepared and tasted at the demonstration."

Scooting back into the chair, I tell him everything I know. He takes notes and then asks, "Did you assist Mr. Boucher in preparing his food?"

"No. I offered to assist anyone who needed help, but Amy said that wasn't allowed. So, I just watched."

"Why did you offer to help?"

I shrug. "I felt uncomfortable watching everyone work so hard while I did nothing. It made me feel rather useless. Besides, I love to cook, so I always offer to help when I'm in a kitchen."

"So, you didn't like being left out?"

Boy, he likes to twist words. I shake my head and clarify, "That's not what I meant. I was willing to pitch in. Nothing more."

"Did you see anyone tamper with the food?"

My body stiffens as I wonder if that's the real reason the detective is here.

"No, of course not. Why would someone tamper with the food?"

Detective Fielder stops taking notes and locks eyes with me. "Ms. Edwards, what food was Mr. Boucher allergic to?"

"I wouldn't know."

In disbelief, the detective questions, "Really? How can that be? All the participants were told to avoid certain foods because of allergies, correct?"

"That's correct. We were given a list of foods that either contestants, judges, or staff were allergic to. However, we weren't told who was allergic to which ones."

The detective drops his gaze to his notepad. "What were those foods?"

"I'm not sure I remember all of them. Give me a minute to think."

"Take your time."

"Let's see. I wasn't participating, so I didn't try to commit the list to memory, but I seem to remember we were told to avoid bleu cheese, sesame seeds, and peanuts."

Following up, the detective says, "So you're telling me that you didn't know who was allergic to any of those foods, correct?"

"That's not what I said. I said that I didn't know Leon had any of those allergies. I did know at least one person who was allergic to bleu cheese."

Snapping his head up, the detective's interest peaks. "And how did you know that and not know about Mr. Boucher's allergy."

"Simple. I'm allergic to bleu cheese. But I don't know if anyone else is also allergic to it."

Annoyed at my benign explanation, Detective Fielder asks, "Do you know why Mr. Boucher chose to make white bean dip instead of something else?"

"Not really."

"Did you hear him say that white bean dip is a good substitute for people who can't eat hummus?"

"No, I don't recall hearing him say that, but that would be true." Then a light bulb goes off in my head. Pointing a finger at the detective, I exclaim, "Wait a minute! Sesame seeds were on the list of prohibited ingredients, so he wouldn't have been allowed to make hummus in the competition. That must be the reason he made bean dip instead."

Eyes focused on my face, the detective asks, "What about sesame seeds would've prevented him from making hummus?"

"Tahini is in hummus. It's made from sesame seeds." I shrug.

"How do you know that?"

"From my cooking experience. It's common knowledge. All the finalists would know that."

"We'll see."

"Leon was the one allergic to sesame seeds, wasn't he?"

Now the questions are starting to make more sense. They must think someone sabotaged his dip. Did they replace it with hummus and essentially poison him?

"I can't share that information. Who, other than you, would want him out of the competition?"

Me? That's absurd. Did I make myself look like a suspect by knowing that tahini is made from sesame seeds? And to make matters worse, I'm sure I was acting nervous when I arrived, which probably makes me look guilty. That's how it is in the movies. The police always suspect anyone who acts nervous. My mind is running at full speed, amping up my nerves again, but I need to defend myself, so I interlace my fingers on my lap to steady my hands.

"First, I didn't want him out of the competition. Second, he seemed like a nice guy, so I have no reason to think anyone else wanted him out either."

"Come now, you were disappointed to be the alternate rather than a finalist, weren't you?"

I turn to Evan, wanting to ask whether he shared our conversation from the night on the balcony where I admitted it was tough not competing. Would he do that? How could someone be caring and attentive one minute and then throw me under the bus the next? I can't believe I thought he might be different and worth risking my feelings on.

Turning back to the detective, I say, "Given that I'm self-trained, it's remarkable the Athena selected me as the alternate. Sure, it would've been great to compete, but I'd never knowingly cause harm to anyone. Further, I never touched any of the food involved. If someone tainted his food, as you're implying, it wasn't me."

"Then why did we find your fingerprints on the container of hummus?"

I gasp as I jump to my feet in utter disbelief. "What? That's impossible!" I shout as my heart skips a beat.

I look toward Evan and almost miss the fleeting look of shock that's instantly replaced by a stoic expression. Sean's face turns stone cold.

They can't seriously think I did this, can they?

Fear swallows me as it becomes clear this isn't a nightmare that I'll wake up from.

22

EVAN

When all the interviews are done, Detective Fielder finally leaves, and Sean pours drinks for us. To say I need one is an understatement. I don't want to talk as I sip my drink and quietly stare into space. Sean gets the message and remains quiet while I process what we know about Leon's death and what the detective said about Cassandra.

The idea that she could have murdered Leon is difficult for me to comprehend. I watched her reactions during the interview. Unless she's an incredible actress, she was genuinely surprised and confused by the detective's accusations.

Eventually, Sean breaks the silence. "I thought the detective would never finish the interviews. Thank god he had other officers interview the bulk of the witnesses in parallel and give us quick summaries. Otherwise, we'd have been here all night."

"Uh-huh."

"Let's go over what we know so far. The staff, crew, and finalists characterized Leon as calm, friendly, and focused on moving to the States. He wore a medical alert necklace, so he was aware of his allergy. He prepped his own food, so he had no reason to think it was hummus instead of bean dip, making an accident less likely. While we still don't know for certain if this was an accident or a murder, it's looking increasingly like someone helped Leon check out. And the fingerprint evidence indicates your new *friend*, Cassie, likely killed him."

"We don't know that, and quit looking at me with that 'I told you so' expression. I don't think Cassandra is guilty. I'm not typically that wrong about someone, and her background check was clean. I didn't ask for the details about her life, but my security guys back home said there were no red flags. Not even any warning flags. Besides, she was genuinely upset last night."

Am I trying to convince myself of her innocence as much as Sean?

A surprised look crosses his face. "Wait a minute. What background check?"

"After we learned Leon died, I had Cassandra checked out as a precaution. The report came back squeaky clean."

"You slept with her!"

"No. But even if I had, we wouldn't be discussing it now."

"Why not?"

"We trade stories about casual flings. She's becoming a new friend."

Referring to her as a new friend seems to undervalue my feelings toward her. I'm not sure what the right label would be, but she's special.

"Friend? Right! You aren't getting off that easy, but for now, you need to open your eyes to the bigger issue. With one of the chefs out of the competition, she'll compete for the prize. And her fingerprints were on the bowl of dip that killed Chef Boucher. If they hadn't also found other unidentified fingerprints on that bowl, she would be under arrest now."

My mind is whirring, trying to think of a benign reason her prints were found on the dish. I'm drawing a blank, but giving Cassandra the benefit of the doubt, I say, "There must be another explanation for the prints. Remember, she may want to be a chef, but she's trained as a lawyer. If she were going to purposefully kill Leon, she's too smart to leave fingerprints on the bowl."

"Maybe she thought she wiped them off but missed one."

"I doubt it. I can't help feeling something is very wrong here. I've spent my whole life on alert for people trying to trick me or pull something over on me. I don't get that vibe from Cassandra. I'm never this wrong."

"Are you really that into her? You would usually walk away from trouble rather than defend it."

Sean gives me a perplexed look, squinting his eyes as if trying to read me. That won't do him any good though. I'm confused about my feelings for Cassandra. The only thing I'm sure of is that she needs protection from the forces mounting against her.

Leaning forward, elbows on my knees, I say, "You know I'm not interested in serious relationships, but I enjoy spending time with her. During the past few days, she's been a helpful distraction from some heavier, personal issues I'm sorting through. I also don't want to see her life ruined. That's all this is."

Sean's forehead scrunches. "You never did tell me what brought you here for a break from your family."

I wave his comment off with a flip of my hand. "I was going to tell you sooner, but you're dealing with too much. My problems can wait."

Leaning forward, his voice serious, he says, "We're friends. Tell me what's going on."

Sighing, I say, "It's going to sound trivial in comparison with murder, but I'm struggling with whether I'll ever have a place or purpose of my own. You're running a major business now, whereas I'm posing for photos. I need to do more. I want to make a difference."

"I had no idea. I should've noticed," he says, shaking his head.

I shrug. "I'm well-trained to hide any discontent from the world."

The downside to that talent is that no one thinks to check on me. By design, everyone assumes I'm the most content, well-adjusted man in the world. Sean is one of the few people I dare open up to about my reality.

"What can I do to help? Aren't you expected to do the bidding of the king? Isn't that important work?"

His view isn't surprising. I've tried to convince myself that it's true but failed.

Shaking my head, I explain, "It usually amounts to little more than handshaking, ribbon cutting, and endorsing charities. Granted, those things are important to the people involved, but those tasks could be done by anyone in my extended family. I want my university degree to matter and my life to have more meaning and impact than what currently lies ahead. I need to be useful as *me*, not merely because I have a royal title."

"Look how you've jumped in to help me review financials and run this cooking competition. Your title has absolutely nothing to do with that."

"Exactly."

"I assume you're not wanting to disavow your title, right?"

My eyes go wide in surprise. That thought had never crossed my mind.

"Of course not. I'm fine with using my title to help people, but I need to work on more substantive projects than what tradition dictates."

"Got it. We need to brainstorm."

I'm relieved that Sean understands and doesn't try to convince me that I'm wrong. It's a reminder of why we're best friends.

"Thanks. You're one of the only people who can understand my predicament and not judge me for questioning my situation. I can't talk with my family without hurting their feelings, and most outsiders would naively trade places with me in a heartbeat."

"It's funny. When we were younger, our only goal was to do nothing other than travel and party. Look at us now." He chuckles, lightening the moment.

"I'm not giving up those things entirely." I smirk.

"We'll figure this out. Now, are you going to tell me what's really going on with Cassie?" He grins, raising his eyebrows.

Palms up, I say, "Nothing really. I'm not looking for a relationship, and she's not the one-night-and-done type. Like I said, we enjoy spending time together, and she's in a similar place to where I am. I understand what she's going through. It's hard to watch her be so close to her dream but stuck as merely the spare. Being drawn into a murder investigation is too much. It could ruin her life."

I've spent my life as the alternate—around just in case they need a substitute for my older brother. I'm happy that my brother will be king one day, but my position is a double-edged sword. On one side, I have a special role, which is an honor. It's the other side that's difficult to handle. If I'm never needed as a replacement, why am I needed at all? I don't want Cassandra to experience even a modicum of these same feelings, but I know she does. If I could make them go away, I would.

"I'm not buying that you don't have something brewing with Cassie, but I know you don't do serious. Back to Leon's death, if Cassie isn't the murderer, it probably was one of the other finalists trying to eliminate a key competitor. They're the only ones with anything to gain," Sean says, handing me a refill.

I'm preferring Sean's new direction of thinking. At least, he's seriously considering that someone other than Cassandra may be the killer.

"That's a real possibility. The other main player here is the host, Amy. But she seemed genuinely shaken. I don't think she was faking it, and I'm not sure what her motive would've been."

"I agree. Amy was upset. Of course, she's used to being on camera and could be a good actor," Sean says.

"Perhaps. I would guess most of these people aren't used to a homicide detective interviewing them, so that would agitate them as well. As for the finalists, all three were either upset, pissed off, or both. In fact, they seemed more focused on whether the competition would continue than the fact that Chef Boucher was dead."

Sean frowns. "I noticed that and found it unsettling. They came across as a selfish group, but they have a lot to gain if the competition goes forward. They also benefit directly from Mr. Boucher's demise, so one of them may be responsible for it."

If I were Sean, I'm not sure I would want any of them as my guest chef given their attitudes. Cassandra would be much more pleasant to have around. The Athena's guests would love her, but I'll keep that to myself for now. Sean already thinks I'm too biased.

Instead, I say, "I was impressed with how professional Cynthia was. She held it together well."

"Yes. My father hired her two or three years before he died. She can be a little dramatic at times, but overall, she's always had a professional approach."

"Hold on. I have an idea. Did you consider that maybe the assailant didn't intend to kill Mr. Boucher but rather wanted to make him sick enough to drop out?"

"That's an interesting angle. If that's the case, then the killer could be anyone we interviewed. If you're right, the murderer would've been genuinely upset that Leon actually died rather than just becoming ill. Hopefully, the police will find something in the rest of the video footage. I'm still wondering when the hummus was switched for the bean dip. Did you notice if one of the finalists lingered in the fridge when they took their cart in? I couldn't tell when we watched the videos."

"No. Too bad there isn't a camera inside the refrigerator. Though come to think of it, maybe it was an accident after all."

"What do you mean?"

"What if Leon planned to demonstrate that bean dip is a good substitute for hummus? The best way to prove that would be to prepare a taste test where people could compare his bean dip with hummus. Perhaps he accidentally grabbed the wrong container to taste."

"Interesting. I don't remember seeing him prepare hummus on the prep video though."

"He could have used pre-made hummus and grabbed it from the fridge when he rolled his cart in."

"True. We should check the video of the cart at the pool. But there's another problem. He knew sesame seeds were on the 'do not use' list. Using that ingredient would have disqualified him."

"He could have interpreted the rules differently. He didn't actually use the ingredient in his recipe. He would've been using the hummus for comparison."

"You're sounding like a lawyer. Do you think he would take that chance? I still think we would've disqualified him, but it's possible he didn't see it that way."

"What should we do next?"

"Most importantly, you need to stay away from Cassie."

I should've seen that coming, but that's not what I want to hear.

"That doesn't seem right."

Staring directly at me until he has my full attention, Sean points his finger at me. "I will not have you endangering yourself while at the Athena by consorting with a murder suspect. If something happens to you, I don't want to be the one to call your mother, the queen, to explain."

Turning away, I stare out the window. "I'll be careful. I must admit that I don't know what to think about Cassandra right now, but my gut is still telling me that she wasn't involved."

Sean laughs. "Are you sure it's your gut talking?"

"For fuck's sake, let it go. I'll be careful. If Leon's death wasn't an accident, then his death, Chef Bernard's death, and your increased expenses may be linked."

"But we don't have any evidence tying them together." He frowns.

The more we've talked about these issues, the more strained his voice has become. Understandably, the stress is getting to him.

"No actual evidence, but there are too many bad things happening to keep writing them off as unrelated. You need to quickly explain the higher food expenses."

"I agree. The coincidences are adding up. This situation is incredibly frustrating, and, in the unlikely event the deaths are related, it's a dangerous situation. Hopefully, the police will resolve the two deaths quickly. Their involvement should dissuade anyone from further criminal activity for fear of being caught."

"Let's hope. What's the plan on the accounting side?"

"Tomorrow, the finance guys are giving me a detailed summary of invoices for each F&B supplier for the past year. That should be enough information for me to identify the problem or at least figure out a pattern that will explain the expenses. I need answers because other than you, there's no one I can trust now," he says, rubbing his bloodshot eyes.

"I understand."

Sean's plan is a good start, but I have a nagging feeling it may not answer enough of his questions. I suspect that whatever is going on at the Athena is more complicated than we know. That means he's right not to trust anyone.

23

EVAN

I wake up to a text from Sean.

Finishing breakfast, I shower and put on a suit.

As I'm walking to Sean's office, the irony of my situation hits me. I'm wearing suits as much on my vacation as I would at home doing my parents' bidding. It's not that I mind, but I thought more casual attire would have the added effect of helping me think outside my usual box. Perhaps Sean wouldn't mind if I adopt business casual as my attire for some of the upcoming competition events.

"Evan, thanks for arriving early. You didn't have to be here, but I'd like your opinion."

"No worries. How can I help?"

"I have a tough decision to make about Cassie, and I'm under the impression you'd kill me if I don't let you weigh in."

"What decision?"

"I have to decide whether to allow Cassie to compete in Leon's place."

I may not be able to prove Cassandra's innocence, but my time with her is telling me that she deserves my support.

"What's hard about that? She's the alternate."

"She's also the number one murder suspect in Leon's death. While the presence of her fingerprints on the bowl is far from conclusive, it's the only physical evidence and the best lead the police have so far. Considering the bad publicity if she's arrested and the responsibility to keep everyone safe, it's not an easy decision."

"What happened to being presumed innocent until proven guilty?"

Before Sean can answer, we hear a brief knock on the door, and Emily shows Detective Fielder in.

Sean asks the detective to sit on the white sculpture-like chair across from the leather sofa where we're seated.

"Detective, have you figured out what happened?" Sean asks impatiently.

He pulls out his ever-present notebook and calmly responds, "Not yet, but we're making progress. However, we need some additional fingerprint samples."

"Does that mean you haven't been able to identify the remaining prints on the bowl of hummus?" I ask, surprised. For Cassandra's sake, I'd hoped the detective would have at least one more suspect today.

"Not all of them. Ms. Edwards turned up quickly because when she became a lawyer, they recorded her fingerprints. As I mentioned yesterday, we have at least one more set of fingerprints that we haven't been able to identify. We understand that the Athena has biometric data for its employees and guests that includes fingerprints. Mr. Cartwright, could you send us that information for everyone we interviewed yesterday, so we can compare them to the unidentified prints? That would speed up the process."

I wasn't excited about the Athena having that data until now.

Sean shakes his head. "Unfortunately, we can't share that data without a court order. It would violate our privacy policy. However, Emily can arrange for you to meet with those people to take their fingerprints directly, if they agree. What else are you doing?"

That'll be useless. No murderer would provide their prints. And what if the guilty party is someone who wasn't interviewed? I bloody wish that Sean could turn over the prints for everyone in the hotel.

"We're running checks on everyone involved and having our video experts analyze all the footage more carefully. It'll take time to get through it. In the meantime, what have you decided to do about the competition?"

"That's why I asked for this meeting. I'd prefer to proceed with the competition, but I want your input about Cassie. Technically, she should be stepping in to compete now. However, if you're about to arrest her, then that would change how we proceed."

I glare at him in horror, but he doesn't look at me. Arrest her? Why would Sean suggest such a thing?

"Ms. Edwards is a person of interest, but we're not ready to make an arrest. However, while we finish the investigation, everyone involved in the competition should remain in Las Vegas. Therefore, letting the competition continue may be the best way to do that."

Quietly letting out the breath I was holding, I ask, "Are you convinced Mr. Boucher was murdered?"

"We don't have another explanation, so more likely than not, we're looking at a homicide."

I guess I'll have to provide a possible scenario, so I say, "What if Chef Boucher was planning to let the guests compare the bean dip with hummus? It's likely the Athena stocks pre-prepared hummus in the walk-in fridge. He could have grabbed it and put it on his cart when he was in there. He may have tasted the wrong dip. It could've been a simple accident."

"That's an interesting thought, but we didn't see two serving bowls or a preprepared container of hummus in the videos."

That's not definitive, and I'm not giving up on Cassandra. I doubt they were looking for an extra bowl when they watched the videos.

Sean says, "Let's turn back to the toughest decision. If we're going forward with the competition, what should we do about Cassie?"

My fists clench. I'm frustrated trying to balance Sean's concerns with my feelings. He already knows what I think, but Detective Fielder doesn't. I can't stay quiet any longer, so I lean forward and argue, "This shouldn't be a tough decision. According to the rules, Cassandra should replace Leon. Not only would it be entirely unfair to exclude her, but it would also irreparably harm her reputation. It's uncalled for when the police aren't even sure Leon's death was anything more than an accident. If Cassandra doesn't compete, everyone will assume it's because she's the prime suspect. That accusation and the associated gossip will follow her forever. As they say, you cannot un-ring that bell."

Detective Fielder holds up his hand to stop me. "I agree the competition should proceed according to the rules. If that means Ms. Edwards competes, then that's what should happen. With your permission, we'll have two undercover officers on hand during the competition to keep an eye on things and ensure everyone's safety. Continuing with the competition will keep the competitors and crew here, and it may force the guilty party to show his or her hand."

With Cassandra here, we can work together to protect her reputation. At least that's one reason I'm glad she'll be staying.

Sean says, "Okay. The Athena will also take extra security precautions. I'll call a meeting tomorrow morning for the crew, staff, and finalists to restart the competition. Can you have your people in place by then?"

"Yes, but I want to make sure no one outside this room knows we have undercover officers here."

"Understood. I'll only tell Emily and Cynthia." Sean stares a hole through me, making sure I receive the unspoken message that I can't share this information with Cassandra.

Detective Fielder responds, "No. I mean absolutely no one other than you and Mr. Catalinius. There's no reason anyone else needs to know. We can give the undercover officers real jobs in the kitchen, and they'll do the actual work while also acting as security. I can't risk another leak. I'm already concerned that information about the allergic reaction and fingerprint may have leaked to the press."

I'm instantly on my feet, livid. "What do you mean the info about Cassandra's fingerprint was leaked to the press? Are you trying to ruin her career?"

"Please calm down. I said it *may* have been leaked. One of the officers told me that a reporter from the local newspaper was lurking in the police station when the fingerprint analysis came back from the lab. He feared the reporter may have overheard the discussion before they realized who was present. We've asked the newspaper not to print any details at this time."

I pace, trying to rein in my fury. How dare they let something like that leak to the press? There's no way it won't end up in print.

"Asking the newspaper is not the same as ensuring that they don't print such speculation. You need to make certain this story doesn't show up in print."

"Mr. Catalinius, we don't have the level of control over the press that some other countries do, but we've taken the steps we can. Now, Mr. Cartwright, what do we need to do to get our undercover officers in place here?"

"If you want them to have the employee badges and access, then we need to at least tell Emily. She'll need to work around some systems to make it happen. We could have one of them help with the kitchen set up. The other one could be on clean-up duty during the events. I think they could easily fade into the background that way."

"Okay. That works. And you may tell Emily since she hasn't been involved in any of the events. But let me make it crystal clear—no one else can know—no exceptions."

"Please coordinate with Emily."

"Great. Make sure she understands that someone's life may depend on her discretion."

"Understood."

Am I the only one concerned they're effectively setting the finalists up as bait for a potential killer? But I don't say anything. The only way Cassandra can compete is if this moves forward, and I want that for her.

24

CASSIE

As I arrive at the competition meeting, Trenton is talking with Kai in the hallway. Before they see me, Trenton says, "I overheard Cynthia telling Amy the police found Cassie's fingerprints on the bowl."

Damn. They've all heard the rumor that I'm the prime suspect.

My stomach clenches as I'm overcome with anguish and uncertainty. How did I end up in this situation? All I did was apply to a cooking competition. This is unbelievable. I have no family for support, and I'm not allowed to call Lowri. It's me against the world with no one to turn to. Somehow, I have to prove my innocence because everyone has already tried and convicted me based on rumor alone.

I fight off the urge to run and hide because I can't untangle this knotted mess if I'm secreted away in my room. I need to keep my eyes and ears open, hoping someone will divulge a helpful clue as to who the real killer is.

Pretending like nothing's wrong, I walk into the conference meeting. The aroma of freshly baked bread and coffee draws my eyes to a table with breakfast foods. I'd normally fill a plate with samples, but I can't eat now. My stomach is churning so much I'm not even sure hot tea will stay down.

I find my spot at the empty conference table. Leaning forward with my hands covering my face, I try to hold it together. It's ironic—I thought my regular job was stressful, but this is a whole new level. Never in my wildest dreams would I have thought I'd be a murder suspect.

My heart pounds, threatening to explode, as I think of what my law firm will do if they catch wind of this fiasco.

Soon, the room is filled with talking and the clinking of cups and plates as the other competitors and crew fill the chairs around the conference table. None of them approach me. In fact, they are visibly keeping their distance, pretending not to notice my presence. But, from all the sideways glares, they aren't actually hiding their opinions of me. What a shit show!

When Sean and Evan enter the boardroom, I hazard a glance at Evan. With tousled hair, he's smoldering hot in a dark-blue blazer, cream-colored polo shirt, and khakis, but he has dark circles under his eyes. I do too.

I haven't spoken to him since the interview with Detective Fielder. I'd hoped Evan might reach out to me, but he hasn't. He must think I'm guilty too. Or at least, he doesn't want to be associated with a murder suspect, innocent or not, and I can't blame him.

I hear Sean whisper to Cynthia and Amy that he's going to run the meeting.

Standing at the head of the table, he says, "Thank you for meeting us here this morning. We appreciate the patience you've shown while we worked through the procedures and logistics in light of Chef Boucher's tragic death. After careful consideration, we've made the decision to proceed with the Guest Chef Competition. Round 1 will take place this afternoon."

Questions start flying. "Does that mean the investigation is over?"

"Was it an accident?"

"Has the murderer been arrested?"

"What's the new competition schedule?"

I don't say anything, but I have a different question running through my head: *Does this mean they believe I'm innocent?*

In his characteristic signal for silence, Sean holds up his hand and says, "While I'm not going to take individual questions, I'll go over a few details, so please let me continue."

The room quiets.

"First, the investigation is ongoing. The police haven't made a final determination about the accident, but they hope to have the case closed quickly. We've decided to proceed with Rounds 1, 2, and 3 of the competition as planned. Each round will feature one of the three traditional courses of a meal. That means Round 1 is appetizers, Round 2 is entrées, and Round 3 is desserts. However, we won't be doing any more demos, given the delays. That said, there will still be interviews and photo shoots around the property that you'll be asked to participate in. I'm also pleased to announce that because none of the actual competition rounds had taken place, Cassie Edwards will be competing as the fourth finalist."

My head shoots up in reaction. Did Sean just say I'm competing? Hopefully, that means I'm no longer a suspect.

But before I can bask in that positive thought, Trenton's brusque voice interrupts as he blurts out, "Why are you letting a killer compete?"

I flinch at the harsh verbal punch that stings like a real one. I'm not sure what to do. Should I speak up in my defense or sit here pretending I don't know that he's referring to me? I'm ill-equipped to handle this situation, having been the rule-follower throughout most of my life. Not that I'm perfect, but I've never set out to break rules or get in trouble. The fact that these people don't know me is little consolation.

I could withdraw from the competition, but they'd twist that into an admission of guilt. I can't imagine having to live the rest of my life in this shadow. But unless the actual culprit is caught, this is going to follow me forever.

Sean responds, "No one here has been accused of anything, so I don't want to hear another comment of that nature. As far as we know, Mr. Boucher's death was a tragic accident. I expect each person in this room to treat everyone else with respect and courtesy. Deviation from that expectation is grounds for disqualification."

Trenton's question simultaneously pisses me off and makes me feel like an outcast. How can I stay here? My mind is racing and foggy at the same time. I can't think straight. How am I supposed to compete after everything that's happened?

Trembling, I crave the touch of the only person in the room who could provide solace. I want to snuggle against Evan's warm body for a comforting hug and feel his strong hand against my back, pulling me close, even if just one more time. Can't he sense that I need him? Why won't he look at me?

But that doesn't seem likely, and even if the rules allowed it, I don't want to call Lowri and pull her into this mess. She's already seen me through enough tough times.

Sean continues, "As originally planned, the competition will conclude with what we're calling the Final Dinner, which will occur in the Athena's Wine Cave. We'll announce the winner then. At 2 p.m. today, we'll meet in the kitchen at Trendz for Round 1 of the competition."

He and Evan leave the room.

I close my eyes to gather my thoughts, but I can hear others collecting their belongings, followed by their soft footsteps on the carpet as they exit the room. A few of them whisper not-so-kind words as they leave. I hear "Murderer," "She doesn't stand a chance," and "She should leave the competition to the pros."

I don't bother to open my eyes. I don't want to know who uttered those words.

Soon the room is silent, but I don't think my legs are stable enough to walk. If I sit here until everyone has time to leave the conference floor, no one will notice. I'll return to my room where I can figure out what to do next.

About five minutes later, I open my eyes and put my hands on the table to push myself up. That's when I see Evan. He's leaning against the wall across the table from me with his hands in his pockets. His tired eyes focus on me as if he's trying to read my mind.

"Evan, I saw you leave. What are you doing here?"

"I came back. We need to talk."

"About what?"

"What do you think? This cocked-up mess."

"Oh. Okay."

I sit back down, propping my arms on the table and massaging my temples.

"How are you doing?"

"Not well. Everyone thinks I'm either the murderer or unqualified to be here. While the latter may be true, I'm not a killer! However, I have no clue how to prove I'm innocent. I should've already hired a lawyer, but I was afraid that would make me look even guiltier."

"Aren't you a lawyer?"

"I am, but my specialty is corporate law, not criminal law. Despite what Sean said about it being an accident, if the case remains open, I suspect my innocence is still in question."

Hands remaining in his pockets, Evan approaches the table, stopping directly across from me. "Your instincts are right, and because of that, Sean is telling me to stay far away from you. However, my gut isn't sure he's right. A big part of me wants to find a way to help you."

A tear escapes and trickles down my right cheek. "How can you help me? Besides, I can't imagine it's good for your family's business, whatever it is, to associate with a murder suspect."

As I wait for Evan to respond, he looks everywhere except at me. He must be rethinking his desire to help me. He strides to a small table in the corner of the room and quickly returns, placing a cube-shaped box of tissues in front of me. He pulls out a tissue, rotates my chair to face him, and sinks to his knee. He gently reaches up, drying my tears as his eyes study me intently.

I've been alone for a long time, so I'm not used to someone taking care of me. It's exciting but raises my recurring fear that I'll be left again.

I analyze Evan's face as he says, "You have no idea how right you are about my family and its business. But I stand by my friends when they need my help. And I'd like to think that we've become friends."

His statement of support means a lot. I'm relieved he still considers us friends. I hope we're more than that. Maybe he does too. But even if our brief time together has been a true romantic connection, I don't want to be the cause of friction with his family. Family is something you shouldn't take for granted.

"Thanks for wanting to stand by me, but you need to protect your family and its reputation. I didn't do anything wrong. I just have to figure out how to prove it. Doesn't the Athena have security videos that would show if someone tampered with Leon's food?"

Leaning back in his chair, Evan shakes his head. "They haven't found anything on the videos yet, but they're still going through them."

"This whole mess is so confusing. How did my fingerprints get on the serving bowl? Do you remember seeing me touch Leon's bowl? Do you think someone is setting me up? You won't believe what's running through my head. I started wondering if this is like a movie plot where someone used sticky tape to transfer my fingerprints onto the bowl. My mind just keeps running through all these outlandish possibilities because I know I didn't kill him. If I don't clear my name, this is going to follow me for the rest of my life, even if I avoid prison." I take a deep breath, needing air after my rant.

In a soft, calming voice, Evan says, "Slow down. I don't know how your fingerprints got onto the bowl. I don't remember seeing you touch anything the chefs were using, but we can go over everything we both remember from the prep session and the poolside demo. However, you need to focus on Round 1 and the appetizer you plan to prepare right now. The competition starts in a few hours. Afterward, we can discuss whether there's anything we can do to help the police find the truth quickly. Let's meet in my suite at 8 p.m. tonight."

"You mean you still want to help me? You believe me? What about upsetting your family?" I'm overwhelmed with gratitude and emotion. As I attempt to dry the remaining tears with more tissues, Evan walks around the table. His strong hands clasp my upper arms. He gently helps me to my feet, turns me toward him, and pulls me against his chest.

His right hand steadies my back, and his left cradles my head. "I'm probably too trusting, but yes, I believe you. Let me worry about my family. If all goes well, your name will be cleared without them ever hearing about the events here. Now, focus on the competition. Keep your eyes and ears open this afternoon. And be careful. If Leon was killed, then you may be in danger too."

Snapping my head back to look Evan in the eye, I gasp. "I hadn't thought of that."

Shit. Someone could be trying to eliminate more of the finalists, not just Leon. And now I'm one of the targets.

25

CASSIE

After talking with Evan, I know it's time to take action. I wouldn't have survived the death of my parents, university, and my job if I weren't capable. It's time to toughen up and take control again. I have a once-in-a-lifetime opportunity to compete against outstanding chefs, so that's what I'm going to do. I'll also take Evan's advice to listen and learn. It's possible that someone will say something that clues me in to what's really going on around here.

With renewed hope and a sense of empowerment, I walk into the Trendz kitchen.

When we're all assembled, one of the crew has us draw casino chips to determine which station each of us will use. I draw the $100 chip and get to pick first. I select the station closest to the pantry and walk-in fridge, and as a bonus, they tell me I get to keep the chip!

After we're settled in our positions, the cameras start filming.

Amy says, "Welcome to the prep session for Round 1 of the Grand Athena's Guest Chef Competition. You'll each have sixty minutes to create an appetizer that reflects something special about you. Remember, Trendz is a fun, upscale restaurant, but it's not pretentious. Its chef has wide latitude to express their style. For example, a prior chef once offered a sampler that paired three high-end wines with three versions of short-rib sliders. So, relax and let us learn something about who you are—not who you think we want you to be. That means your appetizer doesn't need to be fancy—just delicious, eye-catching, and personal.

We've installed a timer on the wall. Keep an eye on it. I'll count you down to the start: five … four … three … two … Wait! I forgot to tell you about the twist. You must use the dip you made for the demo as part of your appetizer. Cassie, you must use the dip you wrote down at the first meeting. What was it?"

"Tomatillo Pineapple Salsa Verde," I answer while internally panicking. It's going to be a time crunch to make the dip and the rest of the appetizer.

Holding up the slip of paper, Amy confirms, "That's right! Okay, everyone, get ready. Five … four … three … two … one … COOK!"

The other three finalists brush by me in a mad rush to the pantry and fridge. Rather than be trampled, I let them pass before following to grab tomatillos, onions, and jalapeños to roast for the dip. First lesson: when Amy says COOK, run for the pantry. The clock is ticking, so don't waste time.

As I fill a large bowl with the ingredients, I rack my brain for the best way to incorporate my dip into the lobster and avocado bruschetta that I plan to garnish with thinly sliced strawberries. I could puree the dip and drizzle it on top, but that doesn't seem very creative. Hmm.

I'll figure something out, but I need to get these ingredients prepped and under the broiler quickly. It's going to be tight to get everything done in an hour.

A cacophony of pans clanging on cooktops, oven doors opening, and knives chopping fills the kitchen as the aroma of sautéing garlic from Trenton's station competes with the smell of Jayden's food frying in a vat of oil.

As we cook, Evan watches from the sidelines, while Amy goes from station to station asking questions. With a camera hoisted on his right shoulder, one of the crew follows her to capture the exchanges. It's hard to concentrate while also wanting to listen to what the other finalists are saying. Over the kitchen noises, I hear Trenton explain he's serving his roasted tomato and kale dip on miniature, fried cheese ravioli. I admit that sounds good. Kai tells Amy that he's using his papaya tapenade as a relish on pork sliders. Who wouldn't like those? The competition is definitely stiff.

As I finish prepping my salsa ingredients, I wonder what Jayden is going to do with his Texas Fondue gravy. Then I hear him say he's making mini chicken tenders served on bamboo toothpicks with a drizzle of the fondue. He's limited to what works with the gravy, so it makes sense. I'm just relieved that my appetizer will fit in and won't be the simplest one.

Amy comes to my station as I'm closing the oven door. "Cassie, what are you making for your appetizer?"

"I'm making Lobster and Avocado Bruschetta."

"That sounds delicious. Tell us more."

"I'm spreading a thin layer of avocado butter on toasted baguette slices. Then I'll top them with bite-sized pieces of lobster and garnish with cilantro leaves and a slice of strawberry or radish."

"I can't wait to taste them. How are you incorporating your dip?"

Fortunately, as I was prepping the dip ingredients, I figured it out. "I'm mixing my Tomatillo Pineapple Salsa Verde with the avocado butter, which will enhance the flavor and complement the lobster. I may also drizzle a little on top of the lobster. I haven't decided yet."

"I'll let you keep working."

Addressing everyone, Amy says, "Don't forget to keep your eye on the clock! You only have forty minutes left. We can't wait to see your finished appetizers."

Confirming with the wall clock that twenty minutes have already passed, I run to the fridge to grab the lobster tails. Having forgotten to grab a bowl to carry everything, I try to balance the lobster in my arms as I grab the rest of the ingredients I need. If I can hold everything, I'll save a couple of crucial minutes.

Barely making it back to my station with my armload of food pressed against my chest, I bend forward to let everything gently fall onto the prep table. Then I rush to my oven to check on the tomatillos and other veggies.

I sauté the lobster in butter and lemon and move it off the heat to cool while I prepare the avocados, strawberries, and radishes. That leaves me just enough time to toast the baguette slices. Shit! I forgot to grab a baguette from the pantry! Running, I grab one and race back to my station.

I smell something burning and panic, thinking it's my tomatillos. I check them and sigh in relief. They're browning with a few charred bits, which will be perfect. However, someone else screams "Fuck!" Looking around, I'm surprised to see it came from Jayden, who's always quiet and introverted. Then I understand why he's so upset. He's pulling small, black lumps of coal from the deep fryer. Those were supposed to be his fried chicken bites. Hopefully, he'll have time to fry another batch.

When Amy announces we have fifteen minutes left, I'm already hustling to mash the avocado.

Each time I check the wall clock, another five have gone. I throw the tomatillos and other dip ingredients into the food processor and pulse it a few times. After a quick taste, I add a little more salt and then spoon some dip onto the smashed avocados. I run back to the pantry, dodging a camera guy who's trying to follow me. I quickly grab plates and a squeeze bottle for the salsa. Returning to my station, the clock indicates I only have five minutes to assemble everything and make it look good.

When the buzzer sounds, we stop and step back from our stations, hands held high to indicate we're done. Smiling broadly, I high-five Kai, who's at the station next to me. I did it! That was a wild adrenaline rush. I actually completed a competition round, and my appetizers look great! It's a dream come true.

I haven't felt this alive in a long time. I've also never known sixty minutes to fly by so fast. I barely got the last cilantro leaf and drizzle of salsa in place when Amy called time. But now that it's over, I realize just how hot the kitchen has become with the cook-tops, ovens, and intense lights for the cameras. I'm dripping with sweat, with random wisps of hair escaping my ponytail. I must look like a mess, but I wouldn't change a second of this experience!

Once the cameras stop recording, Amy explains, "Judging will start in fifteen minutes, so stay nearby. When the judging begins, the cameras will be rolling here in the kitchen and the judging room. You'll each meet with the judges individually. According to the rules, you won't know what they think about the other chefs' appetizers. Unlike many other competitions, there are no eliminations. You'll be cooking in all three rounds but won't know any results until the Final Dinner. We want to keep the information about how everyone is doing a secret until the very end to build suspense so that the final results will be a complete surprise to everyone. You can be disqualified if you discuss the judge's comments with each other. Do you understand?"

We nod. At least I don't have to worry about being eliminated. Everyone will compete in all the rounds. That takes a little pressure off.

Amy continues, "Don't go near your station or anyone else's. Feel free to grab a cold bottle of water while you wait for the judging to start. There are also stools set up where you can wait. Any questions?"

Silence. After the intensity of the cooking round, we're too tired to ask anything at this point.

As I take a bottle of water, I wonder how well my appetizer will compare to the others. Regardless, I'm determined to hold my head high and be an active participant in this competition.

The other finalists are at the table chatting with each other, so I join them and wish everyone good luck. At first, I mainly listen because I'm not sure what their reaction to me will be. But Kai pulls me into the conversation, asking if I've tried any fruits other than pineapple in my salsa. He thinks mango or papaya might work well. Trenton is still cold toward me, but he's reasonably civil. At least the common bond of the Round 1 experience seems to make my presence tolerable to them.

Slightly reassured, I ask what they know about the judges. This is the first time we're interacting with them, so I'm nervous but also excited. I follow most of the cooking shows on the FFT Channel and a few other chefs with famous cookbooks, but I don't know much about these judges. They all have successful restaurants, so I'm kicking myself for not having a broader knowledge of well-known chefs in general. After this competition, I'll pay more attention.

The other finalists know everything about the judges and are quick to share. I think they want to scare me, but information is power, so I absorb it all.

Apparently, Judge Gerard is super picky about presentation. Even one stray drop of sauce annoys him. Judge Holden loves salt and wants everything over-salted. That's not good for me because I tend to err on the lighter side when it comes to salt. Judge Indigo replaced Chef Bernard when she died in the car crash. They say he hates cilantro.

These preferences may not bode well for me. I don't like a lot of salt, and there's cilantro in the salsa. I can't change that now.

One of the crew members taps me on the shoulder and says, "It's your turn. Follow me to the judging area."

Before we leave the kitchen, the crew member instructs, "When you go in, the camera will already be running, so walk slowly and stop on the big red X. Amy will welcome you. Then the judges will taste your appetizer. They may ask you a few questions and give you feedback."

"Got it."

Pushing the door open, he says, "Good luck."

Letting out a deep breath, I say, "Thanks," and walk in.

While we cooked, staff transformed the restaurant into a set for the judging. It's dark except for carefully focused spotlights, illuminating the three solemn judges seated behind a long table on an elevated platform. They look ready to attack anything that offends them in the least, so I prepare myself to smile through the worst!

The table is draped with a black cloth that skims the floor, and a mirror-like silver dome sits in front of each judge. Cameras and crew are positioned along my path toward the judges. On autopilot, I abruptly halt when my sneakers land on the illuminated X. Taking another deep breath and clasping my hands in front of me to avoid fidgeting, I smile and try to soak in the moment. I can't believe I'm really standing here.

When I notice Sean and Evan standing off to the side, my smile widens. It hadn't occurred to me they would be here, but it makes sense. Evan returns my smile, but Sean's face is neutral at best.

After Amy welcomes me, the judges ask where I'm from.

"San Diego."

Why did I start cooking?

"My grandparents encouraged me and sent me to a culinary summer camp in high school. After that, I was hooked."

What does the competition mean to me, and what will I do with the money if I win?

"It's a chance of a lifetime for me as a home cook to compete against these professional chefs. The money would allow me to pay off student loans and pursue a career that is more in line with my dreams rather than what others have expected of me. It's a chance to start fresh and leave behind some baggage."

I'm not sure why I shared the part about others' expectations and my baggage. I rarely even admit those things to myself. But I tell myself to keep smiling—no regrets.

As the judges taste my appetizer, I cross my fingers that the toasted baguette slices didn't get soggy during the wait.

The judges point out things they like and things that could be improved. Fortunately, Judge Gerard doesn't criticize my presentation, which for him is the same as complimenting it. However, he would've preferred one larger piece of lobster rather than the multiple, small bites I used. I expected Judge Holden to want more salt, but she wants "a lot more salt." At least she likes the way I incorporated the dip.

Judge Indigo looks at my cilantro-laced appetizer, then at me, then back to the appetizer. This roller coaster goes downhill fast when he starts with "I absolutely despise cilantro. Never have liked it. Never will."

Not good.

Remember to keep smiling. I can handle this. It's just a taste preference, not a personal attack on my food. Although it was difficult, I worked hard to learn how to accept criticism and learn from it in my regular job. I need to use those techniques to control my emotions here. I can't argue with the judges or be defensive. That never looks good. And I don't want to start crying, so I grit my teeth behind my smile and try to breathe evenly. For extra measure, I push a fingernail into the palm of my hand, which usually staves off tears.

After a dramatic pause, Judge Indigo says with a huff, "However, you're fortunate that I'm not one of the people for whom cilantro tastes like soap, which according to experts may be as much as fourteen percent of the population. I just don't care for the flavor. Therefore, overlooking my personal taste preferences, I can appreciate your work today. It's pleasing to the eye and uses a smart combination of texture and colors. Just be careful about using ingredients, such as cilantro, that are commonly disliked."

Whew! I thank the judges for their feedback. Amy thanks me and tells me to return to the kitchen while the judges finish evaluating the other appetizers.

As I enter the kitchen, I'm met with focused stares from the other finalists, who are obviously trying to read my body language to know how the judging went. I'm guessing that I'm exuding relief because, overall, that's exactly how I feel.

The judges liked the concept of my appetizer and the flavor combination. Fortunately, even Judge Indigo was reasonably positive, which was surprising given that he hates one of my ingredients.

I smile and sit down at the table with the other finalists, simply saying, "Glad that's over."

26

CASSIE

With Round 1 complete, the crew and finalists pack up to leave. This is my best chance to investigate. It's risky, but I want to know if they keep hummus in the walk-in refrigerator.

I hang back and sneak into the fridge unnoticed. As I'm searching, I hear voices in the kitchen and tiptoe toward the fridge's door to see who's talking.

I recognize Jayden's soft, Texas drawl as he says, "I need to get out of here. Why did you summon me back?"

A second, deeper male voice says, "Do you want another advantage in the competition?"

What!? *Another* advantage? In shock, I lean closer to the door, pressing my face against the cold metal.

"I can use all the help I can get, but it depends on what I have to do. After you gave me an advantage before, Leon ended up dead. I hope his death wasn't connected to what I did for you. I don't want anyone to get hurt." His voice is shaky and trembling.

"Of course not. Don't worry. You simply have to sabotage one of the other finalists in the next round. It will only cause them to do poorly in Round 2."

"Okay. If you're sure no one will be hurt. What do you want me to do?"

"When the time comes, I'll let you know. Don't forget, when you win, you'll owe me."

"I won't."

I'm frozen in place by more than just the chill of the fridge as the deep-voiced man says, "You'll regret it if you do. Now let's get out of here."

"Where are you headed? The door is in the opposite direction," Jayden says.

"I don't want to be caught on camera, and we shouldn't be seen leaving together. I'm going to use the Maze. But you need to exit via the front door."

Just when I think they're about to leave, I hear Jayden again. "Hey, it looks like someone left the fridge door open again. I'll close it."

I quickly take off my shoes and move into a corner behind some crates. Crouching down as low as I can, I hide my face.

Deep Voice asks, "Is anyone in there?"

"Nah. Everyone left earlier. Someone was just careless."

"Check it out before you close the door to make sure. We don't want any eavesdroppers."

"You're being paranoid, but I'll check."

Hearing footsteps approach, blood rushes to my ears, pounding with each beat of my rapid pulse. I cover my mouth with my hand to muffle the noise from my fast, shallow breaths as I anxiously hope Jayden doesn't discover my hiding place.

"Okay. I'm out of here," says the unidentified man.

From the fridge door, Jayden calls out, "Is anyone in here?" I hold my breath as he wanders inside and quickly looks around. Then he turns off the light and shuts the heavy door behind him.

At first, I panic, hearing the loud thud as the fridge door closes. I'm stuck inside this frigid box without my phone. I could send a text to someone at the Athena via the TekCuff, but I don't want to risk a message going to the bad guys, whoever they are. I start taking deep breaths so I can think.

Then it hits me. In today's litigious environment, the manufacturer must provide a way out. They don't want to be sued if someone dies from being stuck inside.

With the faint light from my TekCuff, I move toward the door and feel for the light switch. Relief floods through me when I find a safety knob that will open the door. As my hand grasps it, ready to open the door, I hesitate, deciding to wait a little longer to make sure Jayden and Deep Voice are long gone.

Now that my pulse has slowed a little, I'm shivering all over. It's about 38 degrees Fahrenheit in here, and I don't have a jacket. I look at the time on my TekCuff and decide to wait five minutes. Hopefully, that will be long enough for it to be safe but not cause hypothermia.

I remind myself that I'm lucky. There's no telling what would've happened if they had found me.

As the five minutes count down, I think about what to do with this new information. I should call the police. But technically, the two guys didn't mention an actual crime. In fact, Deep Voice denied having anything to do with Leon's death, and I'm not sure rigging a private competition is illegal. It's hard to believe that all the strange happenings around this competition aren't related. At least I've finally found a lead that may help remove me from the list of suspects.

I wish Cynthia hadn't taken my phone. I could've recorded the conversation. Instead, I go back over what they said, trying to ingrain it in my memory.

Should I believe Deep Voice? Was the prior advantage related to Leon's death despite what he told Jayden? Or was it something simpler, such as Jayden knowing ahead of time that we had to use our dip in the appetizer round? That information would have given Jayden more time to decide what to make, which would be an advantage. It might explain why he made gravy for his dip.

It's also interesting that Deep Voice has access to the Maze and knows where the cameras are located. He must be an Athena employee, and for some reason, he wants Jayden to win this competition. But why?

Maybe I should tell Cynthia or Amy what I heard since they're in charge of the competition. The problem is that I can't prove that the conversation actually happened, so they may not believe me. They'll think I'm trying to get another chef tossed out.

I could tell Evan what I heard, but can I trust him? What do I know about him other than he works in his family's business and he's Sean's friend from college? He hasn't even told me what that business is. I could keep quiet about this a little longer and see if I can prove what's going on.

I have time to decide. I'm not meeting Evan for another hour or so.

Slowly opening the fridge door and exiting, I'm relieved the kitchen is dark and empty.

That was a close call.

27

EVAN

When Round 1 ends, I'm happy for Cassandra. She handled the judges' questions well, and her food looked delicious. As Sean and I leave the judging area, I ask, "Do you have time to chat?"

Between the murder investigation and Cassandra, my mind has been somewhat preoccupied, but there's still this burning need to figure out my future, and talking with Sean is the first step in solving at least that dilemma.

"Come with me to my office. We can have a drink before I turn back to work. I'll be up all night sorting through the rest of the F&B data."

"Okay. Anything interesting in the data so far?"

"Based on my initial review, it looks like we've been slowly dumping all our old suppliers and going with new ones. When we get to my office, I need to call my friend Wes. We quit using his company several months ago. I'm hoping he can shed some light on what's going on. Someone must have told him why we quit ordering from him. I'm surprised he didn't reach out to me directly when we dumped his company. I also want to know what he was doing at the pool the day Leon died."

"There's nothing particularly sinister about trying out new suppliers, but why would you do that if they cost more?"

"Exactly."

We arrive at his office a few minutes later.

"Let me get us drinks, then I'll call Wes. You can listen."

As I sip my Boulevardier, Sean dials.

Wes answers hesitantly, "Hello, Sean. What's up?"

"I just learned we quit ordering from your company. Can you tell me what happened?"

"Don't you know?"

Hearing the disbelief in Wes's voice, Sean slowly responds, "No. I wouldn't be asking if I knew. It recently came to my attention that we've made a number of changes in our F&B department that don't make sense to me. That's why I'm following up."

Sighing, Wes says, "Sean, I should've known you weren't involved, but I assumed you knew. I don't have all the answers, but we should talk in person."

"Okay. Do you have time for lunch tomorrow?"

"That works."

Sean replies, "Do you want to meet me at the VIP lounge here?"

"Definitely not. Let's meet at our favorite Mexican place downtown at one. It's been a long time, but you know where I mean, right?"

Why is he being so mysterious? Why not name the stupid restaurant? But Sean goes along and says, "Of course I know. See you then."

"That was strange," I say.

"It was. I've known Wes for much of my life, and that's the oddest conversation we've ever had. He usually can't wait to get past business to discuss the latest sports news, but he didn't even mention how his favorite baseball team is doing. Even more out of character, he turned down lunch in our VIP lounge. I can't remember him ever doing that. Something is seriously wrong."

"I'll be interested to hear what he says when you meet."

"You can go with me and hear it firsthand. How do you feel about Mexican food?"

"As long as it includes a margarita, it's good."

28

CASSIE

It's after 6:30 when I escape the walk-in fridge. I need a piping-hot shower to warm up.

Practically running, I rush through the door to my room and straight into the bathroom. I turn on the shower and peel off my clothes as steam quickly fogs the mirror. I'm a wimp when it comes to being cold, so I step under the waterfall shower and let out a satisfying moan. The warm water feels sooo good.

It would feel even better if Evan were here. I close my eyes, imagining all the things that gorgeous man could be doing to me. If only I could let myself give him a chance. Then I remember I've got bigger problems—I'm an effing murder suspect.

Damn. That put a halt to my sexy daydream.

As I'm toweling off, my TekCuff dings with a message.

Evan: I'll pick you up at 8.

That gives me an hour to dry my hair and then dress.

I pull my purple-and-white sundress from the closet and lay it on the bed.

Huh. The housekeeper left a copy of today's newspaper on the side table.

As I pick it up and see my face staring back at me, my legs give out, dropping me onto the edge of the bed. My whole body trembles as I take fast, shallow breaths, struggling to get air.

With sweaty palms staining the paper, I read the headline: "Lawyer Named Person of Interest in Athena Chef's Murder."

Shit! Shit! Shit!

An overwhelming sense of dread consumes me as I continue reading. The article states that my fingerprints were found on the bowl of hummus that *poisoned* Chef Boucher due to his food allergy.

My chest constricts in pain. This can't be happening. It's a complete disaster. This journalist has destroyed my reputation. I have to clear my name and make the newspaper print a retraction. Of course, papers usually don't put retractions on the front page, so I don't know how much good that will do.

I don't know how long I've been sitting here worrying about losing my job when someone knocks. In a state of confusion, I go to the door and open it. Evan is standing there smiling. Too upset to talk and wiping tears from my eyes, I thrust the newspaper at him.

He wraps his arms around me and guides me to the couch. "What happened?"

"I'm an emotional mess. Where's the newspaper?"

"I tossed it on the coffee table."

"I hadn't dressed yet when I found the newspaper with a front-page article accusing me of murder. Then you knocked on the door."

"Tell me about the article."

"I don't even know what to say. You need to read it."

"It can't be that bad."

"It is."

I watch Evan attempt to hide a scowl as he reads the horrible article. I'd sue them, except they stick to the facts and quotes from anonymous sources.

When he finishes, he throws the paper on the table and pulls me against his chest, saying, "It's going to be okay. Tonight, we were already planning to work on a strategy to clear your name. As much as I hate to say this, put some clothes on and let's go to my suite. We'll have more space to work there."

"Give me a minute."

Wrapped in my towel, I take my sundress into the bathroom and pull myself together.

A few minutes later, Evan places his hand on the small of my back, guiding me down the hallway and into the elevator. The moment those doors close, he turns to me and backs me against the wall, his nose tracing my neck, his hand smoothing the tiny straps of my sundress and then down my arm. Goosebumps follow in the wake of his fingertips. He pulls back, his gaze focused on me, one hand cupping the back of my head, his fingers laced into my hair.

I stare into his eyes, emotions muddled. I'm stupefied and relieved, turned on and unsure.

Evan says, "I know we said we can't do this right now. But I just needed to touch you. I have a feeling you needed it too."

I nod. He's right. It feels so good to be held that I sink into his arms, and thankfully, he doesn't let go.

I want so much more. I can't believe my body is reacting to his after seeing that horrid article. My heart is racing, and my skin tingles from his touch. I can't get close enough to him. I want to rip his shirt off and slide my hands over the peaks and valleys of his warm, muscular chest and forget about everything else.

I know he wants to help me because I'm his friend, but I want more than friendship, and, based on his tender touch, he does too.

With that thought, I pull my head back and look into his eyes. He meets my gaze with an intense stare, and his lips capture mine like he can't get enough of me either. Any thought of us being merely friends evaporates.

After a couple of minutes, he steps back, places his hands on my shoulders, and rests his forehead against mine. "Cassandra, I should apologize for diving into a kiss straight away, but I'm just not sorry. We need to focus on the real reason we're here though. Let's put this on hold for now."

Still panting, I manage to say, "Evan, you're right, but no need to apologize. After that article, I don't have the luxury of waiting for the police to figure this out. We have to find a way to prove my innocence and piece my reputation back together."

"I know. Let's get started."

"First, I need to know something. Why do you believe I'm innocent when no one else does? Even Sean wouldn't return my smile during the judging, and now the newspaper has put the allegation in print."

"There are a number of reasons. To begin with, you and I were in the same room most of the time on the day Leon died. I can't recall any time you had an opportunity to tamper with his food. Second, you were calm throughout the day. If you were planning something like that, I would've sensed your mind was elsewhere. Third, and most importantly, I may not have known you long, but I'm a good judge of character, and unless I'm horribly mistaken, you wouldn't intentionally harm anyone, except maybe in self-defense. Let's sit down on the sofa and come up with a plan."

Evan sits close enough that our knees are touching. He hands me a pad of paper and pen off the coffee table, saying, "Let's start by making a list of what we remember each finalist doing at the prep session. Who went near Leon's station, and who went into the fridge after he put his cart in there?"

With our heads together, I write down the name of each finalist.

Pointing to Jayden's name, Evan says, "He was more nervous than any other finalist when Detective Fielder interviewed him. Of course, that may not mean anything."

"I think Jayden has reason to be nervous, but I'm not sure it has anything to do with Leon's death. I stayed in the kitchen after I thought everyone had left today to check whether they stock hummus in the refrigerator. Jayden returned while I was looking around, and I overheard him talking to someone I'll call Deep Voice because his voice was so distinctively low. He offered Jayden an advantage in the competition."

He grasps my thigh.

"Cassie, what were you thinking? Sneaking around the kitchen alone was dangerous. You need to be more careful. What if they'd found you?"

"I knew it was a little risky, but it's driving me insane that I'm a murder suspect. I had to at least figure out where the hummus may have come from."

Evan closes his eyes and drags his hands down his face. "I under-stand your stress, but please promise me you won't put yourself in situations like that again. These people are dangerous."

Trying not to be mad at his bossiness, which is admittedly a little sexy, I place a reassuring hand on his shoulder.

"I'll be careful, but you don't have the right to tell me what to do. My whole future is on the line, even more so after that article. I can take care of myself. That said, I appreciate that you worry about my safety. It's sweet. Now, can we talk about what I overheard?"

He pats my leg and says, "Okay, but I'm not sweet. Pick another descriptor next time. Now, tell me what you overheard. What advantage did the guy you call Deep Voice offer Jayden? Did Jayden take it?"

Evan listens intently as I share the details of the conversation, including that Deep Voice exited via the Maze.

"Interesting. Someone is trying to manipulate the outcome of the competition. But who and why?"

"If Deep Voice has access to the Maze, doesn't that mean he works for the Athena?"

"Likely. We need to tell Sean about this."

"Not yet. First, we need proof. Aren't there cameras in the kitchen? Can you check with security to see if they have videos from this afternoon? Also, won't they have records of who used the Maze door in the Trendz kitchen? Shouldn't we check that data before bothering Sean? He thinks I'm a murder suspect, so he may not believe me. I'm also worried that Sean, Cynthia, and Amy will think I'm trying to get another chef kicked out. Besides, it's not clear this has anything to do with Leon's death."

"We need Sean's help to accomplish most of those things."

"I hadn't thought of that."

The doorbell rings.

"I hope you don't mind, but I ordered dinner. I gave Eduardo the evening off so we could have privacy for this discussion, but we both need to eat."

"You're right. I haven't had much to eat today."

"I assumed as much. We can talk over dinner."

Evan opens the door and directs room service to serve dinner at the dining table. As the server is readying the food, it occurs to me that someone could live here full time. The two-story suite is enormous. There's a kitchen, a dining area with a table for eight next to the living room, and who knows how many bedrooms and bathrooms there are. The curved marble staircase leads to an open loft-like area with a pool table visible from the lower level.

After the server leaves, Evan ushers me to one end of the modern, glass-and-chrome dining table where our dinner awaits. My mouth waters as my eyes feast on the perfectly plated food, featuring a crisp summer salad, grilled halibut, and steamed asparagus. Sitting down, I moan when a whiff of the warm, yeasty dinner rolls reaches my nose. The smell reminds me of my grandmother's kitchen. What a perfect moment for such a comforting memory. It's like she's sending me a warm hug.

Evan pours glasses of a lightly sparkling Vinho Verde wine from Portugal. The crisp white wine perfectly matches the halibut and will, hopefully, lower my stress level a notch too.

I take a sip of the soothing beverage. "This is delicious. It's just what I needed."

"Excellent. I want to learn more about you. Why did you sign up for this competition when you already have a successful career?"

I sigh. "It's complicated. Until now, I've taken the safe route to ensure I could pay my own way. After law school, I thought I'd be happy after securing the job my parents always wanted for me at a well-respected law firm. It's stable and pays well. It's also monotonous, and my boss doesn't show any consideration or respect for the younger attorneys. He expects us to be available 24/7, and anything less crushes our chance for a promotion."

"That sounds awful."

"It can be. I'm goal-oriented, so for a long time, I've been laser-focused on exceeding expectations. I haven't had much time for fun or for seriously exploring my passion for cooking."

"That's sad."

"I know. When I saw the application for this competition, I was burned out and craving an adventure. This was a chance to regain my zest for life, so with a little nudge from my best friend, Lowri, I took the plunge and applied."

Evan places his hand on my forearm and gently squeezes. "It's important to be passionate. I admire that you took the initiative to explore a new path. Most people aren't willing to take chances or make changes unless forced to."

"Thanks for the support. What are you passionate about?" I ask as I butter a roll.

"If I had to pick only one thing, it would be the charities that my family supports. We have a foundation whose goal is to make sure no family in our country goes to bed hungry."

"That's a noble and worthy cause. How successful have you been?"

After finishing a bite of the halibut, Evan lays his fork on the plate. "Moderately successful, but we have a tremendous amount of work to do. I'd like to expand our efforts to improve employment opportunities, education, and training to make sure the next generation will be less likely to suffer from hunger. However, it's a difficult and complicated problem to solve," Evan says, scrunching his brow.

"I'm sure it is. Tell me something else about yourself. What do you like to do for fun?"

As much time as we've spent together, I don't know much about his life.

Evan replies, "I enjoy visiting new places and experiencing different cultures. As for hobbies, sailing is my favorite. What about you?"

"Other than cooking for friends, I've always wanted to travel, but I haven't had many opportunities yet. Growing up, my parents were workaholics who rarely took time off. Even when we went on trips, it was usually somewhere they needed to go for work. That meant I spent most of my time at the hotel while they went to meet their clients. I missed out on sightseeing, so that's what I look forward to."

Old habits are hard to change though. Hearing Evan mention sailing, it dawns on me that I've lived in San Diego for several years and have never been on a sailboat. I'm going to have to work harder not to become my parents.

"Where would you go first?" he asks.

"I've been making a list of my top ten dream vacations, but I'd love to hear about your favorite places."

"That's a good excuse for another dinner. I asked first, so tell me about *your* top ten list. Is there a common theme to the places?"

"Actually, there is. I already mentioned that I love beaches. My list also includes trips to the countries that influence my cooking so I can take cooking classes to learn more about their food. Do you prefer warm weather or cold weather?"

"Warm weather unless skiing is involved. Do you ski?"

"A little. I've only been skiing a couple of times. I could use some lessons and more practice."

"I can help with that," Evan says with a glimmer in his eyes.

It seems that we have many of the same interests. I can only imagine how much fun it would be to travel with him.

I laugh. "Sounds like fun. When you aren't playing, what type of work do you do?"

Evan's eyes turn somber. "I help with the family business. With my father retiring, I don't want to let the family down, so I'll be busy supporting my older brother. He'll be taking over for my father." He stares into the distance as though transported somewhere else.

Noting the seriousness in Evan's voice, I put down my utensils and gaze at him. Hoping to pull him back to the present, I say, "It sounds like you have a close family. Do all your siblings work in the family business?"

With a quick nod, the trance is broken. "Yes, we do. I hate to cut this conversation short, but if you're going to get any rest tonight, we need to get back to our main focus for the evening. Let's take our dessert to the sofa," he says, pushing his chair back.

"You're right, but I'd rather talk about vacations than murder and sabotage."

Evan's so easy to talk to. There's an easy connection between us that I'd like to explore more. I hope we'll have more moments like tonight's dinner. I've thought about telling him about my family, and I'd love to hear more about his family's business. It's clearly successful given his lifestyle and time for charities. I'm not sure why he hasn't talked about it more, but then I held back about my parents too. People don't realize that simple questions can be painful. Based on my history, I've learned not to press for details. I'll leave it to him to share when he's ready.

When we're seated on the couch, Evan says, "We need to talk with Sean about the conversation you overheard, but I understand your hesitancy and wanting more proof. Let me call Sean to see if we can gain access to the videos from this afternoon. I'll try not to divulge too much of your story. Would that be okay?"

"I don't think we have a choice but be careful what you say."

He nods and pulls his phone from his pocket. He and Sean talk for several minutes, but I only hear one side of the conversation. Evan's succinct comments don't tell me much.

Ending the call, Evan smiles. "Good news. Sean's going to give me access to the videos from the kitchen camera and the data showing who used the kitchen's Maze entrance. The bad news is that we can't access them until tomorrow morning."

"Thanks, Evan. You're amazing."

Evan pulls me against him as we stare out the wall of windows that face the Strip. Neon lights and a parade of cars and people fill the view. He reaches up, brushing the back of his hand against my cheek. Gently turning my head toward him, our lips collide. I melt into his warmth as his hand wanders down the side of my torso.

"Mmm. I need you closer." With one hand against my back, he slides the other under my thighs, and lifts me onto his lap with my legs sideways across his. Keeping his one arm around my back, he deftly positions his other hand between my thighs. I ache for more as my hand grips his strong bicep.

When our kiss breaks, he nuzzles my neck and nips lightly at my skin. I softly moan, begging for more. His warm breath tickles as he moves his lips to my ear. His tongue lightly teases my earlobe before he sucks it into his mouth. His teeth barely graze it as he continues to taunt me with his welcome attention. I'm squirming on his lap as he wraps his arm around my waist to firmly hold me close, whispering in my ear, "Stay with me tonight."

"Evan, I already told you that I'm not used to moving this fast."

I'm conflicted though, which means I'm at a decision point. Do I push him away like I have others, or is now when I tackle my fear of getting close to someone? He's making me want to try.

Evan peppers my neck with soft kisses as he murmurs, "Tell me you don't want to stay."

Breathing heavily, I gasp. "I can't. Our chemistry is the most intense I've ever experienced. There's a problem though. For me, staying the night implies we're serious. You travel the world, dress like a male model, clearly come from money, and are best friends with the owner of a major Las Vegas resort. I'm sure you're accustomed to women just throwing themselves at you and begging for even one night. That's not me. I'm sorry."

"Cassandra, you have nothing to apologize for. I like that you're different. And I want to be with you tonight. We won't do anything you don't want. I promise."

"That sounds so tempting. I spend most of my time by myself. That's usually fine, but I don't want to be alone tonight. I want to be in your arms, but I'm not sure I'm ready to give you everything that you want. What if I can't? Do you still want me to stay?"

Moving me off his lap, Evan says, "Yes. It's settled. We'll sit here and finish our wine and fruit while we take in the neon extravaganza on the Strip. If you're interested, I'll tell you about the trip I've planned to New Zealand."

After learning about Evan's love of sailing and his plans to go to New Zealand to watch the America's Cup yacht race, I fall asleep on the couch with my head snuggled against his chest. At some point, I'm vaguely aware that he's carrying me to a big bed and gently placing me on the softest mattress ever. He crawls in beside me, spoons me against his warm, hard body, and covers us with a fluffy comforter. I'm in heaven.

29

EVAN

I wake up around 3 a.m., pleased that Cassandra's next to me. Propping up on an elbow, I watch my sleeping beauty, who's still wearing her colorful sundress. I didn't want to wake her to change when I carried her to bed. I normally wouldn't sleep in anything, but out of respect, I wore shorts—not that they're hiding much right now.

What am I going to do about her? I was first drawn to Cassandra by her natural beauty and her plight as the back-up in the competition. Now, I've learned she's also smart, charming, and caring even in difficult situations. She's been through some tough times, but she's not bitter. Instead, she's a loyal friend and, from what I can tell, a good person. Before her, I wouldn't even consider the idea of opening my life to someone, whereas now, I can't fathom the idea of walking away from her. I'm just not sure I can keep her close given my family obligations and uncertain future.

"Mmm. Where am I? Is someone there?" Cassandra asks, a tinge of fear in her voice.

"It's me. You're safe."

I gently push the hair off her face and watch as recognition dawns.

"Evan, it's you." She smiles.

"Yes, my goddess. You're beautiful."

"Why are you looking at me that way?"

"What way?"

"I don't know—all warm and fuzzy or something."

"What if that's how I'm feeling?" I ask.

"When I decided to come to Vegas, I vowed to adopt a new mantra: *don't look back*. I meant that to apply to the cooking competition and my career. Now I want it to apply to us. Kiss me. Now."

Our lips meet, at first our kiss is soft. She gently rests her warm hand on my bare chest. As heat builds between us, our kiss intensifies. She's so responsive as our tongues tangle and breathing grows heavier. Her hand moves to my back and down until it reaches the elastic waistband on my shorts. Is she relieved or disappointed?

I playfully say, "I'm at a disadvantage. You're wearing far more clothes than I am. What do you think about evening the playing field?"

"We can work on that."

"Good girl."

I gently nudge her sundress over her head, revealing a lacy purple bra and knickers.

I moan. "Please tell me you wore these for me."

"Maybe." She grins.

"I'm going to taste every inch of you, starting here." I kiss the tender spot behind her ear, eliciting a shudder of pleasure.

"Mmmm, I like that," she whispers.

My mouth explores her soft skin as I slip my hand under the lace of her bra. Running my thumb over her nipple, it pebbles beneath my touch.

"Keep doing that," she begs.

I squeeze her perfect breast, circling her nipple and letting my fingernail graze across it as she moans for more.

She's so bloody amazing.

Ripping away the thin fabric, I growl, "No one else will ever see you in this. It was only for me."

I suck her nipple, letting my tongue tease it as my other hand reaches underneath her, cupping her ass and pulling her against my hardness. She needs to know what she does to me.

She groans. "Please. More. Now. I can't wait any longer."

"You can. It'll be worth it." I move my mouth to her other breast and let my teeth graze her nipple. Reaching between us, I slip my hand into the top of her knickers and down over her bare skin. I've been dreaming about this since she accidentally dropped her towel. It feels just as heavenly as it looked.

I whisper, "Is this what you planned? Is that why you wore these fuck-me knickers?"

She gasps. "No. I didn't plan this, but I've wanted you so badly. I've been fighting my inner demons. That's why I kept pushing you away."

"Let's kill those demons tonight. They need to disappear forever."

"They do."

"I need to taste you," I say as I slide down her body.

"Yes. Please," she pants.

I reach between her parted legs, slipping the fabric aside, and press my mouth to her warm, wet center. I lick and suck her nub as she squirms beneath me. She laces her fingers in my hair, holding me in place, saying, "Please don't stop. I'm almost there."

Adding my fingers, she topples over the edge, screaming, "Yes, Evan. Oh, my god, yes."

I kiss a trail up her exposed skin and reach for a condom from my nightstand.

Her moans and whimpers drive me to the brink with need for her. I've been with more women than I'd care to count, yet this time feels so vastly different.

Her hand roams down my torso until it reaches the bulge in my shorts. She gasps as she strokes it through the fabric.

"Princess, I hope that means you like what you found. But if you don't stop, this will be over way too soon."

"Oh. That wouldn't be good."

I show her the foil packet, my eyes silently asking permission.

When she nods in agreement, I don't waste any time. I remove my shorts in one motion.

Reaching between her legs, I tear off her knickers.

She throws her head back, gripping my shoulders as my finger traces tiny circles around her swollen clit. I stare at her beautiful body with amazement. She's stunning, all breathless and flushed, glowing from her first orgasm and aching for another. I want to make this so good for her. Taking my time, I continue circling and stroking her while sucking her nipple into my mouth. She's so wet.

"Please don't make me wait. I need you," she begs.

She deserves whatever she wants, so I slip on the condom. Positioning my body over hers, I fill her with one slow thrust. I give her time to adjust and then move in and out, savoring every sensation.

"You're so fucking tight. I'm not going to last long."

"Oh, Evan, you feel so good. That's perfect. Keep doing that."

I want to make it last for her, but I've never been this far gone on a woman. I can't hold back.

My movements become faster and rougher, spurred on by Cassie's pleas for "Harder. Deeper."

I struggle to hold off as long as I can. Suddenly, I feel her tightening around me.

Thank fuuuck!

We go over the edge together, soaring to unimaginable heights.

Floating back to earth satiated, Cassandra falls asleep wrapped in my arms.

That was hotter, more exciting, and hell, more meaningful than I've ever experienced.

She doesn't hear me whisper, "Love, I think you're the one."

30

CASSIE

The next morning, I wake spooned against Evan's warm body. It brings a smile to my face. I should have regrets, but I don't. I'm not looking back. Maybe the future isn't like my past.

Evan stirs and stretches. He pulls me closer and kisses me hungrily, saying, "I could get used to having you in my bed."

"Mmmm," I murmur.

"Let's order breakfast and stay here the rest of the morning. Last night wasn't enough."

My body agrees. It wants to stay under the covers nestled against Evan. But the image of the newspaper headline flashes in my head, and I know there's work to do today.

"Last night was beyond fantastic, and I'd love to spend the morning in bed with you. But we need to review the videos."

"I know, but breakfast first. I'll order food and check with Sean to see when the videos and Maze entry data will be ready."

We eat breakfast in bed. This pampering is new to me. We indulge in croissants with apricot jam, thick slices of bacon with brown sugar and coarse black pepper, old-fashioned hash brown potatoes, blueberry pancakes with pure maple syrup, and hot tea with lemon.

How did he know my favorite breakfast splurges without even asking? Then the light bulb goes off. Christian! He must have asked Christian to send up one of everything I've ordered for breakfast since arriving at the Athena. But I never ordered them all at once.

Damn. He's thoughtful and clever.

When we finish, Evan says, "If you want a shower, you can use the one in the adjoining bathroom. I'll shower in the bathroom down the hall. As much as I'd like to join you, we don't have time for that today."

Stepping under the rainfall showerhead, I have mixed feelings. On the one hand, meeting Evan and spending last night with him was like a fairytale. He makes me feel like a princess. On the other hand, I have this constant uneasiness and fear from the cloud of being a murder suspect. Will my law firm fire me if, and more likely when, they see the news article? I highly doubt the negative publicity will be overcome by the truth that I'm innocent. With that thought, I turn the shower to scalding, trying to clear my head.

As I'm using one of the fluffy white towels to dry off, I hear the doorbell. Quickly, I throw on my clothes from last night and hurry to the suite's living room.

"Who was that?"

"Sean sent a flash drive with the data, along with a printed layout of the kitchen showing where the cameras are and the location of the entrance to the Maze."

"Great. Let's look at the layout first. I'd like an idea of how much area the cameras cover. I think the Maze door wasn't too far from the walk-in refrigerator, but I don't remember ever seeing it."

"It must be hidden like the other Maze entrances," Evan says as we study the layout.

"Let's see. The fridge takes up a large portion of the back left corner of the kitchen. I heard Deep Voice's footsteps pass along the front of the fridge. That means the Maze door must be somewhere along the left side of the layout, not too far from the fridge."

"This must be it. See the little circle with a small capital M inside?"

"You're right. That has to be it. Let me think. I remember a door in that area. There's a sign on it that says 'Electrical Room. Danger. Keep Out.'"

"That must be the Maze entrance. Now that we know where to look, let's watch the video."

We fast-forward the video to the time when I was stuck in the fridge. The video is grainy, so we both lean in close to the laptop screen. When Jayden's mouth starts moving, I say, "See, Evan. Jayden is talking to someone. I wish we see could who it was. Do you believe me now?"

Evan puts his arm around my waist, pulls me close, and presses a sweet kiss to the top of my head. "Princess, I never doubted you."

"That's the polite thing to say, but you wouldn't be human unless you had at least a little doubt. My unexplained fingerprints on Leon's bowl would be enough to make anyone question my innocence."

"Sean's responsible for my only doubts. My gut always told me he was wrong. We're past that now. I believe you, and I never questioned your story about what you heard while trapped in the refrigerator. Let's keep watching and figure out who's behind the sabotage."

After watching all the videos, we realize none of the cameras captured anyone but Jayden. And unfortunately, the videos don't have audio.

I ask, "Do you think Deep Voice knew where the cameras were and purposefully stood where he knew he wouldn't be captured?"

"That's possible. You said he mentioned cameras before leaving the kitchen. Let's check the Maze entrance data. Unless he's a magician, he should show up there."

Evan accesses the entry and exit data for the Maze entrance in the kitchen. It shows the door was only opened six times that day.

Excited, I point to the screen and exclaim, "There, Evan. Those two entries have to correspond to Deep Voice. They're the only times the door was opened while I was in the fridge. One must be when he entered and the other when he left. But there isn't a name, only a number. Is it an employee number?"

"Finally, some progress. It's probably an ID number. We need to match it to the employee. I'll call Sean."

Grabbing his phone, Evan dials and puts it on speakerphone. He holds his finger over his lips, indicating that I should stay quiet. When his friend answers, he says, "Sean, if I know the number for a person who entered or exited the Maze, how can we match that to a name?"

"That's easy, give me the number."

"7583928."

I'm wringing my hands as we wait.

Sean eventually says, "That's Mitch Hendricks. He works in security. Why are you asking? Did he turn up in the data I sent you?"

My mouth falls open. Why would a security guy be trying to sabotage and rig the competition? It doesn't make sense.

Evan replies, "Yes, he did. What type of security does he do? Would he have reason to be in the kitchen in Trendz?"

"According to our records, he's a mid-level employee in the security department. He could be anywhere at almost any time. He may have been assigned to secure the kitchen after the competition today."

Agitated, I push my chair back, scraping it against the marble floor.

Evan moves a finger to his lips, reminding me to be quiet so that Sean won't know I'm listening.

I nod in understanding but start to pace while I listen. Sean won't hear my bare feet against the cold marble.

"I see. So, it wouldn't surprise you that he was in the Trendz kitchen late yesterday afternoon?"

"Not particularly."

"What do you know about him?"

"Not a lot. He's worked here for a couple of years or so. I recognize his photo. I've run into him on occasion when he's worked an event. You clearly have concerns. What's going on?"

Returning to my chair and sitting on my hands, I nod, indicating to Evan that he has my permission to share more.

"I have reason to believe that Mitch offered an advantage to one of the finalists yesterday, and it may not have been the first offer of that type."

Sean almost screams through the speaker, "What? Where did you hear this?"

Evan wraps his arm around my shoulders. "That's not important. What is important is that Mitch offered Jayden 'another advantage' in exchange for Jayden sabotaging one of the other finalists. Even more disturbing is that Jayden accepted the offer, saying he was happy to go along with the plan as long as no one is hurt."

"Do you think Mitch and Jayden had something to do with Chef Boucher's death?"

"I don't know, but maybe."

"That doesn't make sense. Mitch isn't in a position to give someone an advantage."

Evan replies, "Mitch must be working with someone else who is."

"What would he have to gain?"

"I don't know, but we need to keep a close eye on Jayden and Mitch."

After a long pause, Sean concedes, "Whether I like it or not, I need to share this with Detective Fielder. Then I'll deal with the Athena's security team."

"We don't know who Mitch's partner is, so I wouldn't mention this to anyone involved with the competition."

"You're probably right. But I need to know where you got this information. Is your source credible?"

"My source is highly credible, but that's all I can say for now."

"I see. You didn't heed my warning to stay away from Ms. Edwards. How do you know she didn't make this up?"

Deflating, my shoulders sag. I'd hoped this new information would change Sean's opinion of me. But he still doesn't trust me and doesn't want Evan anywhere near me.

Squeezing me closer, Evan says, "The videos back up my source, but we'll talk when we meet for lunch. Goodbye."

Ending the call, Evan looks at me with apologetic eyes as he pulls me from my chair onto his lap, pressing my head into his chest. I fight to hold back tears of frustration, sadness, and fear for what the future holds.

After regaining my composure, I say, "I'm not surprised. I knew Sean wouldn't believe me, but at least he agreed to keep an eye on Mitch and Jayden."

"Don't worry. We'll solve this."

Evan's alarm goes off.

"What's that?"

"My reminder that I'm going to lunch with Sean to talk with one of the food distributors. Do you want to wait here and order room service?"

"No, I'll go to my room and prep for the interviews at three. Will you be at the photoshoot? It's at the Olympic Torch Bar."

"Yes. It should be fun."

With Evan around, it'll be easier to keep a smile on my face. I'm in a strange predicament though, and I'm not sure how I should be reacting and feeling. My time with Evan is wonderful and special, but I'm suspected of committing a heinous crime. How is my mind not focusing one hundred percent on the bad part and getting out of this messy situation? I can't explain it. All I know is that I want to spend as much time with Evan as possible.

"I do know a little about the photoshoot, but it's a surprise."

"They said to wear a shirt and shorts over a swimsuit. Are we going sailing on the Aegean? Can't you give me a teeny clue?" I tease.

"You'll have to wait to find out."

31

EVAN

Thanks to the spectacular night with Cassandra, I'm heading to the meeting with Sean in higher spirits and a more hopeful mood than I've experienced in a long time. An unexpected sense of optimism is permeating my thinking even amid this chaos. I'm becoming convinced that we'll clear her name. She needs me, and I won't let her down.

I dutifully arrived at his office ten minutes early to leave for lunch with Sean and Wes. I argued that Wes may be hesitant to talk in front of a stranger, but Sean insisted that I accompany him.

"Emily, please have them bring my car to the VIP driveway. Evan and I are going downtown for lunch with Wes," Sean says.

"I'll take care of it. Your car will be waiting for you."

"Great, we'll head down there now."

Turning to me, Sean explains, "Wes owns one of the best gourmet food distribution services in Las Vegas, so I don't understand why we aren't using his service anymore. Hopefully, our lunch will shed some light on the reason."

We arrive at the upscale Mexican restaurant that Wes loves. As Sean gives instructions to our driver, I take in the cream-colored stucco building. Hand-painted tiles decorated with rust, blue and yellow patterns outline the distressed wooden doors for an old-world feel.

I chuckle, "You've got your knickers in a twist, and he hasn't even touched your car."

"Don't give me grief. I'll tip him well, but I don't want any nicks on the paint."

There are more important things than a paint chip, which I'd point out if his stress level wasn't already off the charts. Instead, I shake my head and follow him inside, where the aroma of slow-cooked meats and spices makes me almost forget the large breakfast I shared with Cassandra.

"There's Wes," Sean says, pointing to a guy with brown hair and glasses at a table in the back corner.

As we walk across the restaurant, my mouth waters, and my hunger grows. If the food is as good as it smells, I'll have to bring Cassandra here.

Reaching the table, Sean says, "Wes, it's great to see you. This is my close friend, Evan Catalinius. He's visiting and helping me with the Guest Chef Competition."

When Wes stands to greet us, he's an inch or two shorter than Sean and has a slightly stockier build.

"Evan, it's nice to meet you. Have a seat," he says.

As Sean and I sit, I can't help noticing that Wes is being cordial but reserved. It's as if he's not sure how this meeting will go. What's up with that? I thought he and Sean were friends.

"Wes, what was it you couldn't tell me on the phone?" Sean asks, getting right to business.

"Let's have drinks and order before we get down to business," Wes says as he calls the server over and orders a Yellow Diamond Margarita with an extra shot of tequila on the side.

"What the heck is a Yellow Diamond Margarita?" I ask.

The server explains, "It's our newest and most popular margarita. It's made with premium agave tequila, simple syrup, lime juice, a splash of pure cane rum, and a lemon twist."

"Wes, that sounds like an afternoon hangover in a glass," Sean says.

Wes looks at him and says, "For this discussion, you're going to need at least one."

I say, "It sounds fabulous to me. I'll take one."

"Me too, but hold the extra shot," Sean says.

While we wait for our drinks, Wes insists on small talk, but I can tell that Sean's patience is running thin.

After downing his shot of tequila, Wes says, "I didn't reach out to you before because I don't have proof of what I'm going to share."

"Wes, don't play games. We both know it's strange that your company is no longer one of the Athena's suppliers. You own the best gourmet food distribution service in Las Vegas, and we'd be foolish not to source from you. Plus, you're not the only one who was cut off. I need to know what's going on, and I need to know now."

He leans back against the booth and narrows his eyes, hesitating before saying, "There are rumors that if suppliers don't give kickbacks, the Athena cuts them off."

"What the ever-loving fuck? Kickbacks to whom?" Sean growls, fire in his eyes.

Wes's comment is shocking. Sean prides himself on playing business by the rules. If someone working for him isn't, he won't tolerate it.

"I'm not even sure the rumor is true. We've never been approached for a kickback. Orders from the Athena just slowly decreased until eventually we weren't getting any of your business. When our account manager asked why, he was told that Chef Maurizio was in charge of approving all suppliers and all orders."

"Did your account manager speak with Chef Maurizio directly?"

Shaking his head, Wes says, "No. Apparently, your chef wouldn't return his calls or take a meeting." He throws his hands up in frustration.

Sean squints his eyes, mystified. "That's strange. You've been one of our suppliers for years. Why would Chef Maurizio suddenly cut you off?"

I can't help but wonder if the kickback rumor is true. If so, it would explain why the people behind the scheme quit doing business with Wes's company. The risk that Wes would mention the scheme to Sean would be too great. I'd bet that Sean isn't good friends with the other suppliers the Athena is currently using.

"Our account manager said he heard your former chef was reaching out to other suppliers, offering them business if they kicked back money to him."

Sean chugs the rest of his margarita, looking away. Based on the tenseness of his jaw, he's attempting to harness his anger. In his place, I'd be upset that my friend hadn't brought this to my attention.

After a minute or two, Sean asks, "So, Chef Maurizio was behind this?"

"I'm not sure. Like I said, I heard the story from Eric, our account manager, soon after we lost the Athena's business. If he hadn't been with us so long, I would've questioned whether Eric made up the story to cover for a mistake that caused him to lose your business."

"Did Eric tell you anything else?"

"Yes. The other suppliers told him their conversations with Chef Maurizio were awkward, like the chef wasn't comfortable asking for the kickbacks. I'm not sure what that means."

"After Chef Maurizio left, did you try to get our business back?"

"Of course, but we were told that the Athena wasn't looking to change suppliers at this time."

"Who told you that?"

"I'm not sure. I can check with Eric. But rumors are circulating that kickbacks are still a requirement to do business with the Athena. That makes me think your former chef was not the only one involved."

Bloody hell. Wes is suggesting there's a conspiracy operating right under Sean's nose, and they're successfully stealing from him. It's not a surprise that Sean's face is beet red and the veins in his neck are pulsing.

I say, "Wes, we're both friends with Sean. You must know he would never be part of something like you describe. I think we could all use that shot you originally suggested."

Wes must be communicating with our server telepathically

because shots mysteriously appear, and we down them in silence. It gives Sean a moment to lower his blood pressure.

Sean says, "Wes, I wish you had come to me about this."

"I was planning to talk with you, but it was awkward. I didn't have any proof. Then Chef Maurizio left shortly after we were cut off. Like you, I assumed we would be able to get the business back when you got a new chef. Besides, it's not in my nature to beg a friend for business. If you didn't want to use us, that was your prerogative."

"But we've known each other almost our whole lives. Like Evan said, surely you didn't think I'd put up with someone skimming or taking kickbacks."

"Without any proof about the kickbacks, the conversation I needed to have with you was going to be uncomfortable. But when we didn't get the business back after Chef Maurizio left and the rumors continued about the kickbacks, I decided we had to talk. I was planning to corner you at the reception for the Guest Chef Competition."

"Why didn't you?"

Wes sighs. "Well, this is another awkward part. I noticed the food at the reception was lower quality than what we had been supplying you with in the past. I decided that we lost the business because you needed to save money and were cutting corners where you could."

Sean's eyes go wide in shock. This is clearly news to him. And I can't comment because I didn't pay attention to the food. My focus was on my newly found interest: Cassandra.

Sean asserts, "I wouldn't do that. I didn't have a chance to sample the food at the reception, so I didn't notice its quality. Now I'm embarrassed that we apparently served our VIPs crappy food. What a shit show."

"The differences in quality were small. I doubt your guests noticed."

"I can only hope, but it was a discerning crowd. Can you give me examples?" Sean asks, rubbing his eyes.

Now Sean also has to deal with any fallout from less-than-stellar food at a premier event. It looks bad. Not only is the publicity bad for the Athena, but also, the stress is dangerous for Sean. His father passed away from a heart attack. I don't want to lose my best friend to one.

Wes explains, "The cheese wasn't the best. It was a lower-quality Gouda instead of an aged Gouda. Instead of caviar, they served salmon roe, which is much less expensive. Instead of champagne, they poured prosecco. Nothing was wrong with the food, but it wasn't up to your past standards."

"But I was served champagne. I saw the bottle."

"Of course, *you* were given champagne. Everyone knows you can tell the difference. But the guests received prosecco, which was nice but less expensive."

I remember thinking my first glass of "champagne" at the reception tasted off.

"Sean, have you spoken with Chef Maurizio?" Wes leans in and asks.

"Not yet. I'm trying to gather as many facts as I can first. I'd hoped the problems left with him, but it looks like that may not be the case."

"It would make sense to talk with him."

"You're right. I have another question though. What were you doing at the pool the day of the cooking demonstration?"

"My wife and I had friends visiting from New York. They were staying at the Athena and invited us to have lunch with them at the pool. Why do you ask?"

"No real reason. I was just curious why you didn't stop by to chat."

"That's simple. As you entered the pool area, we were being hustled out because of the accident. It wasn't the time for a friendly chat."

"That makes sense."

Our food arrives, providing a welcome excuse to stop talking about unpleasant business issues and focus on the best enchiladas de mole in the city.

When we finish, Sean promises to mend the business relationship with Wes, and we say our goodbyes.

As we're walking out of the restaurant, Sean says, "Evan, I need to talk with Chef Maurizio as soon as possible. I'd prefer to talk with him in person, but I don't have time to fly to Europe until after the competition. A call will have to do. Until then, I need to figure out who else was part of this kickback scheme."

I nod, not knowing what else to say. He's had quite a shock. And with what we just learned, I'm more convinced than ever that Cassandra is innocent. If there's a complicated plan in place to steal from Sean, murder may have been part of it.

Sean's driver pulls in front of the restaurant, and we head back to the Athena.

32

CASSIE

"We need each finalist to have a seat at one of the high-top tables," Amy says, gesturing to four tall tables in the Olympic Torch Bar.

Cynthia's assistant, Cameron, hands out pens and notecards to each of us.

Amy continues, "For Round 2 of the competition, you'll each be making an entrée that fits our chosen theme. Once I give you that theme, you'll have fifteen minutes to write down the entrée you'll make and list any key ingredients you need in addition to the basic pantry items."

What? Only fifteen minutes? That's impossible. I thought we had another full day to figure out ideas for a special entrée to wow the judges. I should've been giving it more thought. Instead, I've been focused on clearing my name, and of course, Evan was a significant distraction last night.

Taking a few deep breaths, I remind myself that while I'd prefer to be fully prepared, I perform well under pressure. Let's hope that works for me today.

Surveying the reactions of the other finalists, they look stunned as well. Trenton is scowling, and Kai looks perplexed. Interestingly, Jayden smiles smugly. He must have taken the advantage.

My thoughts are interrupted when Amy says, "Are you ready?"

We all nod like robots. What else can we do, right? Sean did say this competition would require us to think fast on our feet and tackle unexpected challenges with a smile.

"Great. As a word of caution, I won't answer any questions about the theme. You must decide what it means to you and create an entrée that reflects that meaning. Also, write down a one-sentence description explaining your interpretation of the theme. The theme is 'Comfort with a Flair.' Your fifteen minutes start now."

What the heck is "Comfort with a Flair"? It could mean different things to different people. It could be comfort food with an unusual twist. It could be comfort food plated in a fancy way. Neither of those seems quite right for the Athena, which is about luxury in everything. Maybe we're supposed to create an upscale experience that is based on a comfort food. What if I can deliver all three? Is that what they want?

I start racking my brain for ideas. When I think upscale, I think lobster, crab, shrimp, filet mignon, and fancy sauces. Those don't scream comfort food though.

To me, comfort food is mac and cheese or beef stew on a chilly winter night. That's it! An upscale version of beef stew. Instead of a traditional version, I'll make beef in a red wine sauce. I can serve it with mashed potatoes and puffed popover rolls. Roasted rainbow carrots will add color and fit with the idea of a stew.

Amy calls out, "You have three minutes left."

How did the time pass so quickly? Hurriedly, I scribble my list of ingredients.

I've barely finished when Cameron takes the card from my hand, and Amy starts interviewing each of the finalists.

Suddenly, the room grows warmer, and a tingling sensation runs down the back of my neck. Turning my head, I see Evan standing behind us, discreetly watching everyone. I should've known where the warmth came from. It's mysterious how I can always sense when he's in the room.

Evan's always dressed for business when I've seen him in public, so my heart skips a beat or two when he shows up in his swim clothes. While I've seen him naked in private, which is sexy as hell, he's sizzling hot in his dark-blue swim shorts and taut red-and-blue polo shirt with designer sunglasses tucked into the front. I still don't know why they insisted that we wear bathing suits and cover ups, but I won't complain if I can see Evan shirtless again.

After Amy interviews us for the promotional video, she announces, "It's time for the photo shoot at the Olympic Tower."

We follow her toward the balcony overlooking the Aegean and walk down the wide staircase that leads to a pathway at the edge of the water. A security officer opens the gate, allowing access to the path. As we approach the tower, my eyes fixate on the staircase that winds up its exterior like a clinging vine. My pulse quickens, and I begin sweating uncontrollably as thoughts of falling from the stairs consume me.

No. I can't have a panic attack now. I focus on my breathing and picture a happy place, hoping the coping mechanisms I've learned work this time.

I avoid looking up as we round the base of the tower where another security guard holds open a hidden door in the back. Peering inside, I exhale a relieved breath when I see an elevator. If we have to go to the top of the tower, I'll be okay in an elevator. I squeeze into it with Amy, Evan, and the other finalists. When we reach the top and exit, a guy hands me a helmet and gear as another person directs us to step out onto the balcony encircling the tower.

So much for being relieved. I start trembling as panic returns.

A warm hand caresses my back, and Evan whispers, "Are you okay?"

"No. I hate heights. What's this harness for? Why do I need a helmet?"

Before Evan can answer, Amy says, "Welcome to the Athena's Thrill Ride. While this is a cooking competition, the Athena is also using it as an opportunity to show off the fun activities that guests can enjoy when they visit. Today, we're going to highlight the Athena's zipline. We have drones ready to take videos, and we also have camera crews here and on the other side of the Aegean to capture you zipping across the water. Since you'll land in the water, we had you wear bathing suits, so please hand your cover-up clothes to one of the crew members. We know you're going to love this exhilarating experience, so please remember to smile for the cameras."

I can't believe I never noticed the zipline connected to the tower. I'm really freaking the hell out now. I can't do this. Heights terrify me. I can't step off the platform. What if the wire breaks or I fall off?

Apparently, I'm the only one who finds this frightening. Kai and Jayden are laughing and ready to go. Trenton seems annoyed, as though this is a waste of his time, but he's not balking.

"Why aren't they scared?"

Evan answers, "It's going to be okay. Breathe slowly and deeply." He's peeling off his polo shirt, revealing his ripped abs that I want to run my hands over like I did last night. My pulse was already high, but staring at him is another level.

His gaze fixes on my black-and-gold bikini, looking like he wants to devour me here and now. We're in big trouble. If we don't quit staring at each other this way, everyone will figure out something is happening between us.

Fortunately, Amy breaks our spell when she says, "I need a volunteer to go first."

Kai quickly steps forward.

"Excellent. I also need two people to show off the tandem option for couples. Cassie, would you be willing to do a tandem ride with Evan?"

Before I can explain that I'm not going on the zipline at all, Evan says, "That sounds perfect. We'd be happy to do it."

I give him a look of sheer terror. "I can't do this."

"It'll be fine. Close your eyes, and I'll hold you the whole way down."

Amy claps her hands. "That's perfect. The two of you will go last. Now, everyone, put your helmets on. The instructor is going to show you how the harness works and go over the safety information. Have fun."

After a quick safety lesson, we watch a relaxed Kai, soar through the air, signaling "hang loose" with his left hand. He lands on a platform that's submerged a foot or two under the water on the far side of the Aegean Sea. Jayden is naturally meeker, but he pumps his fists and steps off the edge of the tower, hurtling toward the platform as if it's no big deal. I guess this brought out an adventurous spirit in him. Trenton steps up next, looking annoyed but unfazed as he silently slides along the wire.

I'm relieved they all survived. I tell myself that means it's safe enough. This experience could help me overcome my fear of heights. Las Vegas certainly is making me face my fears whether I want to or not. That said, I'm still scared to take that first step.

Evan and I are connected to the zipline cables with me in front of him. The ride operator tells Evan to put his arms around my waist. His muscular arms encircle and comfort me. The next thing I know, we're flying through the air. Rather than scream, I close my eyes tightly, tense my body, and grip Evan's arms.

Almost immediately, I hear a ripping and cracking sound. I scream, "My harness is tearing! I'm going to fall!"

I feel myself dropping farther below the zipline cable and slipping out of Evan's arms.

Evan says, "Stay still. I've got you."

"Please don't drop me," I cry.

"I won't. My arms are locked around you. Don't move."

I hear more tearing as the webbing on my harness continues to rip. Tears run down my cheeks as I say, "I can't hold still. I'm falling!"

My fear escalates when people below scream in horror. Unless Evan can hold onto me, I'm going to die.

I continue to slip down Evan's body. He holds me under my arms with his hands locked together across my chest.

Evan says, "We're almost to the landing platform. Try to hold your legs up and get ready for the splash."

I'm tightly gripping Evan's arms just as my harness completely disconnects from the zipline. My whole body dangles precariously. I hope he can hold me the final few yards because I'm not sure the water is deep enough to survive a fall onto its concrete bottom.

As the zipline trolley connecting us to the cable smashes into the block designed to stop us, we're splashed with water as my shins drag across the rough underwater platform. Workers quickly surround us, shouting instructions and removing our equipment. Towels appear, and someone checks us for injuries. I hear someone call for medics.

Evan lifts me out of the water, cradling me in his arms, and carries me to the side.

"You're going to be okay," he reassures in a soft but firm voice as he buries his nose into my hair, not caring who's watching.

As he holds me close, I feel the pounding thump of his heartbeat and hear him taking quick breaths.

Trying to catch my own breath, I manage to say, "Are you okay?"

He assures me he's fine. As the medics arrive, he lays me on the ground.

I stare into his eyes, whispering, "You saved my life. I would've died if I'd gone by myself. Thank goodness we did the tandem ride."

"You're safe now, but we need to let the medics look at your legs."

I raise my head and see blood covering the front of my legs. Now that the initial shock is wearing off, they're starting to burn, but another thought dominates.

"Did someone just try to kill me?"

"To be honest, I'm not sure. Let the medical people check your legs. Then we'll deal with security."

I lie back down, exhausted, and let the medics evaluate my wounds. They explain that the bones are bruised with protruding bumps. Both shins have floor burns and scrapes from being dragged along the platform.

It's taking them a while to clean and bandage the wounds to prevent infection, so I have no choice but to lie on the ground and let them do their job.

Fortunately, the injuries aren't serious, even though they're starting to hurt like hell. It could have been so much worse. I hear Evan demand the zipline supervisor shut down the ride and check all the equipment immediately. He also tells her to set aside my gear for Mr. Cartwright to see.

With both legs bandaged from knee to ankle, I'm instructed to take an over-the-counter pain reliever as needed. Evan helps me to my feet. He offers to carry me, but I refuse, so we slowly head toward the other finalists and crew. As we walk, Evan and I decide to be careful what we share with the others.

Once we reach the group, we're peppered with questions about what happened. Pointing out that we've had two outdoor events and two "accidents," Kai questions whether someone is sabotaging the competition or whether it's just bad luck. I'm thinking sabotage, but I don't share that thought.

Trenton wants to know if I unclipped myself. Really? Does he think I'm that stupid? Jayden is quiet and just asks if I'm okay.

I'm not sure what to make of Jayden. He's more than willing to sabotage the finalists for an advantage, but he seems to be concerned about me. His voice was shaky like when I overheard him asking about Chef Boucher. If he really doesn't want anyone to be hurt, he needs to wise up and cut ties with the bad guys.

Rather than divulge what I know about him, I reply in a clipped tone, "I will be, but I need a shot of something strong to drink."

Amy, on the other hand, shocks us all when she glibly says, "Glad the accident was minor, Cassie. We shot some fantastic videos. Mr. Cartwright and Cynthia will be thrilled. Thank you, everyone. Round 2 is tomorrow. We'll meet in the Trendz kitchen at 2 p.m. You'll have four hours to prepare your entrée. Then you'll meet with the judges for their evaluation. See you then."

My jaw hangs open. Really? I almost die, and all she can say is that they shot some great video, and management will be thrilled. Is she clueless? We stare dumbfounded, watching her walk away as if nothing unusual happened.

33

CASSIE

Cassandra and I stay behind while the rest of the group disperses. I don't want to talk while others can hear.

As we wait, worry fills my thoughts. Seeing the blood on her legs is like a knife to my heart. I want to scoop her up, put her on the royal jet, and take her as far away from here as possible. I have to keep her safe.

When the others are finally out of earshot, I say, "We need to find Sean and have him put more security in place. I don't think he was particularly worried about the photo shoot today because it wasn't a cooking event. But clearly, you and the other finalists need security all the time."

"We don't know that my equipment was sabotaged. Besides, anyone could have been given that faulty harness."

She's in denial. That's another reason I need to protect her. She may not recognize the next threat in time.

"I wish that were true, but it's not. Did you notice that all the helmets had names on them and were connected to the harnesses when they handed them out? More likely than not, someone wanted you to get the bad one."

"You're right! My name was on the helmet. It still could have been an accident if the equipment was defective. Maybe I was just unlucky."

"That's one explanation, but we can't take that chance. We have to assume this could have been the sabotage that Mitch mentioned to Jayden. Having you out of the competition would be an advantage."

"But Jayden said he wasn't willing to hurt anyone."

"True, but others may also have been offered advantages, and they may not have been concerned about the safety of their competitors."

"This is out of control. I'm tempted to quit the competition and go home. It isn't worth my life. But if I quit, Detective Fielder may arrest me to keep me from leaving town, and that would follow my name forever."

"The competition isn't worth your life, but I agree that Detective Fielder will insist you stay in Las Vegas until he closes Chef Boucher's case. And if you're here, you might as well continue with the competition. We just need to ensure there's more security."

We rush to Sean's office to tell him about the zipline "accident." Sean promises someone will be looking out for Cassie, but he refuses to tell her who it is. He does share that they have undercover police in place but thought it would be better if Cassie didn't know who they were. That way she wouldn't accidentally expose their identity.

Leaving Sean's office, Cassie asks if I'll walk her back to her room. When we arrive, I start to follow her in, but she says, "Thanks. I'm going to try to rest now."

Leaning against the open door, I nod in understanding. "Okay. Why don't you pack up your stuff so we can move it to my room? You can rest there."

She shakes her head. "I can't do that. I need time alone to process everything."

Baffled, I spread my arms, palms up. "Why not stay with me? You'll be safer in my suite."

"I'll be fine here. I can't thank you enough for keeping me close when I was upset, but now I need alone time to clear my head and rest. If I stay with you, there won't be much time for sleep. I'll lock my door and stay in for the evening. I'll see you tomorrow."

I wrap my arms around her, pulling her tight.

"Are you sure?" I don't want to leave her alone, but ultimately, it's her choice.

"Yes, I'm sure. Sean activated panic codes on my TekCuff that will directly alert you, him, and security if I'm in trouble. Sean promised that Mitch isn't part of that aspect of security, so I'll be safe."

"If you insist. I'll call the concierge desk and ask Christian to escort you to the competition tomorrow afternoon. Please don't open the door for anyone other than me, Sean, or Christian. We don't know if we can trust anyone else."

"That seems like overkill. I have the panic code now, so I feel much safer. Besides, I'll need meals between now and then, so I'll need to open the door for room service."

I give Cassandra a final squeeze and step aside.

"Christian or I will bring you food. Please don't let anyone else in. I couldn't bear it if anything else happened to you."

I lean back and push a strand of hair out of Cassandra's eyes but resist the urge to attack her luscious lips with mine. Instead, I gently kiss her forehead and tell her to lock the door, murmuring, "Stay safe, Cassandra."

I chose not to share with her the insane fear I felt when she almost fell forty feet to her death today. First, I didn't want her to realize how close I came to dropping her. Our bodies and arms were slick with sweat from the sun's heat, so she kept slipping further and further. Second, I'm confused about my feelings. The thought of losing her was shattering.

Am I falling for her? Would I have felt the same way about anyone in that situation? Given that I've never been the type to fall in love in the past, this is new to me.

All I know is that Cassandra is different.

34

CASSIE

At 1:45, Christian knocks on my door to escort me to the competition. I thank him again for all his help. Not only did he deliver dinner last night, but he also brought me ice packs to soothe my swollen legs. Then with brunch this morning, he handed me a bag with antibiotic cream and new bandages. After he left, I found the note he'd tucked under the napkin on the tray.

The antibiotic ointment includes a pain reliever so you'll be able to concentrate on cooking today rather than on your aching legs.

I'm cheering for you. Good luck today!

Christian

I make sure to let him know how much I appreciate all the extra work he's doing to look after me. I know this isn't part of his job. The true professional, he tells me that it's his pleasure.

As we walk to Trendz, we talk about the competition and what I'm planning to cook this round. He offers sincere words of reassurance and support, which I find soothing. He must be an amazing person to have as a friend if he can provide a relative stranger like me with such comfort. Looking after people seems to come naturally to him. No wonder he's head of concierge services. It's the perfect job for him.

When we arrive at the kitchen, we part ways.

I should be nervous about the competition, but I've been too busy trying to stay alive and clear my name for cooking to scare me. However, the other chefs seem wound up tighter than a spring. Strangely, my bad experiences may give me an advantage. Surrounded by Sean's undercover security team, the idea of cooking for a few hours sounds like a relaxing break from my real concerns.

But where's Evan? I could use a smile of encouragement from him before we begin, but he isn't anywhere in sight.

When the cameras and lights are in place, Amy directs us to our stations and reminds us of the four-hour time limit. At exactly 2:30, Sebastian signals for the crew to start filming.

Amy explains Round 2 to the camera. She stops at my station, asking me what I'm cooking.

I explain that I'm transforming a comforting beef stew into an elevated meal with a flair. My entrée will be braised beef with red wine and mushroom sauce, mashed potatoes, and roasted baby carrots. I'm serving it with my favorite homemade rolls, called popovers. They're similar to England's Yorkshire pudding.

I'm working as fast as I can because I know the four hours will go by quickly, but I'm still a little distracted by the interviews of the other finalists. Trenton says he's stuffing manicotti with roast beef, spinach, and béchamel sauce. Then he's topping the manicotti with marinara sauce and baking it in the oven. I hear him tell Amy, "Nothing is more comforting than pasta."

Kai is creating a macadamia-coated fish filet on top of pineapple fried rice. As Amy asks Kai to explain how it fits the theme, someone turns on a food processor, so I can't hear his answer.

Jayden explains he's making Texas comfort food with a flair. He says that enchiladas are comfort food where he comes from, but for a flair, he's making seafood crêpes filled with crab, shrimp, and spinach, topped with a cream sauce, and accompanied with a side of wild rice. I give him credit for capitalizing the similarity between enchiladas and crêpes.

My beef is braising in the oven, and my popover batter is ready. It's almost time to roast the carrots and bake the popovers. The hard part is making sure they're ready to plate at the same time. Double-checking the clock, I calculate that I need to wait ten minutes, so I walk toward the pantry to collect dishes for my entrée.

On the way, I hear Kai call out, "Jayden, watch where you're going. I almost stabbed you." Looking toward Kai's station, I see he's holding up a long, sharp knife for fileting his fish. Jayden must have bumped into him.

Why was Jayden walking by Kai's station? Jayden's station is closer to the pantry than Kai's. Was Jayden trying to sabotage Kai? Hopefully, security is watching closely. For now, I have to grab my plates and hurry back to guard my own food.

Amy repeatedly distracts us with questions about how things are going, which makes it difficult to concentrate. To stay on track, I keep running through my mental checklist as I continue watching the clock.

I also scan the kitchen, trying to figure out if there really are undercover officers here. And I keep expecting to see Evan. He still hasn't shown up, which doesn't make sense. He may be upset that I turned him away last night. But that wouldn't keep him away from the competition, would it?

Amy pulls my attention back when she calls out, "You have five minutes to plate your dishes."

I chose dishes that are a cross between a plate and a shallow bowl to keep the red wine sauce from looking messy. I slice a popover in half, place one half on the bottom of the plate, and spoon mashed potatoes into its hollow center. Carefully placing tender chunks of beef on top, I make sure that some of the mushrooms and pearl onions are visible. I add three whole baby carrots across the top, letting one end of each rest on the rim of the plate. As a final touch, I angle the top half of the popover on the edge of the plate.

I'm putting the last popover in place as Amy says, "Fifteen seconds."

At the last second, I remember to sprinkle chopped parsley on top.

Amy yells, "Stop! Step away from your stations."

Whew! The last few minutes flew by. I wish there had been time to clean up the rims of the plates, but they don't look too bad.

My main concern is whether the judges will think my entrée has enough flair. I'll find out soon.

35

CASSIE

Kai's exiting the judging room as I'm about to enter. As our paths cross, he mumbles, "How could my entrée have been so salty? I didn't add any because the macadamia nuts were extra salty. It doesn't make sense."

"Kai, are you okay?"

"No. Salt ruined my entrée, and I don't know how."

"That's terrible."

We aren't supposed to discuss the judge's comments, so I don't ask more. Then panic strikes me. Did Jayden sabotage it? If so, did he destroy mine too? I didn't have time to taste my food before I plated it.

Kai is about to say something else, but Amy's assistant hurries me into the room. I'm surprised to see Evan standing on the right side near the front. That makes me smile as Amy announces my name and describes my entrée. The judges remove the silver domes from atop their plates to reveal my creation. I hope it's still warm.

As they lift their forks for a sample, Amy says, "Cassie, please explain how your entrée fits today's theme."

"A warm beef stew is comforting, so I started with that concept in mind. To add flair, I transformed the basic ingredients of a stew—

beef, potatoes, and carrots—into what you have before you. The beef was braised with mushrooms, pearl onions, and red wine. For a special touch, I served it nestled inside a popover with mashed potatoes and roasted rainbow carrots. I hope you enjoy it."

Not a single smile crosses any of their faces as their eyes squint in judgment of me and my food. First, they close their eyes and take in the aromas of the stew, and then they taste their initial bites. I'm watching closely but can't tell whether they're enjoying it.

Out of the corner of my eye, I catch a hint of a smile on Evan's face, which is reassuring. It also reminds me that I'm supposed to smile whenever the camera is running. Amy and Cynthia pounded that into our heads.

The judges finally set their forks down, and Amy asks Judge Gerard for his comments.

He says, "Overall, I like the idea of transforming stew into something more interesting. The red wine sauce is subtle, the beef is tender, and the popover is a nice, light addition. However, I would have preferred more salt and a little more flair. For example, you could have used medallions of tenderloin instead of cubes of beef. Your entrée is closer to comfort than flair."

I'd worried about that.

To my relief, Judge Holden chimes in, "I disagree. I'd be happy to order this dish at an upscale restaurant. It's the perfect balance between comfort and flair. However, I agree it needs a little more salt. Did you taste it before you served it?"

"Unfortunately, I ran out of time and didn't have a chance."

"Don't make that mistake again. Never serve food you haven't tasted."

She's right. "Understood. Thank you for the feedback."

Amy turns to Judge Indigo and asks, "What are your comments for Cassie?"

"I agree with Judge Holden. Personally, I would not braise tenderloin. It would be a waste of that cut of meat. Cassie, you made the right choice. And I like the sauce and flavors you developed from the slower cooking method. The dish Judge Gerard proposes would have had to be prepared entirely differently to work. That said, you could have elevated the mashed potatoes with some add-ins, but overall, good job."

"Thank you."

Not too bad. I know people hate under-salted food, but I'll take that over Kai's situation.

WHEN THE JUDGING IS OVER, AMY, CYNTHIA, AND EVAN RETURN TO THE kitchen and tell us that we have tomorrow off except for a one-hour promotional event in the afternoon. Round 3 will be the following day.

After yesterday's Thrill Ride fiasco, I'm not too excited about another promotional event. My legs are sore and aching even with the ointment and over-the-counter pain medication. At least Sean promised security for all the events, so hopefully, there won't be any more injuries.

As I'm about to leave, Cynthia reminds us that the Final Dinner is black tie.

Oh! I love an excuse to wear a long formal dress, but I'll need to find one. I brought a cocktail dress for the opening reception, but they didn't tell us to bring anything formal for a black-tie dinner.

I'm trying to decide where I can find an affordable dress on short notice when Cynthia says, "Unless you brought formal attire, please stop by the Tux & Tiara Chalet tomorrow. It's located in Aphrodite's Way, the shopping area. They will loan you something appropriate."

Thank goodness.

On my way out of the kitchen, Evan surreptitiously slips me a note. When I start to say something, he shakes his head and keeps walking.

I wait a minute or two before leaving. With the note hidden in my fist, I find the nearest restroom and enter one of the stalls. Unfolding the note, I read.

> *Meet me at my suite at 8:30 tonight. Sean arranged for your handprint to give you access.*

I check my TekCuff and see it's 7:30 now. That gives me time to change from my sweaty, black-and-white competition clothes to something nicer.

As I'm about to exit the bathroom stall, I turn back and decide to flush the note down the toilet, like I've seen in spy movies.

Over-dramatic? Probably. At least I stopped short of eating it—I've seen that too.

36

EVAN

assie is thirty minutes late. I'm pacing, and my palms are sweating. Why didn't I send Christian to escort her? If someone intercepted her, I'll never forgive myself.

I text Sean.

> **Me:** Track Cassie. She's missing.

The doorbell rings as I hit send. Rushing to open it, I sigh in relief. Cassandra's leaning against the doorframe out of breath.

"Are you okay?" I ask.

"Yes. Sorry I'm late. I accidentally fell asleep when I went to my room to change. Today's competition was exhausting."

Reaching for her hand, I yank her in for a hug, whispering, "I was worried."

My phone dings.

> **Sean:** She's in your suite. It's not that big. You should be able to find her. Try under the bed.

Why's he being such an arse. Hasn't he ever worried about anyone?

"Who was that?" Cassandra asks.

"Nothing important. I'll fix drinks."

"Thanks. Do you have sparkling water?"

"Is champagne okay? It sparkles."

"I'll always say yes to champagne, but water first. By the way, where were you while we were cooking today? I was surprised not to see you until the judging room."

"I watched the live video feed from here. Sean had extra cameras set up in the kitchen last night and hooked up monitors here. That way, I could watch the competition from several angles as well as pause and rewind when something interesting happened. With multiple camera angles at the same time, we hoped to learn more than I could in person."

"How did you listen? I thought the cameras didn't have audio?"

"There's audio now. He used an outside tech company. They installed microphones as well as additional cameras last night."

"Good move. Did anything out of the ordinary happen?"

"Yes. Did you notice when Jayden bumped into Kai's station?" I ask while carefully balancing two champagne flutes and a glass of sparkling water.

As I walk toward the sofa, Cassandra meets me partway, taking her drinks.

She explains, "I didn't see what happened, but I heard Kai tell Jayden to be more careful. Wait a minute. I didn't understand why Jayden was walking past Kai's station in the first place. The pantry was in the other direction. It made me suspicious."

We sit next to each other on the sofa as I say, "Your instincts were right. It was sabotage. When Jayden bumped into the station, he grabbed the top of Kai's food processor to balance himself. The video shows him opening his fist and releasing a handful of granules into the bowl of macadamia nuts."

Cassandra places her hand on my thigh and squeezes. "Oh no! Could you tell what the granules were? Was it salt?"

"Yes, but how did you know it was salt?"

"As I was entering the judging room, Kai was leaving. He was extremely upset and talking to himself. He said something about not knowing how his food could have been too salty."

"That makes sense."

"How could you tell from the video that it was salt rather than something more dangerous, like poison?"

Wrapping my free arm around her shoulder, I explain, "I immediately rewound the video that showed Jayden's work area. Right before he moved toward Kai, Jayden poured a bunch of salt into his hand. He sprinkled a little on his food as he looked around the room to see who was watching. Then, instead of throwing the leftover salt away, he closed his fist and walked toward Kai's station. Given that we still don't know the identity of Mitch's partner, if he has one, I thought I should let it play out."

"But Jayden destroyed Kai's chances of winning."

"When the time is right, I'll make sure everyone knows what happened. Just not yet. Have you picked up any clues as to who besides Jayden is working with Mitch?"

Cassandra sits back and nestles against my shoulder. "No, but the new cameras and audio may help if Mitch meets up with Jayden again. They may mention someone else. Did you learn anything?"

I hesitate before responding because I'm not sure how much Sean wants me to share with Cassandra. I take a long sip of champagne and excuse myself to the bar to retrieve the bottle as I weigh my options. Deciding she deserves reassurance that Sean has made progress, I say, "Sean learned a little more about how someone is skimming profits, but he doesn't know who is involved or if it's connected with the competition's accidents and sabotage."

"Something tells me all these things are connected. If there's money involved, that would be the motivation. Do you think Mitch is the one skimming?"

Before I can respond, she shakes her head and continues, "No. That doesn't make sense. Mitch works in security. He wouldn't be involved with the F&B suppliers."

Setting my glass on the coffee table, I agree. "Good points. Maybe they are connected. That would tie all this together, but Mitch's involvement is a mystery."

After a brief pause, I ask, "You have tomorrow off, right?"

"I do, except for the short promotional event, and I need to go by the Tux & Tiara Chalet to borrow a dress for the Final Dinner."

"That should leave you time to decide what to make for the dessert round."

"I hope so. I want to have several ideas in mind because I'm sure there'll be a twist."

"That's likely."

"Do you think Jayden's advantage for Round 3 will be knowing the twist ahead of time?"

"Possibly. That would definitely help him in the dessert round. But how would Mitch know what the twist is?"

"He's in security, so he might be good with computers. He could've hacked someone's account and found the info. Otherwise, he has a partner who has access to the plans for the competition."

"I hadn't thought about the computer angle. That would explain it, but we can't ask too many questions of his supervisors without risking him finding out. Let's see if he meets Jayden again before Round 3."

"How will you know if they meet again? You can't watch the video feed all the time, so you might miss it."

"Sean's tech team installed cameras with motion sensors, so I'll receive a notification on my phone if someone enters the kitchen. The video will be recorded, and I can watch it anytime. Detective Fielder also has access to the videos and receives the same notifications."

"Do you think Mitch will ask Jayden to sabotage Round 3? Or is Mitch out of things to offer as advantages?"

"Mitch could always offer him money."

"True. Who would know about a twist and what it will be?"

"Good question. No one was discussing it during the judging today. I would assume that at least Cynthia, Cameron, and Amy know. For that matter, the whole crew may know. I can ask Sean, but I'm hesitant to raise the question with anyone else."

"I agree. At this point, we need to be careful about who we talk to about our suspicions."

"Definitely. I do have a great idea. Stay here tonight. We can order dinner and wait to see if anyone enters the kitchen. If they do, we can watch the video together."

I want her in my bed, but even more importantly, I don't want her out of my sight when I'm convinced someone is trying to kill her. I can't let that happen.

Cassandra laughs for the first time this evening. "You're just looking for an excuse to convince me to spend more time in your bed. Besides, you said the police are watching the videos, so why do we need to watch them too?" she teases.

"Can you blame me for wanting to share a bed with you? And while the police can watch the videos, I highly doubt they'll watch them tonight. This is not their only case. But you won't be safe until we have more information. We need to know if Mitch and Jayden meet again tonight. If they do, we need to hear what they say. I don't want to wait a day or two for the police to watch. So, will you stay?"

"I guess another evening with you isn't too much of an inconvenience. You're wearing me down but in a good way." She grins.

Smiling, I stand up and reach for Cassandra's hand. "Fantastic. Let's take our drinks to the hot tub on the balcony. Dinner should be here in about an hour."

"You already ordered? A little over-confident, huh?"

"I call it optimistic. Now let's climb into the hot tub and work up an appetite for the steak and lobster."

We strip off our clothes and slip into the bubbling, steamy water.

By the time the doorbell rings, we've left the hot tub and are cooling off on a double lounge chair as we enjoy the dry night air. I grab my robe and hand one to Cassandra before letting room service in.

They quickly set up a beautiful candlelit dinner on the balcony. The inviting aromas draw us to the table, and we quietly devour the food.

When we finish, Cassandra walks to the balcony wall and leans against it, admiring the view. Forget the neon lights, I can't take my eyes off her.

Walking up behind her, I wrap my arms around her waist and nibble on her ear. "You're irresistible, my love. I can't get enough of you."

Sliding my hand inside the front of her robe, I caress her soft breast. It's the perfect handful. With my other hand, I move her hair aside to expose the back of her neck. Kissing from one side to the other, I don't let a single spot go unattended.

"We should go inside," she says without conviction.

"Relax. We're on the top floor and wearing robes. No one but us will know what we're doing."

She nods and moans, arching her back and pressing her beautiful ass against my hard, needy length. "Evan, do you have any idea what you do to me?"

"Can't you feel what you do to me?"

"Mmmm."

Moving my hands to the top of her shoulders, I slowly let them roam down her robe-covered arms. Reaching her hands, I interlace our fingers and move them to the balcony rail, whispering, "Hold on tight."

Pulling my hands away, I reach for the bottom of her robe and lift it up in back just enough to slip my hand between her legs, finding her soaked. With my foot, I gently nudge hers, saying, "Spread your legs apart for me."

As she does, I reach into the pocket of my robe for a condom and quickly roll it on.

Wanting her more than I've ever wanted a woman, I enter her. She's so tight. Reaching around her, I slip my hand inside the bottom of her robe and find her sensitive nub. As my finger circles her, I increase the intensity of my thrusts.

She pushes against me, moaning, "Yes, yes, ohhh, it's sooo good."

Using every trick in the book not to lose it too soon, I don't let up. I give her everything I have, pushing as deep into her as I can and slowly pulling back, over and over again.

"Please don't stop."

When I feel her tighten around me, I add pressure to her clit, and she lets go, trembling in my arms.

I growl, "Fuuuuck, Cassandra," as my own orgasm consumes me.

Wrapping my arms around her, I hold her tight while we catch our breath.

I whisper, "That was incredible."

"That was more than incredible. Between the hot tub and this, I'm exhausted."

"Then it's time for bed," I say as I pick her up and carry her inside.

I tuck her into bed and crawl in beside her. She sighs and nuzzles her head against my chest as we doze off.

I WAKE UP IN THE MIDDLE OF THE NIGHT, SPOONING HER. OUR LEGS ARE intertwined, and my hand is cupping her bare breast. I whisper, "Do you have any clue how special a woman you are? You're not like the other women I've dated—my guard lowers around you. Others try to convince me they'd make the perfect wife or that I should fly them around the world on a luxury vacation. You're happy with a simple dinner on the balcony with me."

Cassandra stirs, murmuring, "Are you calling me a cheap date?"

I rub my hand through my already tousled hair. I'm an idiot. I was trying to tell her she was different in a good way. Man, did I blow it if that's what she thinks I said.

"That's not what I meant. What I was trying to say is that being with you feels comfortable and real. I can be myself with you without feeling like you're trying to take advantage of me. Most women see a blank check or a black AMEX card when they look at me. I was trying to thank you for being different. Neither of us knows where this will lead, but I look forward to spending more time with you. I'm sorry it all came out wrong. Shite. I'm making it worse. I've never had this type of conversation with a woman before, so I clearly don't know how to express my feelings properly. Please, forgive my clumsiness. I need you here with me."

As she snuggles closer, I sigh in relief. Then Cassandra softly says, "I'm sorry other women have jaded you. We don't all pick our friends or dates based on their bank accounts. I've learned that money is replaceable. People and memories aren't. But I have my issues too. Because of my past, I'm hesitant to become involved with anyone. My reasons are just different than yours."

Sensing that Cassandra wants to share more, I ask, "What happened?"

"I grew up with successful, driven parents who made sure I had everything I needed. When I went to college, they cut off all monetary support. They wanted me to be financially responsible and earn my way in the world. That wasn't a surprise, so I didn't begrudge them. I wanted to make them proud. I took out student loans, made a budget, and lived frugally like most college students."

"That must have been hard."

"I learned a lot about managing money. Then my parents died five years ago. That's when I discovered they had left our home to charity, along with the rest of their assets. Don't get me wrong, my parents had always told me they were planning to leave most of their estate to charity, so that wasn't a surprise. I admired their generosity, but they had also said they would make sure I could always come *home* to our family memories. Instead, I barely had time to retrieve a few mementos before it was gone."

"That's terrible."

I had no idea she had suffered so much heartbreak. I'm in awe of this woman's strength. She was left all alone in the world, without a home or any real mementos to even remember of her parents or childhood. It must have been devasting for her. It's remarkable that she's accomplished so much and become such an amazing person who is able to laugh and empathize with others. I feel guilty that I've been complaining about my life.

"It was devastating. My parents were both talented lawyers. Most people assumed I was taken care of for life because of their success. Other than my best friend Lowri, no one understood the pain I felt from first losing my parents and then our home. It wasn't about the money. It was the loss of the only family left in my life and the lifetime of mementos. Everyone thought I decided to sell the house. I was too emotionally wrecked to explain it. To make matters worse, my parents died in a car crash on the way to my law school graduation. In a twisted way, I've always blamed myself for their deaths. They were workaholics and never took time off, but I wanted a long weekend with them before starting my new job. If I hadn't guilted them into coming a couple of days early, they would still be alive."

I stroke her arm, saying, "Love, I'm so sorry. Wanting extra time with your parents doesn't make you responsible for their car accident."

"The logical side of my brain knows that, but on lonely nights, it's sometimes hard to be rational. It got worse though. A few weeks after the accident, my boyfriend dumped me because I wasn't fun anymore."

"What an arse!"

"I know that now. At the time, it felt like everyone I loved had left me. Through everything, I learned it was easiest to portray myself as strong and try to hide my vulnerabilities. I'm horribly afraid of getting close to someone and then losing them to another tragedy. That's part of the reason I've had trouble letting myself get close to you. Over the last few years, I rarely went on a second date, much less a third one. I protect myself by pushing people away. If I don't let anyone get close, I won't feel the pain of loss again. Do you understand?"

"I do. I'm not sure how I would feel if I'd been through what you have."

"For some inexplicable reason, I find myself wanting to share more with you, but it's still hard. You have no idea how difficult it was for me to admit the other night that I didn't want to be alone. It made me feel weak to need you. I'm not typically the damsel in distress, but that doesn't mean I don't sometimes crave a hug. It just scares me to get close."

Turning her to face me and holding her tight, I say, "We're quite the pair. We both want to get closer to each other, but our pasts are in the way. We could help each other, which leads me to the reason I started this conversation. I'd like to invite you to my father's retirement party. It's going to be stressful for me and my family, but it would be so much easier if you are there with me. Will you be my date?"

I don't want to attend it alone, and there's no one I'd rather have with me than Cassandra.

In a hushed voice, Cassandra asks, "When did you say the party is?"

"In a few weeks."

"Didn't you say it will be in Europe?"

"Yes. You can fly over with me on our private jet. It'll be a special celebration. I'd like to share it with you."

I should have already told her that I'm a prince and Dad's the king. Then she'd understand why this celebration is so important, but now's not the right time to share all those details. I don't want to scare her away. I'll tell her soon though.

"I'd love to go to Europe and have more time with you, but I don't know how I can take more time off from work. I already had to take unpaid leave to be here, and now I've told you why I need a job. My inheritance was lost, and my student loans are enormous."

She doesn't know that I could fix her money issues instantly, but even if she knew, I doubt she would let me. Instead of offering my help, I say, "If you win the competition, you'll receive the prize money and you'll quit your job to work here, right?"

"True, but that's beyond unlikely. At best, I have a one-in-four chance of winning the competition. And it looks like it's rigged for Jayden to win. That's not fair, but it also lowers my chances of winning to practically zero. In fact, I'm certain that if the other finalists knew about Jayden's advantages, they'd have quit by now."

"Trust me, Sean will find a way to make the outcome of the competition fair. Now, please reconsider my question. If you win and Sean agrees to give you the time off, will you go with me to my father's celebration?"

"Evan, even if I were to win, which is a Las Vegas long shot, Sean won't give me the time off. I'll be expected to start work immediately. But I have nothing to lose by agreeing that if all those things were to happen, then I'll happily go with you."

"Excellent. Goodnight, love."

I close my eyes and smile, relishing the possibility of more time with Cassandra.

Did I really just think that?

37

EVAN

The next day, In khakis and a linen shirt, I pick up Cassandra at her room, and we're off to select a dress for her to wear to the Final Dinner in the Athena's Wine Cave.

We follow the signs to Aphrodite's Way, the Athena's luxury shopping area. Stopping along the way, we peer in the windows of various shops and comment on the displays. When we reach a boutique with formals, I say, "Let's go inside."

"This isn't Tux & Tiara."

"No, but let's look anyway."

"Why not? We just have to allow enough time for me to borrow a gown at Tux & Tiara."

"We have plenty of time. Come on."

Walking in, we're greeted by an elegant, silver-haired woman. "Welcome. We have everything ready for you."

Cassandra looks at me with brows raised. "What is she talking about?"

The woman backs away, sensing we need privacy.

"I want you to have a special dress for the Final Dinner, so I had Christian arrange an appointment for you to try on a few dresses."

"I make a good salary, but, as I told you, I'm still paying back a small fortune in student loans. I can't afford to shop here. These gowns will be thousands of dollars."

"I understand your need for independence, but you've already proven you're capable of taking care of yourself. I admire that you don't expect anything from me in terms of money. However, I have loads of it, and I'd be extremely happy if you let me spoil you today. Besides, they've spent their morning selecting dresses specifically for you. We don't want to be rude, so please, at least try them on."

"I'll try them on for fun, but we're not buying anything. Does that work?"

"I can live with that for now."

Just then, another woman approaches carrying a silver tray with two flutes of champagne. I hand one to Cassandra and take the other for myself. The woman then escorts us to the back of the shop. There's a large dressing room for Cassandra and a separate sitting area with a comfortable sofa where I can wait.

I clink my glass against Cassandra's, saying, "A toast to having fun!"

I hope this relaxes her. She deserves to enjoy a little pampering. I can't help but shake my head and grin. I've never had to work this hard to spend money on a woman. No one I've dated—even titled, royal women—had any problem letting me dump insane amounts of money on them.

Cassandra is refreshing.

38

CASSIE

I model several dresses for Evan.

The last one is a gorgeous, floor-length, black one with thin spaghetti straps and crystal accents. It fits perfectly but shows a lot of skin. While there's an inch-wide strap across the back at bra level, the rest of the back is open and plunges so low it barely covers my backside. Evan insists on buying it for me. I decline, telling him it's too expensive, but he explains that pampering me gives him pleasure.

He makes me feel like a princess, and it's not about the money. He treats me like a treasure to be cherished, and dare I say, loved. The way he treats me is more intoxicating than the champagne, so eventually, I relent, and he arranges for the dress to be delivered to his suite.

Walking back through the casino, I ask, "Would you mind if we stop and play a couple of hands of blackjack? I've never played before, but I've studied the rules for basic strategy."

"I love blackjack, and the High Roller Lounge isn't too far."

"I can't afford to play in the High Roller Lounge. I can barely afford to play two or three hands at the $20 tables here."

"You can play with my money."

"That would take all the fun out of it. Let's play here."

We sit down at the nearest table, my excitement building as the dealer passes out the cards.

I'm doing okay—winning some, losing some—when Evan's phone dings.

He whispers in my ear, "We have a video to watch."

"Let's hurry." I quickly collect my chips, and we walk toward the elevators.

When we arrive at Evan's suite, he logs into his computer to access the video feeds from the kitchen in Trendz. This time we have audio and more camera angles that cover the entire area. Sure enough, Jayden is in the kitchen talking to Mitch. Jayden says, "I took care of Kai's food, so give me the advantage."

Slapping a white envelope into Jayden's outstretched hand, Mitch says, "Relax, buddy. Here it is. Use it wisely. We need you to shine in the last round to ensure you win this competition."

Jayden responds, but his voice is soft, so we can barely make out what he's saying. Evan increases the volume and replays it. We rewatch the grainy video and move closer to the laptop, straining to hear as Jayden asks, "Do you think this advantage will be enough? Trenton has been doing well. His food always looks great. Hell, Cassie's an amateur, and her food looks good. Rumor has it she has the inside track because of her relationship with Evan."

Staring at the computer screen, we watch Mitch lean against a counter as he inquires, "What have you heard about Cassie's relationship with Evan?"

I grab Evan's leg, worried what the rumors are.

"Well, one of the crew said they seem really close. Some think she's sleeping with him in exchange for a good word with Mr. Cartwright."

I gasp, and Evan hits pause on the video and wraps his arm around my shoulder, kissing the top of my head.

"For crying out loud, how can they say that? I would never sleep with anyone to gain an advantage!"

"I know you wouldn't. Don't pay attention to those arses. Let's keep watching."

When the video continues, Mitch says, "Don't worry about Cassie or Trenton. They won't be a problem. Just make sure you take care of your dessert."

"Okay. What else do I need to do?"

"Make a great dessert tomorrow. When you win, you'll owe us though."

"Understood."

"We won't be meeting again. After the contest, my partner will be your contact."

"Who's your partner?"

"Win first. Then you'll find out."

They both leave the kitchen, and the video goes silent.

"That's ominous. What did he mean by 'They won't be a problem?' I'd convinced myself that the panic code on my TekCuff was enough, but after hearing this conversation, I'm afraid. It's creepy to know someone wants me out of the competition."

Evan leans over and kisses me. Staring deep into my eyes, he says, "Love, I promise to keep you safe. I'd fight to my dying breath before I let anything happen to you. I'll also call Sean to make sure he watches the video and keeps security on alert."

"Thank you. I don't know what I'd do without you."

My TekCuff chimes, and within seconds, Evan's phone beeps with the same message. We need to be at the Olympic Torch Bar in thirty minutes for a mixology promotional event. I'm always up for tasting new cocktails, and it would be a fun event if I wasn't worried. Instead, a cold chill runs through me, knowing I'm walking into an event where someone may be scheming to eliminate me from the competition.

39

EVAN

When we arrive at the Olympic Torch Bar, the film crew and staff are ready to start.

Sebastian shouts, "Action," and Amy introduces Sean.

He explains, "We're here for a fun afternoon of mixology. My college friend has been helping me with this competition, so I want to do something as a thank you to him. We're going to learn how to make his favorite drink, a Boulevardier."

There is mumbling among the finalists and the crew. No one has ever heard of the drink, much less has a clue how to make it.

Sean continues, "It's a somewhat unknown drink here in the States, but it's my best friend's favorite. He'll be the judge of your efforts today. To get started, Ray, the head bartender here, will give you a quick demonstration. Then you'll have ten minutes to make your version. Any questions before we start?"

Kai asks, "Will the competition judges also be tasting it? Do we need to make extra drinks for them?"

"No, this is just for fun. You only need to make one drink. However, I'd suggest making two so you can taste it. That will give you a chance to make adjustments before serving it. I should add that while this mixology event doesn't matter in the overall competition, there'll be a small prize for the chef who makes the winning drink today. If there aren't more questions, let's begin. Ray, show them how it's done."

While Ray explains the steps, I approach Sean and whisper, "Thanks for the tribute to my drink of choice, but please keep me off camera. It is a miracle that no one has recognized me yet, and I'd like to keep it that way."

"Don't worry, I brought you an Athena baseball cap and told Amy to have the crew film your back. Your face will never be shown. Regardless, they're going to concentrate on the finalists. Are you okay with having your voice on the video?"

"That should be fine."

"By the way, when are you going to tell Cassie who you really are? I'm told that she's practically moved into your suite."

"Soon. I'm waiting for the right time. It's a pleasant change to get to know someone without them realizing who my family is, so I'm not in a hurry to tell her. It would also be best to wait for the police to close the murder investigation first."

"In other words, you don't want your family to know you're sleeping with a murder suspect. I warned you to stay away from her. She's adding unnecessary complications to your life."

"She isn't guilty, and you know it. I have new information for you. Mitch met with Jayden again today. You need to watch the video because Mitch essentially threatened Cassandra and Trenton. He also gave Jayden an envelope that supposedly contains an advantage for tomorrow's competition."

"Damn. I'll watch it when this is over. I'll also increase the security on the finalists."

Applause draws our attention to Ray, who is putting on quite a show. He tosses a drink shaker in the air and catches it behind his back. As he strains the amber liquid into a glass with one giant ice cube, Ray reminds the finalists that the traditional version of the drink contains bourbon, Campari, and sweet vermouth. The finishing touch is a garnish of orange peel.

Taking over as host, Amy says, "Let's thank Ray for his fantastic demo. Now it's time for you to make your versions for our judge, but guess what? There's a twist. You must add or change an ingredient to make the cocktail your own. Your goal is to convince Evan that your drink is even better than his favorite version. You have ten minutes, and the time starts now!"

While watching the bedlam of everyone scurrying to the bar to pick up their ingredients and return to their tables, Sean asks, "I assume Cassandra has this one in the bag, right? You must have shared your favorite add-in with her."

"No, this will be completely fair. Until now, she didn't know this was my favorite cocktail. We've only shared champagne or other wines."

"Then this should be interesting. Have you seen the unusual ingredients the finalists are picking? Is Trenton adding rosemary?"

"It looks like it. That doesn't sound very appealing. Are you sure this is a thank you, or are you punishing me?"

Amy calls time, and I taste each of the drinks in turn. Trenton's sprig of rosemary overpowers the orange twist, giving the drink a strong herbal scent that effectively kills my taste buds. Jayden decided that Texas tequila would be a good substitute for the bourbon. It wasn't.

Kai and Cassandra had better ideas. Kai added a cinnamon stick along with the orange twist, which provides a note of warmth. Cassandra added a pineapple spear. It's a little acidic but still extremely good.

Making my decision, I write down the winner's name on a slip of paper and hand it to Sean, whispering, "It was a close call."

"I'm told that this was a tough decision, but the winner is Kai with his cinnamon Boulevardier. However, none of you added the extra ingredient that Evan always requests. He insists on three Luxardo cherries, not to be confused with the bright-red maraschino cherries. And yes, for some undisclosed reason, it must be exactly three."

Everyone laughs.

Sean continues, "Now for the prize. Kai, please come forward to accept your gift certificate for a day at the spa. Congratulations! We'll see everyone for Round 3 tomorrow at 2 p.m."

Cassandra's drink was great, and I would have loved to give her the win. But Kai's creation was just a tad better, which was not a bad result given the rumors about my relationship with Cassandra. And after what Jayden did to him with the salt, I was happy to see Kai come back with a win.

40

CASSIE

I arrive at the kitchen for Round 3. Cameron immediately asks me to draw a chip from a chef's hat. Today, we'll use the station adorned with the color that matches our chip. I draw the green $25 chip, so I take my place and pocket the chip. I'll save it for another hand or two of blackjack.

I examine the ingredients on my table, making sure no one swapped the salt and sugar or sabotaged the equipment. I don't find any obvious problems. Trenton and Kai are double-checking their ingredients too. I'm not the only one concerned. Meanwhile, Jayden is organizing his prep area before we even hear the requirements for our desserts.

When the crew is ready, Sebastian signals for the cameras to start recording.

Amy asks everyone, "Are you ready for the final round?"

We all smile and respond that we are.

"As you all know, this is the dessert round. But as we have said from the beginning, the Athena is looking for a guest chef who can think on his or her feet, deal with last-minute changes, and present beautiful plates of food to the guests. That's why we've had various twists that you've had to deal with in each round.

                    J. D. CAROTHERS

Therefore, it's probably no surprise that the same is true today. In this round, you must make a dessert that includes both chocolate and fruit. You have three hours, and your time starts now! Good luck."

Relief washes over me. Planning for this round, my imagination ran wild. I feared the twist would require me to use something like mushrooms or olives in my dessert. I also worried they might tell us we couldn't use chocolate or a key dessert ingredient like sugar. But I can deal with this twist.

As I begin assembling ingredients, Amy stops by and asks, "Cassie, I see you're melting butter. What are you making?"

"I'm making mini molten chocolate cakes in individual ramekins," I say as I grab a whisk and bowl.

"That sounds delicious. How are you going to incorporate fruit?" Amy asks as she steps closer.

Moving the pan of melted butter off the heat, I look into the camera and answer, "I'm using strawberries. They'll pair well with the chocolate."

"That is a fantastic combo, but I have another twist for you. This hat is filled with four chips. Each one has an additional ingredient written on it. You must draw a chip and use that ingredient in your dessert. And you cannot change what you have just told me you're going to make. The final twist is that you'll have thirty seconds after you draw the chip to tell us how you'll be using the new ingredient. Think fast."

Shit. Shit. Shit.

Attempting to hide my panic, I keep smiling as I draw a chip.

"Show us what ingredient you drew."

I take a deep breath and read, "Almonds."

Whew! That was lucky. I know exactly what to do.

"How will you use almonds in your dessert?"

"I should thank my gluten-free friends. I'll use almond flour in place of regular flour. It works great in a molten cake and will be delicious."

Amy wishes me good luck and moves on to talk with Trenton. He's creating individual chocolate swirl cheesecakes with orange rind. He drew cinnamon, but the whir of Kai's food processor drowns Trenton's explanation of how he plans to use the cinnamon.

Kai is making chocolate coconut tarts, and he reminds the camera that coconut is a fruit. His extra ingredient is mascarpone. He can use it to stabilize the whipped cream topping or as an addition to the chocolate filling.

I can't resist a quick pause to watch as Amy interviews Jayden. He draws rum and must use it with his chocolate and raspberry ice cream. While he may have had an advantage in knowing that we had to use chocolate and fruit, there's no way he could have known that he would draw rum as his extra ingredient. However, to my surprise, Jayden immediately says he'll make chocolate rum ice cream with raspberries and almonds.

Then it hits me. At first, I thought ice cream was a lame choice, but it's the perfect base and can be easily adjusted to accommodate any of the twist ingredients.

Shaking off the distraction, I return my focus to my dessert to make sure it isn't under- or overcooked.

As I place the last ramekin on a plate and garnish it with a strawberry, the timer goes off, and Amy announces, "Time is up. Step away."

Wiping my damp brow, I smile because my molten cakes look perfect.

When I look up, Detective Fielder's glaring eyes erase my smile and cause my stomach to flinch. While I know there's plenty of evidence pointing to others, I still can't explain my fingerprints on Leon's bowl. I'm not off the hook yet.

Finally, Sebastian yells, "Cut," and filming temporarily stops so they can reset for judging in the main area of the restaurant. The detective uses this time to corner various crew members and ask questions, but I can't hear what they're talking about.

I'm up first for judging this time, so I walk into the restaurant, hoping my molten cakes are still warm and gooey.

Amy announces, "Cassie made a molten chocolate cake."

"Why didn't you turn it out of the ramekin for a more elegant presentation?" Judge Gerard asks. But before I can answer, he adds,

"And merely putting fruit on top doesn't impress me as a creative use of that requirement either."

He's the presentation-centric judge. Staying as calm as possible, I politely say, "Unlike a standard molten cake, I not only garnished with fruit but also hid fresh strawberries in the center for a special twist, which I hope you'll enjoy. Given the weight of the fruit in the center, I didn't believe it would work to remove the cake from the ramekins. I worried the cake would collapse."

Returning my smile with a huff and intense stare, Judge Gerard sinks his spoon into the warm chocolate and scoops up a combo of cake, strawberries, and, to my relief, runny chocolate. Placing the spoonful of dessert in his mouth, he never takes his eyes off me. After a long pause, he says, "I rarely admit it, but I was wrong. I'm impressed with your use of the ingredients. However, I would have garnished the plate with chocolate drizzles."

"Thank you for the feedback. I'll do that next time."

After tasting the dessert, Chef Holden then says, "Please remind us which extra ingredient you drew."

"Chef, it was almonds."

Rather sarcastically, she asks, "Where are the almonds? Did you forget to sprinkle them on top?"

This is a tough crowd. They're looking for anything to criticize.

"To incorporate almonds into my dessert, I used almond flour, so you're sampling a gluten-free dessert," I answer, trying to keep any annoyance from my voice.

"I must say, I had no idea this was gluten-free. Great job," Chef Indigo compliments.

Turning to leave, I'm smiling from ear to ear, barely holding back from doing a fist pump.

When the judging is over, all the finalists are smiling, so I guess the judges universally liked our desserts. No disasters or sabotage this time. Now, we must wait until the Final Dinner tomorrow night to learn who will be the guest chef. That also means Detective Fielder needs to hurry up and solve the murder because most of the suspects will be clamoring to leave town soon after the winner is announced. I need my name cleared before it's too late.

41

EVAN

The morning light streaming through the windows nudges me awake, but Cassandra's still sleeping peacefully. Tonight, the winner of the Guest Chef Competition will be announced. I hope her dream comes true.

The sad part is that means our time together is running out. I invited her to go with me to Catalinius if she wins, but she may not have been serious when she agreed. And it's not like I could, or would, hold her to it. I can only hope that she wants more time together too.

Based on what I've seen, Cassandra has done quite well. She thinks her chances of winning are low given that the other finalists are professionals and someone is handing out advantages to one or more of them. However, she doesn't know Sean the way I do. Having dealt with cheaters in the casino industry, he loathes them. I have no doubt he'll ensure the result is fair.

Regardless, I've told Sean I don't want to know the outcome before he announces it. Until then, my goal is to take Cassandra's mind off the competition. I've planned a little surprise for her.

I hate to wake her when she looks so beautiful snuggled next to me with one arm splayed across my torso and the other hugging her pillow. Unfortunately, I have no choice for my surprise to work. I kiss her gently on the cheek and pepper more kisses down her neck before pulling away. She slowly opens her eyes and finds me propped up on an elbow, staring at her.

"Good morning," she whispers.

"Good morning, princess."

Her sleepy eyes are adorable, and her tousled hair makes her look thoroughly fucked. I want to wake up like this with her every day. It's both frightening and energizing to admit to myself that I'm falling hard and fast for this remarkable woman. I may not have all my future plans ironed out, but somehow, I want Cassie in my life.

"Why are you staring at me?" she asks.

"Because it makes me smile, and I have a surprise for you. Remember that I asked you to let me spoil you a little?"

"Yes. Thank you again for the dress. It's beautiful."

"While I understand it's against your nature to accept gifts, it gives me immense pleasure to do special things for people I care about. Therefore, I'm hoping you'll let me do one more thing for you today. I made appointments for you at the spa this morning. I arranged for you to have a massage and then have your hair and nails done. You can relax and will shine like a star at the Final Dinner tonight."

"That's too much. Besides, we need to figure out who else is behind the sabotage. I'm running out of time to clear up this mess."

"It's not too much. You've been under a lot of stress with the competition and the murder investigation, not to mention the newspaper article. A morning at the spa is my way of letting you know I care and want to see you relax for a few hours. Even strong, independent people let others do nice things for them from time to time, so please let me do this. It's not like it's a diamond necklace. It's just a morning at the spa. Besides, Sean is going to talk with Chef Maurizio this morning, and I plan to listen in on the call."

"You're right. It's a lovely and thoughtful gift, and I need to learn to just say 'thank you' sometimes. Will you tell me what Chef Maurizio says?"

"Of course. You can meet me when you're done. I'll give you an update. How about lunch at the Blue Ramen Bowl at 1:30? I'll send you a message if we need to change plans after the call with the chef."

"Sounds good. I better hustle if I'm going to be on time for the spa appointments."

We dress and take the elevator to the spa level. The doors open, but Cassandra hesitates, deep in thought.

"What's bothering you?" I ask.

"I feel like I've missed an important detail or forgotten something that happened during the competition. Whatever it is could be the key to solving this mystery. I keep thinking I should know how my fingerprints ended up on Leon's bowl. It's like I almost remember something, and then the memory slips away before I can make sense of it. It's stressing me that I can't figure it out, and my future depends on it."

"If you saw something important, I'm sure you'll remember it. Sometimes, it helps to clear your head, so let your mind rest while you're at the spa. Then you can think back over the last few days to see if you remember any new details."

"You're probably right."

"Don't forget, meet me at the Blue Ramen Bowl at 1:30 unless I send you a note with a change of plans."

"Sounds great."

I don't want Cassandra worrying, but we need Chef Maurizio to fill in the missing pieces. If he knows why Jayden, Mitch, and Mitch's mystery partner are trying to rig the competition, I suspect the rest of the pieces will fall into place.

42

CASSIE

Stepping into the spa's circular reception area transports me to a peaceful indoor garden. Soothing music plays in the background, interrupted only by the sound of trickling water from a cherub-topped, multi-tier fountain in the center of the room. It rises almost to the ceiling. Green ivy trails over the edges and down the sides of each tier, and white gardenias float in the water, filling the air with their sweet fragrance. Hand-painted clouds and birds surround a domed skylight.

I close my eyes and take a deep breath to enjoy the floral scent. A peaceful feeling washes over me for the first time in forever. Even my shoulders fall as tension slowly releases. Evan was right. This will be good for me.

The receptionist instructs an attendant to show me to the women's locker room. I change into a fluffy white robe and wander into an adjacent relaxation lounge. Stretching out on a cushy lounge chair, I sip herbal tea while waiting for my massage.

I'm not usually one to sign up for massages, so I'm not sure how comfortable I'll be having a stranger rub oil all over my naked body. But my arm and shoulder muscles have been so tight, I'm ready to give it a try.

As I finish my tea, Ava introduces herself and walks me to the massage room, which is lit with a soft, warm glow from candles and sparkling pinpoint lights in the dark ceiling, simulating a starlit night sky. The room is much larger than I expected, with a massage table and a cozy sitting area with an oversized chair and fireplace.

As Ava gives me time to get comfortable on the table, the scent of lavender and something else permeates the room. It could be eucalyptus, but I abandon all thought when Ava starts working on my tense shoulders. Between the stress of the competition and having my reputation brought into question, my stress level is high. Even if this relief lasts only while I'm here, it's amazing to let my muscles relax as I drift off.

The next thing I know, Ava is gently waking me to tell me it's time for my pedicure and manicure. I slowly climb off the massage table.

Clad in the luxurious Athena robe and slippers, I follow an attendant to another private room. The attendant helps me onto an elevated, heated chair. I let my feet dangle in a pool of swirling, lavender-scented water. I think I'm going to fall back asleep. This is pure heaven.

As they're finishing my nails, an attendant walks in with an envelope for me. I read the note.

URGENT! CHANGE OF PLANS. WE'RE HEADED TO THE LOADING DOCK VIA THE MAZE. THE POLICE ARE ON THE WAY.

SHOW CHRISTIAN THIS NOTE, AND HE'LL LET YOU INTO THE MAZE AT THE OLYMPIC TORCH LOUNGE. THE PASSWORD IS ARES—NER.

WE'VE FIGURED IT OUT, BUT YOU NEED TO HURRY IF YOU WANT TO SEE YOUR NAME CLEARED.

EVAN

That's fantastic news. There's no way I'm missing this. I want to see who's responsible for trying to ruin my life!

My heart races with the hope that my nightmare will soon be over as I scurry to the women's changing room. As I'm yanking on my clothes, I chastise myself for not bringing sandals instead of tennis shoes. My toenail polish is still wet, so these shoes are going to ruin my beautiful pedicure. Oh well. Watching handcuffs snap onto the people who tried to ruin me is much more important.

I practically run to the concierge lounge to find Christian. Arriving out of breath, I gasp between words as I ask for him. Fortunately, he's on duty and soon appears in front of me.

I thrust the note at him, and after reading it, he tells me he isn't supposed to let anyone into the Maze without Mr. Cartwright's approval. I tell him we don't have time and point out that Evan is Sean's best friend. Sean must have given Evan the password.

Christian acknowledges it's the correct password for today. Reluctantly, he admits he may get into more trouble if he doesn't follow the instructions, so he finally agrees to take me to the Maze.

As he's about to walk me down the stairs, he gets a call. He scrunches his forehead and rubs his eyes.

When the call ends, he says, "I'm sorry. There's an urgent problem that I must attend to. The note included the letters NER, which means no escort required. I suppose you can go ahead on our own."

I thank him before darting down the stairs.

That's when I realize I don't know where I'm supposed to meet Evan. Should I wait here or try to find the path to the loading dock? I'd assumed he'd be waiting for me at the entrance.

As I'm looking around for a sign, the Maze's hospital-like smell hits me. The cleaning crew must be exceedingly diligent, but they could learn from the spa and pick a more pleasant-smelling cleaner.

I hear the click of a door opening behind me, and the antiseptic odor grows stronger. As I turn my head, a hand presses a cloth firmly against my mouth and nose, and an arm encircles my neck. I reach up to pull the constricting arms away, but they're too strong.

I can't scream. I can't breathe. In my panic for air, I inhale the horrible-smelling substance that's coating the rag. My head spins. I feel sick.

Mitch's familiar deep voice says, "You aren't going to cause us any more trouble now."

Knowing that fighting is futile, I relax my arms and try to secretly reach for my TekCuff to enter the panic code. I can't see the screen, so I go by feel, hoping I entered the correct 555 panic code. My attacker's left arm tightens against my neck, and everything goes dark.

When I come to, I'm under a blanket on a swiftly moving cart. The cloth that was around my mouth has fallen off. I discreetly check my TekCuff to see if the panic code went through and stifle a groan when I see 222 displayed on the screen.

Shit. I sent the wrong code. I quickly enter 555 and press send, hoping the panic code works this time.

The cart screeches to a halt. I close my eyes, pretending to still be knocked out. Someone grabs me, and I feel a sharp prick on my upper arm.

Fuck! Lights out. Again.

43

EVAN

"Evan, you're here just in time. I'm about to call Chef Maurizio. If you don't mind, stay quiet. I assume he'll talk more freely if he thinks no one else is listening."

Settling back into a guest chair, elbows resting on the side arms, I nod. "No problem."

After a few rings, Chef Maurizio answers with the Italian greeting, "*Pronto*."

"Chef Maurizio, this is Sean Cartwright from the Grand Athena. Thank you for taking my call. How are you and your family?"

"*Bene, grazie.*"

"That's excellent to hear. I'm hoping you can answer a question for me."

"What is it?"

"It relates to your work at the Athena. During the last couple of months that you were here, you replaced several of our suppliers with new ones. Why did you decide to make those changes? It's a mystery to me when the new ones seem to be more expensive."

After a long pause, Chef Maurizio coughs and then hesitantly responds, "Mr. Cartwright, it's no mystery. We were trying out new options."

Huh? An experienced chef doesn't randomly decide to try out new options for an operation as large as the Athena.

Sean continues, "I'm sorry, but that doesn't make sense. We're receiving lower-quality products at a higher price. For the love of god, please tell me why someone with your excellent reputation and training would do something like this?"

Silence fills the phone connection. In a hushed voice, Chef Maurizio says, "I don't think I can answer your questions."

"Chef, you're now at the helm of your family's business, so I'm sure you understand my position. This hotel is my family's business and its legacy. I protect it, just as I assume you're now protecting what your family built. I'm sure if you were in my position, you would do whatever is necessary to resolve these problems and determine the cause, so please be honest with me."

"I understand, but it's not that simple," he says, regret in his voice.

Mystified, Sean asks, "Why not? You made the change to the new suppliers, correct?"

"Yes, that's correct. I made mistakes that I regret, but at the time, I had no choice. It would have been dangerous for me not to make the changes."

Raising his voice in bewilderment as well as frustration, Sean practically screams, "How could it possibly have been dangerous? Please tell me why you changed suppliers. Otherwise, I'll have no choice but to send the international authorities to question you and your family."

The sinister nature of the chef's answer causes an impending doom to loom over me. Sean has no power to have Chef Maurizio questioned, much less his family. If the chef knows that, we're in trouble because we need him to tell us what he knows.

But Chef Maurizio falls for his bluff, responding, "Please don't do that, Mr. Cartwright. I don't want my family involved. I'll explain what I can. As I said, I had no choice. I'm sorry, but I was being blackmailed. I never wanted to take anything from you or the Grand Athena, but I feared for my career and my safety if I didn't go along with it. Then, when my father became ill, I saw an escape path. I could return home to take care of him, and if I kept my mouth shut, I'd be safe. It was my chance to get away from the blackmailers. I'll try to pay what you require for me to make it right for you, but please don't tell anyone you spoke with me. I must keep my family safe."

I raise my hands in question, mouthing "Blackmail?"

Lowering his voice, Sean asks, "Why did someone want you to change suppliers?"

"For the kickbacks. I could only use suppliers who paid us kickbacks. The suppliers would raise the prices of the food and wine and give us a cut of what the Athena paid them. I only got a small portion, but I understand the masterminds behind this plan received a much larger portion. Please believe me. I didn't want to be a part of the scheme. I just didn't know how to get out of it when they kept threatening me."

"What were they holding over you? Who was blackmailing you? Who is behind this mess?"

"Mr. Cartwright, I cheated on my wife, which I deeply regret. They found out, but I have already said too much. I want to avoid further risk to my family. All I can say is look up." Then the line goes dead.

Sean looks at me, saying, "I'm appalled, stunned, and confused. I can't believe blackmail and theft took place under my watch, even if only for a few months."

"It's shocking."

"What the hell does *look up* mean? Does he think the cameras in the ceiling in Trendz recorded something important?"

"I have no idea. Do you even have video from that far back?"

"Not unless it was archived as part of our backup system. Do you think Chef Maurizio is telling the truth?"

"Yes. He sounded remorseful but afraid of someone."

"If we believe him, then we know a little more. Unfortunately, it looks like our problems didn't leave when he did. I hoped for a less ominous cause. I'd also hoped the sabotage in the competition was unrelated. But if Chef Maurizio was being threatened too, the sabotage and blackmail may be linked. Now, I need to figure out what the next step should be."

Standing, I say, "I'm meeting Cassandra at the Blue Ramen Bowl for lunch. Do you want to join us? We can discuss what to do next."

An alert simultaneously goes off on both my phone and Evan's, interrupting our conversation.

"Fuck! Sean, that's Cassandra's panic code. She's supposed to be at the spa. Where's her security?"

"If she's at the spa, security would be waiting nearby. Let me text them to see if they have eyes on her."

Sean types quickly as my worry soars.

"Shit, Evan. She left the spa while my guy was in the restroom. He doesn't know where she is. The tracking on her TekCuff isn't working."

I punch my fist into my other palm, furious that the security guard left Cassandra unprotected. Doesn't he realize how important she is and that someone has already tried to kill her? His only job was to protect her.

"Sean, we have to find her quickly. She wouldn't have used the panic code unless she's in danger. If she's been harmed, I don't trust what I'll do."

"Let's go."

As we leave Sean's office, he calls out, "Emily, it's imperative that we find Cassie Edwards ASAP. Please ask our IT department to text me her last known location and have security search all video feeds to locate her. Tell them to start with the spa exit. This is a Code Red Alert."

Emily's head pops up from her work, jaw slack and eyes popping out, but she recovers quickly like a true professional. She answers, "We rarely have Code Red Alerts. I'll make sure they understand the seriousness of the situation."

44

CASSIE

Where am I? I crack my eyelids open a smidge. When light seeps between them, I'm struck with an intense searing pain. My head spins. I'm nauseous. I clamp my eyes shut to regroup. Taking a deep, cleansing breath, I try to calm myself.

When the pain subsides, I use my other senses to survey my surroundings while keeping my eyes tightly shut. I'm sitting on a cold, hard floor—probably concrete. My hands are bound in front of me, and my ankles are tied together. My right arm is sore, like after a flu shot. I vaguely remember a sharp prick. It must have been an injection of some kind. Whatever it was is upsetting my stomach. I guess it was a knock-out drug rather than poison. Not that I'm complaining, but why keep me alive?

Trying to ease the nausea, I quietly take two more slow, deep breaths. If someone is watching me, I don't want them to notice. Vomiting would be a clear giveaway that I'm awake, which would kill my only hope of getting the upper hand.

The immediate threat of sickness subsides, so I ease my eyes open a sliver, needing to check where I am and who's around. The pain is milder this time, so I let my eyes adjust to the brightness. I'm relieved to see that no one is nearby. I'm tucked between crates in a back corner of a warehouse. There are rows and rows of metal shelves. They must be at least forty feet high. Costumes and props with the Athena logo are everywhere.

Thank goodness I'm still at the Athena. If Evan and Sean received my panic alert, there's a chance they'll find me. My hope evaporates when I think about the concrete and steel surrounding me. What if the signal couldn't transmit it? Even if they didn't get my signal for help, I have to believe that Evan will look for me when I don't show up for our lunch.

I hear footsteps approaching and someone talking, so I close my eyes tightly and still my body as much as possible. It's Mitch, my kidnapper. I recognize his voice. He must be talking on his phone because I don't hear the other side of the conversation.

He says, "Don't worry. I've got her. She won't cause any more problems."

After a pause, Mitch continues, "No, she's safely hidden out of sight and still knocked out cold. I gave her enough meds to keep her quiet for hours. We have plenty of time to deal with her later. Besides, Mr. Cartwright and his friend have no idea what's going on."

He stops talking, apparently listening to the other person.

He says, "I wouldn't worry about that. They'll think the chefs are cutthroat enough to take each other out. Jayden will be the last viable option. They'll have to pick him. Besides, with Cassie gone, they'll think she sabotaged Leon, got scared, and took off. They already found her fingerprints on the bowl of hummus that killed him."

After another pause, Mitch responds, "No. Cartwright's friend won't care. He's not serious about her. It's just a fling while he's in Vegas. He'll head back to Europe soon."

Following another brief silence, Mitch says, "They haven't connected Chef Bernard's death to the F&B increases. We're in the clear. To make sure, I planted opioids at Chef Bernard's restaurant.

The police just haven't found them yet. I guess I hid them too well, but an anonymous tip will take care of that loose end."

My mind whirls at this new revelation. It's devastating to know that they drugged and killed my cooking mentor, Chef Bernard. She didn't die from her own carelessness, but rather at the hands of this evil man and his partner. It's so unfair to her and her family.

Mitch listens longer this time and then says, "Stop worrying, Sis. There's no need to abandon our plan. The competition will end soon, and Jayden will be in place as the chef."

Who is his sis?

After another pause, Mitch reassures, "Yes, I'm sure. I heard they loved his dessert. They should have. He was ready for all the twists. We've got this. I need to go now."

I open my eyes just enough to see Mitch staring at my ankle bindings. Shutting my eyes, I freeze. He walks away, most likely satisfied that I'm still sufficiently bound and asleep.

After the footsteps have faded into the distance, I open my eyes. The nausea and dizziness threaten to overwhelm me again, so I try the deep breathing again. Eventually satisfied that I'm not going to be sick, I use my teeth to pull my long sleeve up so I can look at my TekCuff. It's already 2 p.m. I was supposed to meet Evan half an hour ago. Surely, he's searching for me.

Glancing back at the screen on the TekCuff, I check for signal bars. Shit. No service. There must not be a signal in this warehouse. That probably means the built-in GPS doesn't work. I can't risk waiting any longer. It's time to save myself.

Thankfully, the drugs wore off much faster than Mitch expected. He had no way of knowing that my body metabolizes painkillers and similar drugs extremely quickly. The dentist can't even do a simple filling without stopping to give me at least one extra numbing shot.

I roll over onto my knees. With my wrists and ankles bound with zip ties, I inchworm crawl from behind the crate, looking for something to cut the plastic handcuffs. A thin metal sign on a nearby shelf catches my eye. I crawl to it and use the sharp edge to saw the zip tie around my ankles. The motion causes the narrow plastic to cut into my already scraped-up legs. The process is slow, and I begin to panic that it's taking too long. Working faster, the zip tie finally snaps. My ankles are bleeding, but I'm free.

Holding the metal sign between my knees, I start working on the zip tie binding my hands. Suddenly, I hear someone coming. Able to use my legs now, I quickly return to the hidden spot between the crates. I barely tuck myself behind them before a couple of guys walk by. I let out a breath when they keep walking and don't notice the drops of blood I left behind.

Hobbling back to the shelf with the metal sign, I rub the tie against it until it pops, freeing my hands.

Frantically, I look around for a safe path out of the warehouse, remembering Emily mentioned everything is color-coded. We followed the blue lines on the floor and signs on the walls to get to Sean's office elevator, but I don't see any blue lines. I don't know what the other colors mean. If I head into the Maze's corridors, I may run into Mitch. Running into someone else could be just as dangerous because I don't know who I can trust.

But I can't stay here, so I take my chances and carefully move toward the nearest door. Testing the knob, I'm relieved to find it unlocked. Easing the door open, I enter an empty Maze hallway and slowly walk until the hallway ends, and I have to turn right or left.

I pick right.

Nearing the next intersection, I hear voices, so I approach the corner slowly. Strong arms jerk me back and whip me around.

Mitch seethes, "So you thought you could escape. I'll make sure you don't get away this time."

I scream and try to kick Mitch, but his arms are too strong for me. I try again. This time, aiming my knee toward his crotch. He squeals when it connects, but he keeps his grip on me. Yanking my arms behind me, he throws me onto the floor. He lands a hard kick to my side, knocking the air out of my lungs. It takes all the strength I can muster not to throw up from the pain.

Hurried footsteps and loud shouts rapidly grow closer. Evan, Sean, Christian, and a bunch of security guys round the corner. As

Mitch is about to kick me again, the security guys tackle him, throwing him to the ground with a hard thud.

Evan quickly kneels beside me and pulls me toward him. "I have you. It's over. You're going to be okay."

He holds me as if I'm a fragile porcelain doll that may shatter at any second. His lips gently kiss my forehead, my nose, and my lips. It's almost as if he's reassuring himself that I'm safe.

I am because he saved me again.

Struggling to get air into my lungs, I mouth, "They got Mitch, right?"

"Yes, they got him. Where are you hurt?"

"It's a little hard to breathe, and Mitch injected something into my arm. ... I don't know what it was, but I still feel dizzy and nauseous. ... My head is throbbing like the worst hangover ever," I gasp in spurts.

"Sean, get medical help here fast. The arsehole drugged Cassandra, she may have broken ribs, and her wrists and legs are bleeding."

"They're on the way," Sean replies.

Examining my arms as he cradles me, Evan asks, "What happened to your wrists?"

"Mitch used zip ties on my wrists and ankles."

"Bloody hell. Close your eyes and rest. Medics are on the way."

"Mitch was talking to his partner on the phone ... He called her 'Sis'. ... Tell Sean and the police. ... They need to find out who his sister is," I plead between painful breaths, grasping his shirt.

"Will do," he assures, stroking back my sweat-slicked hair.

"Did you get my panic alert?"

"Yes, but your GPS wasn't working. The tech guys said that someone disabled your device. Luckily, they knew Christian let you into the Maze. He said you had a note from me, but I didn't send one. We guessed it must have been Mitch, so we tracked his phone."

"Thank you. You saved my life." I weakly reach up to touch his cheek, but the EMTs arrive and pull Evan away.

They ask me questions, and when they mention transporting me to a hospital, I beg, "No hospital, please ... Take me back to my room."

"Is anything broken?" Evan asks the EMTs.

"It's unlikely. Her ribs are definitely bruised, and we need to wrap her wrists and ankles."

"Can you tell what the injection was?"

"He originally knocked her out with chloroform. Then he gave her the injection, which we suspect was ketamine, based on her symptoms. It takes time to completely wear off, but she should be fine."

"Does she need a blood test to be certain?"

"That's what we recommend, but she doesn't have to go to the hospital for that. It can be done here."

Looking into my pleading eyes, Evan says, "It's her choice."

"I'm not going to the hospital," I whisper.

Evan yells to Sean, "I'm taking Cassandra to my suite. Are you going to interrogate Mitch?"

"We've called the police. They're on their way, but I'll be asking him questions while we wait."

"I want to hear what he says firsthand. Who can stay with Cassandra?"

Christian steps from the background and says, "I will."

Evan narrows his eyes. "I don't know if I trust you."

"Please let me make it up to all of you. When the note was typed instead of handwritten, I should've known something was off and double-checked before letting her into the Maze. I planned to accompany her. Then I was called away at the last second for what turned out to be a prank call. Since she had the correct password and NER designation, I let her go ahead without me. I feel horrible. I promise I won't leave her side."

I'm exhausted and confused. Why do they think Christian would hurt me? He's gone out of his way to be kind and supportive. I'll let Evan sort this out. Thinking hurts too much.

"Sean, what do you think?" Evan asks.

"He followed protocol by verifying the password, and his story checks out. Security just confirmed it was a prank call. They traced it back to Mitch."

"Okay, but I am going up to the suite with them to make sure

Cassandra is as comfortable as possible. Then I'll be back. Where should I meet you?"

"Take a couple of the security guys with you. I want one posted outside your suite. The other one can bring you to Holding Area C."

"Will do. What about the Final Dinner tonight?" he asks.

"We'll postpone it."

45

CASSIE

I wake from a deep sleep with Evan's arm draped over my stomach. Turning to look at the bedside clock, I do a double take. It's noon. No wonder I'm thirsty and hungry. I'm also grateful that the horrible headache from yesterday is gone. Assessing myself, I find that my ribs are still sore, and my wrists and ankles are tender from the cuts and bruises. Otherwise, I'm better.

Evan's still asleep. He must be exhausted.

As I watch his even breathing, yesterday's frightening events replay in my head. Thanks to Christian and one of Sean's long-time security guards, I was able to rest last night while I waited for Evan to return. Not knowing whom to trust, Evan insisted two people stay with me to ensure this didn't turn into a real horror movie if one of the two turned out to be a bad guy. I told Evan he was being too paranoid, and thankfully, I was right. If anything, they were overly protective. Neither would leave the other alone with me.

When Evan eventually returned last night, my head was still throbbing. Still, I was eager for him to tell me what Mitch revealed, but he said the police had everything under control. I'm not very patient, so I didn't find that answer acceptable. However, I was too exhausted, and my head hurt too much to argue.

I try to slip out of bed without waking Evan, but he immediately stirs. That's my cue to ask again, "What did Mitch tell you? Do we know who is behind the killing and sabotage?"

He rubs the sleep out of his eyes and yawns. "Yes, we know."

"Who?"

"I can't say. We need breakfast."

"I'm hungry too, but I don't understand why you can't tell me who's behind everything. You know what I've been through being a murder suspect. I need answers. Please tell me," I plead.

He grasps my hand and squeezes. "I want to tell you, but I made a promise to my best friend and the police. Please trust me this once. It's for your safety and to ensure that they apprehend Mitch's partner before they get away. It'll be clear soon, so let's enjoy today."

"I promise I won't say anything to anyone."

"I know you wouldn't, but my word counts. I made a promise. The police have it under control and don't need our help. You'll know everything by tomorrow, and I mean everything."

"I appreciate that a promise means something to you, so I'll trust that you had no choice."

"Thanks. Besides, Sean delayed the Final Dinner until tonight. He plans to announce the winner of the competition then."

My eyes pop. "You're kidding, right? I can't believe that Sean's still going to pick a winner after everything that has happened. I assumed he canceled the competition."

"Sean said there was no reason not to move forward. He still needs a guest chef. I don't know who won, but he assured me the finalists will agree the result is fair. Will you feel like going to the dinner?" Evan asks with concern in his voice.

"The good news is that I feel much better today, but you couldn't keep me away, regardless," I say, waving off his worry with a flick of my wrist.

As Evan props up on his elbow, a smile replaces his concern. "I'm glad you're on the mend. The hospital called and confirmed that you were given ketamine, so the effects should be wearing off."

"That's good to know. At least it wasn't something more sinister."

"I'll have the spa send someone up to fix your hair for tonight. It looks like your toenails need to be redone as well. What happened to them? Did a five-year-old paint them?" he teases.

I look at my feet and laugh at the smeared polish.

"You're right. They are a mess. When I received the note to meet you in the Maze yesterday, the polish on my toes wasn't dry yet. But the note said it was urgent and to hurry, so I ignored the wet polish, skipped the manicure, and rushed to find Christian."

"That explains it. The spa can send someone to fix your nails when they do your hair," Evan says as he grabs his phone and starts texting.

Remembering Mitch's phone call with his sister, I frown and hug myself to fend off the chill running down my spine. Mitch's bitter words are lodged in my already fragile heart. They're echoing in my head: *Cartwright's friend won't care. He's not serious about her. It's just a fling while he's in Vegas. He'll head back to Europe soon.*

Evan and I haven't known each other long, so Mitch's comment shouldn't bother me as much as it does. But thinking about it now is like being in the shadow of a dark cloud. Deep down, I started hoping that Evan and I would find a way to stay connected even after we go back to our homes. I'm dreading saying goodbye. He's everything I could want in a partner—smart, caring, protective but respectful of my independent nature, and the best lover I've ever had. He even believed in me when no one else did.

I'm not sure what true love is supposed to feel like, but it's hard to believe it's better than what I'm starting to feel for Evan. That scares me.

I may not like his answer, but it's time to clear the air before I lose my courage, so I blurt out, "Mitch said I was just a fling to you, and you wouldn't care what happened to me. Is that true?"

Dropping his phone and enveloping me in his arms, he says, "That's absurd. I do care what happens to you. I freaked out when your panic code lit up my phone."

Burying my head against his neck so he won't see the tears threatening to overflow, I murmur, "That doesn't mean this isn't just a Las Vegas fling. Regardless, I know this is all coming to an end.

After tonight, I'll be headed home to look for a new job, and you'll be flying to Europe."

Evan pulls back, hands holding my face. "Wait a minute, why do you need to look for a new job?" he asks as his eyes search mine for answers.

"Oh, I haven't had a chance to tell you. The law firm told me to contact the human resources department to confirm my return date. With the competition over, I assumed it was okay to use a phone again, so I called them yesterday."

"At this point, no one would care how many people you called. What did they say?"

"I'm getting to that part. When I called HR to let them know I'd be returning next week, they told me that I've been laid off. The law firm is making cuts and realized that they could cover my workload without me. It makes me wonder if someone saw the news article painting me as a murder suspect. This is probably their excuse to let me go so they can distance themselves from the drama."

"Why didn't you tell me?"

"It was a couple of hours after you'd saved my life. I was still a little drugged, so I wasn't thinking clearly. It didn't really sink in until later. It's not as devastating as you'd think. I'm just so happy to be alive."

"That's terrible. When the police officially announce the name of the killer, the firm will want you back. But you may prefer to look for a position at another firm that's not so quick to judge. Of course, that's assuming you want to return to your law career." Evan snuggles my head against his shoulder, consoling me.

My arm wraps around his waist, and I hold on tight as he rubs comforting circles on my back.

He continues, "I'm confident that the beautiful food you prepared has you in the running to win the competition this evening. But let's not think about the results until then. We'll enjoy the dinner in the Wine Cave tonight, and tomorrow, we'll deal with the problems if any remain."

"I could use a day off from worrying."

"And there is one upside to losing your job. You can join me at my

father's retirement party so we can have more time with each other."
He grins.

"Oh, Evan, I'd love to go to Catalinius with you, but I can't afford
to. I need to find a new job as soon as possible to pay my bills.
Tomorrow, I'll have certainty about my career path. If I don't win the
competition, I'll look for another job in law."

If only I could just say "yes" and run off to Europe with this
handsome, caring, and sexy-as-hell man, it would be a fantasy come
true.

"I'll respect your career choice, whatever it is. But give yourself
time to think and consider your options. You deserve the chance to
pursue your passion. You don't have to make a long-term decision in
the next twenty-four hours."

"You're probably right."

"And one more thing. I'm not ready for what's between us to end
yet."

"I don't see how it continues with us in two different countries,"
I say with a shake of my head.

"I have a few ideas. Give me a little time to see if I can work out
the details."

"What do you have in mind?" I ask, tilting my head to study the
mysterious twinkle in his eyes.

"I don't want to get your hopes up just yet so please be patient
for a day or two. I'm waiting for a message from my parents about
our business. We can talk more after that, okay?"

Grasping his upper arms, I say, "It means the world that you
want *us* to continue, but you know patience is a tough one for me. I
also don't like to be left out of the loop. It's driving me insane
waiting to be taken off the list of murder suspects."

"I know. I'm hoping it will be worth the wait."

"Me too."

Winning tonight would change my life and might make it easier
to date Evan. I doubt that's in the cards, but I hold out a modicum of
hope. I cross my fingers behind my back and silently wish for my
version of a fairytale ending.

46

EVAN

My phone pings with a text.

Sean: Keep Cassie in your suite. Jayden will be in custody by noon.

Me: I'm on my way to your office.

Sean: Hell no! It's too dangerous. Two people are already dead.

Me: Bollocks. I have more training than most security guards. See you in 5 mins.

The spa people arrive to pamper Cassandra as I rush out the door. I stop long enough to instruct the guys standing guard in the hallway not to let Cassandra leave until I return.

I arrive at Sean's office and join him and Detective Fielder in front of a computer screen.

Sean says, "You should go back to Cassie and let us handle this."

"For fuck's sake, don't be an arse. I'm staying. What are you watching?"

"The blue dot blipping across the screen is Jayden. We're tracking his TekCuff. When the dot stops outside Cynthia's office, we'll know it's time to move in."

"Where's her office?"

"Right here," Sean says, pointing to the screen.

We watch as Jayden moves closer.

"Time to go," Fielder orders.

We follow the detective and his backup officers as they stealthily position themselves outside Cynthia's door, which is slightly ajar.

Barely audible, I hear Jayden saying, "Cynthia, I still don't understand why you wanted to talk with me."

Without waiting to hear the answer, Sean shoves the door open with the detective and me on his heels. Jayden flinches in the guest chair across from Cynthia's desk. To conceal the other officers' presence, I push the door partially closed.

Hiding his anger, Sean calmly says, "Hello, Cynthia. Sorry to interrupt, but we wanted to share some information. Jayden, you'll want to hear this as well. We learned that one of the finalists received advantages in the competition in exchange for what they thought were harmless pranks."

A glance out of the corner of my eye reveals Jayden slumping in the chair while white-knuckling its wooden arms.

Cynthia palms her cheek in shock. "That can't possibly be true!"

"It is. Unfortunately, one of the pranks was to substitute hummus for bean dip. Right, Jayden?" Sean hisses, jerking his head toward him.

"What are you talking about? I didn't do that," Jayden barks defensively.

"Oh, but you did. We have video of you in the Trendz kitchen discussing sabotage in exchange for advantages in the competition, so don't even try to deny it."

"There aren't any microphones in the kitchen. You're making that up," Jayden scoffs.

"Wipe that smug look off your face. Originally, there weren't any in the kitchen, but we added microphones and more cameras after we saw a video of you talking with Mitch."

Jayden bolts from his chair, screaming, "Cynthia, is this why you called me to your office? I don't have to take this. I didn't do anything wrong. I'm leaving."

Before he can escape, one of the officers slips through the partially open door and pushes Jayden back into the chair, firmly planting his hands on Jayden's shoulders.

Sean orders, "Stay seated and stop lying. You're not going anywhere. You knew sesame seeds were a banned ingredient, but you still substituted hummus for the bean dip. You're responsible for Chef Boucher's death. You also sabotaged Kai's food in exchange for an advantage. The evidence is clear. Why did you do it?"

Deflated, nervous sweat beads roll down his forehead. Jayden stares at his lap, wringing his hands. Finally, he breaks the silence, saying, "He promised I would win the Guest Chef Competition if I went along with some harmless pranks. I didn't know anyone would get hurt. I thought Chef Boucher died from his head injury when he fell. I thought it was an accident. He was supposed to be disqualified for using the banned ingredient. He wasn't supposed to die."

"Who promised you'd win?" I ask.

My question is met with silence as Jayden refuses to look me in the eye. Staring a hole through his downturned head, I repeat my question louder and add, "Was it Mitch's partner in crime? Tell us now!"

I'm determined to fully clear Cassandra's name, and that means identifying every single person who played a role in the sabotage.

Jayden's voice shakes as he reluctantly answers, "Mitch told me I would win. I don't know who his partner is."

"I see. Well, Mitch doesn't even work in the Food & Beverage department. He works in security and certainly doesn't control who wins. Therefore, it shouldn't come as a surprise that you are officially disqualified from this competition. I'd also like to introduce you to the police officer who's currently restraining you. His name is Ken. You may recall seeing him in the kitchen during the competition. He was the dishwasher who saw you sabotage Kai's food. He'll make an excellent witness at your trial."

"Shit," Jayden mumbles as Ken pulls out handcuffs.

"Stand up. Hands behind your back. You're under arrest. You have the right to remain silent," Ken says as he slaps the cuffs on Jayden's wrists.

Turning toward Cynthia, Sean asks, "Cynthia, did you know about this?"

Rising from her chair, hands on her hips, she asks, "Are you kidding? Of course I didn't know. This is appalling."

Sean raises his eyebrows halfway up his forehead. "As head of F&B at the Athena, you expect me to believe you didn't know anything about the supplier kickbacks?" he asks, sarcasm lacing his words.

Closing the distance between us, Cynthia throws her hands in the air. "Kickbacks? What are you talking about? This is the first I'm hearing about it."

After taking a deep breath, Sean approaches the matter from another direction with a calmer tone. "The kickbacks are the reason for the unacceptable increase in F&B expenses. Did you ever talk with Chef Maurizio to find out if he knows anything about the changes in suppliers and increased costs?"

Cynthia shrugs. "I wasn't able to get hold of him."

Sean squints in disbelief and retorts, "That's strange. Evan and I didn't have any problem reaching him."

A flash of fear briefly flickers in Cynthia's eyes at the news. If I hadn't been watching her closely, I would've missed her tell because she instantly hides her concern.

With a wave of her hand, she explains, "To tell the truth, I didn't bother trying to find Chef Maurizio. Based on my experiences with him, it would've been futile. He's a liar. You can't believe a word he says."

Sean's face reddens as he unleashes his pent-up anger and disgust. "Oh, but I do believe everything he says. You see, Mitch and the chef told us the same story. And the suppliers I spoke with this afternoon identify you as the mastermind behind the kickback scheme. The authorities also got a warrant and searched your home today. They found extremely interesting bank records. It appears you are a very wealthy woman as a result of your thefts from the Athena."

Perplexed, Jayden asks, "You mean it was you all along? You're Mitch's partner?"

"Yes, Jayden. It was Cynthia," Sean says.

"You bastard. How dare you accuse me of such things?" Cynthia seethes, venom in her voice.

Let me tell you what I think happened based on our little talk with your half-brother Mitch and the facts we have pieced together. First, you offered Chef Bernard money if she would use her position as a judge to ensure that the right person won the competition. She refused and was going to tell me about your offer as soon as she had the chance. You couldn't let that happen, so you made sure you were the one who handed champagne to the judges at the press confer-ence. Her champagne had a little something extra so she wouldn't have the chance to tell me about your conversation. Did I miss anything?" Sean asks, balling his fists.

His rage is palpable. It's understandable. A trusted employee murdered his good friend, Chef Bernard.

Like a caged animal, Cynthia's face contorts, eyes flickering between us and the door. Suddenly, she darts toward the door and flings it wide open, yelling, "You don't have proof of anything. I won't stay here and take this."

Before she makes it through the doorway, Detective Fielder and another officer lunge toward her, each grabbing one of her arms and yanking her back.

Shouting obscenities, Cynthia thrashes in their hold and stomps her spiked heels on their shoes, struggling to free herself. With his free hand, Detective Fielder successfully snaps handcuffs tightly around her wrists.

Sean shakes his head in disgust and shouts over her outbursts, "We also know you killed Chef Boucher. Just like Chef Bernard, he didn't want to play your game. You made him the same offer before approaching Jayden. You promised to rig the competition so he would win in exchange for sabotaging other finalists. Instead of grabbing the opportunity, he was going to report your offer. You decided he had to go too. What do you have to say for yourself?"

Cynthia fumes, "I want a lawyer."

Sean nods. "You need one. Detective Fielder, she's all yours. Let me know if the Athena can be of further assistance."

"Thank you, Mr. Cartwright."

As the police drag Cynthia and Jayden away, the officers read them their rights.

Sean and I stand frozen in Cynthia's office as the reality of the situation soaks in.

I pat him on the back, saying, "Everything is finally resolved. You no longer have to worry about the F&B expenses or the murders."

He says, "My blood is still boiling from Cynthia's betrayal, but the anger is mixed with regret. If only we'd pinpointed the kickback issue sooner, those two chefs would be alive. Instead, she orchestrated two senseless deaths and was responsible for Cassie's injuries."

"Cynthia will pay for what she's done. And you're going to apologize to Cassandra for misjudging her."

Sean nods.

47

CASSIE

I'm wearing my new, low-cut, black dress that shimmers when the light hits it. The spa's hairdresser worked her magic, weaving shiny crystals through my long, wavy hair. It sparkles against my almost bare back.

She left me special lotion with glitter for my neck, arms, and back. Evan was more than happy to lightly massage it onto my skin. Based on the hunger in his dark, piercing eyes, he's torn between wanting to tear my dress off and showing me off at dinner. Either way, he makes me feel incredibly appreciated.

As I admire my finished look in the mirror one final time, Evan surprises me by draping a spectacular diamond necklace around my neck. I bring my hand to my throat, touching the gems. It must have thirty carats of diamonds.

"Evan, this is too much. I can't possibly accept it."

"It's not a gift. I borrowed it from the jeweler."

"What if it falls off my neck or I lose it?"

"It's insured. Quit worrying,"

He doesn't stop with the necklace. He silently wraps a diamond-studded, white-gold cuff around each of my wrists, saying, "These will cover and shield your wounds from the zip ties."

I can't muster a response as tears well up in my eyes. That he remembered to protect my wrists is beyond thoughtful.

"Enjoy the evening as my princess. I hope this will be the first of many special events we share."

I nod, not knowing what to say.

He guides me out the door of his suite, and we make our way to the Final Dinner.

As we enter the Grand Athena's Wine Cave, I stop and take in the scene, overwhelmed by the warm and inviting atmosphere. The ceiling is low, the walls are made from rough-cut stones, and the floor is concrete. It's as if we're in an underground cave.

Dim lights with a yellowish glow dance off the various surfaces. The scent of oak and wine fills the air from the barrels that line one wall. A long, formal table with flickering candles graces the center of the room. Nothing could be more perfect.

I pause, wanting to remember every moment of tonight, but Evan places his hand on my back and urges me further into the Wine Cave. One white-gloved server hands us glasses of champagne, and another presents shrimp appetizers on a shiny silver tray.

I had no idea there would be so many people here: the film crew and photographers, Sean, Trenton, Kai, several of the Athena's managers, the three judges, and others. Even Christian is here as a guest. I hope that means Sean isn't going to fire him for letting me into the Maze unescorted. I turn my head in the other direction and notice Detective Fielder, which is interesting. It's probably Sean's way of thanking him.

Evan and I stop to chat with Trenton and Kai. Greetings exchanged, Kai asks, "Have you seen Jayden?"

"No," I say.

I assume Jayden's under arrest by now, but Evan said he couldn't talk about it until after dinner tonight.

Trenton chimes in, "He doesn't have a chance at winning, so who cares if he shows up?"

"That's rather harsh," Kai retorts.

Hoping to diffuse the situation, I interject, "I'm so excited. This is such a beautiful setting for the final event. I can't wait to hear who the winner will be."

"Me, of course," Trenton says with a huff.

Inserting a little diplomacy, Evan points out, "All three of you competed admirably. The Athena would be lucky to have any one of you."

Kai nods. "I agree. We all have a good chance, depending on exactly what type of chef the Athena is looking for."

"You're right," I add.

The difference in Trenton's and Kai's personalities is certainly shining through tonight.

A bell rings, indicating it's time to take our seats. Evan and I part ways to find our assigned places. Oddly, it feels lonely without him by my side.

Trenton, Kai, and I are sitting directly across from Sean and Evan, but with an empty seat between each of us. When everyone is settled, Sean says, "Tonight, we have assembled key people who have been involved in this competition. I want to offer my congratulations to all the finalists! Unfortunately, Jayden will not be able to join us."

Trenton, Kai and I look at each other. Our raised eyebrows and quick looks between each other indicate we are dying to discuss the implications of his absence. But given the cameras, we resist the desire to discuss what Jayden's absence means.

Sean calmly raises his hand, which always silences a crowd. He says, "We have some additional guests joining us tonight. As a surprise, we've invited someone who is special to each finalist to share this dinner with them. Trenton, your father is here. Kai, your girlfriend is joining us. And Cassie, your best friend, Lowri, is here. Welcome!"

We simultaneously turn around and jump out of our seats in surprise. Trenton's father is slapping him on the back as the two giant men embrace. Kai swings his girlfriend in circles as he plants a kiss squarely on her lips.

After all I've been through, I can't believe Lowri is here for me.

Seeing my best friend's smiling face has tears welling in my eyes. We run to each other and hug.

"I can't believe you're here," I say, a smile plastered on my face.

"We have a lot to talk about!"

As the exuberant greetings subside, Sean instructs, "Everyone, please take your seat. There will be plenty of time for catching up later."

Continuing, Sean says, "I also would like to thank our staff and the film crew for their hard work. Please raise your glass and join me in a toast to everyone who made this competition possible. Cheers!"

We all raise our glasses and take a sip of the exquisite champagne.

Sean explains, "Our worthy finalists have been working diligently in the kitchen. It's now the Grand Athena's pleasure to present the finalists and our other guests with a specially prepared meal to celebrate the conclusion of our competition. I'm told our first course is a salad of spring greens, sugar-sweet cantaloupe, and prosciutto, topped with a drizzle of aged balsamic vinegar. It is paired with the Veuve Clicquot champagne we're drinking. Enjoy."

Sean asks Sebastian to turn off the microphones while we eat.

With the cameras still rolling, conversation remains limited. There's always the chance for lipreading, so we're being cautious.

I notice Lowri staring at Sean intently as she says, "I had the pleasure of meeting Sean and Evan earlier."

I respond carefully, "That's nice."

"It was. Hopefully, I'll have time to talk to them again later."

Sean's sneaking glances at Lowri too, so I think she really means she's hoping to talk with him again later.

After our salads are removed, the microphones are turned on again as a second course appears. This time, Evan explains, "For the second course, we have a lobster and ricotta ravioli served with a lemon butter sauce. The ravioli is paired with a crisp sauvignon blanc. *Buon appetito!*"

My mouth is watering. The ravioli is velvety. The lobster has just the right bite. The ricotta adds creaminess, a hint of lemon zest brightens the overall flavor, and the butter in the sauce adds a smoothness that brings the flavors together. I think I'm in love. I should slow down, but it's so good I quickly clean my plate.

The table remains silent as servers arrive with the main course. I wonder if Sean or Amy will start actively encouraging conversation to spice things up for the cameras.

Waiting for my plate, I look across at Evan and find him staring at me with a smug grin on his face. I automatically return his smile. I'm going to miss him when this is over. I wish there were some way we could extend our time together. It's too bad I can't go with him to his dad's retirement party in Europe. Evan says he has an idea for making us work, but it would take a miracle.

Unless I win tonight, I need to start looking for another job before my meager savings are completely depleted. It would be more exciting to look for a culinary opportunity, but with my student loans hanging over my head, that doesn't make as much sense as applying to other law firms.

When the next course arrives, Sean reads from a menu card. "You have a dry-aged prime filet mignon served with roasted asparagus. To accompany our steaks, I selected a Screaming Eagle red wine called Second Flight, from the same winery that makes Screaming Eagle cabernet. Enjoy."

With the mention of Second Flight, there is a gasp among the finalists. I've never tasted a wine that expensive before, and I can't believe we're being treated to such an extravagance.

With Sean and Evan sitting directly across from me, I overhear Evan whisper, "Why did you select this instead of the Screaming Eagle cab?"

Sean retorts, "Why do you think? The wine alone is costing me about a grand per person for this dinner. That would at least triple the wine costs. I want this dinner to be special, not outrageous."

I knew this was an expensive dinner, but that's even beyond my estimate. Taking a sip of the high-end wine, I let the full-bodied, silky liquid envelop my taste buds. Closing my eyes, I detect notes of blackberries and chocolate with what I think is a hint of black truffles. A second sip confirms it's truly amazing. I'm going to savor every sip. I'm not sure when, if ever, I'll be at another dinner that costs thousands of dollars per person.

After the plates are cleared, Sean signals to Sebastian, who yells, "Cut!" Sean demands everyone's attention again, saying, "I've asked for the recording to stop temporarily because we have a little business to take care of before we enjoy a wonderful dessert."

I assume Sean is about to reveal the winner, but why would he want to do that off-camera?

He says, "Before we announce the winner of the Athena's Guest Chef Competition, I want to deal with the sabotage and cheating that have plagued this competition."

Murmurs engulf the space before Sean taps a wine glass with his knife to regain everyone's attention.

Continuing, he explains, "We've learned that one of the finalists received advantages in the competition in exchange for what that finalist thought were harmless pranks. For example, this finalist added extra salt to someone's dish."

Kai exclaims, "That explains it!"

"Yes, Kai, it does. Unfortunately, one of the other pranks was deadly and designed to frame another finalist. The saboteur made use of a bowl Cassie touched when she offered to help during a prep session. I doubt she even remembers handling the bowl."

I say, "So that's how my fingerprints got there. I did move some bowls on that table before Amy told me I wasn't allowed to help. I knew I'd forgotten something important."

"Yes, Cassie. Sometime after you touched the bowl, Jayden retrieved and saved it. Later, he filled the bowl with hummus and switched it with Mr. Boucher's bean dip. But Chef Boucher was highly allergic to sesame seeds. As many of you know, tahini, which is made from sesame seeds, is a key ingredient in hummus. When Chef Boucher tasted the dip on camera, he went into anaphylactic shock and died. We've confirmed that Jayden didn't know that Chef Boucher would die from the hummus. He thought Chef Boucher would be disqualified for using a banned ingredient: sesame seeds."

The room collectively gasps. Instead of feeling shocked, I'm relieved. I finally know how my fingerprints ended up on the bowl.

It's also sad to learn about Jayden. I knew he was given advantages in exchange for sabotage, but I hadn't been sure his actions were so directly related to the murder.

Sean explains, "I'm sure you'll hear the details from the press, so I'll share a few more with you tonight. Cynthia, through her half-brother, Mitch, who was one of our security guards, promised Jayden that he would win the Guest Chef Competition in exchange for performing these so-called pranks."

Turning and gesturing toward a large man seated a few chairs to my right, Sean says, "I would also like to introduce and thank Chef Maurizio, the former chef of Trendz, for joining us tonight and agreeing to share his part of the story as well."

Chef Maurizio stands, dabbing his mouth before placing his napkin on the table. "Mr. Cartwright, thank you for giving me this opportunity to clear things up. Cynthia and her brother blackmailed me into helping with their scheme to take kickbacks from suppliers. When my family needed me at their restaurant back in Europe, I left the Athena to escape their control. That's when they decided to rig the Guest Chef Competition to get someone to replace me that they could control. I never imagined they would go as far as murder to control the outcome."

Questions are flying at Sean, with one common question dominating. "Why did they kill Chef Boucher?"

Sean explains, "Before they approached Jayden to act as saboteur, they first approached one of the judges, Chef Bernard, offering her money in exchange for help rigging the competition. When she wouldn't agree and planned to tell me about the plot, Cynthia spiked her drink, which caused her to have the fatal car accident."

She killed Chef Bernard.

Continuing, Sean says, "Then they approached Chef Boucher for help with their plan, promising him that he would win the competition. He refused, intending to report it to me, so they decided he had to go as well. Rather than drop the plan after two murders, Cynthia and Mitch were emboldened and approached Jayden. He agreed to help. Cynthia, Mitch, and Jayden are all in custody now, and I understand they will be charged with murder."

Evan asks, "Sean, I have one question, if you don't mind. Did Cynthia sabotage Cassandra's zipline equipment?"

Shaking his head, Sean responds, "Mitch took care of that. According to Mitch, Cassie wasn't supposed to be competitive. That's why they picked a home cook as the alternate in the first place. They were hoping to knock out the best chef early through a disqualification and substitute someone who wouldn't be a threat to their intended winner. Cassie turned out to be too good of a chef for their purposes. They were afraid she might have a chance at winning. A zipline accident was supposed to get her out of the way. Fortunately, Amy had you ride tandem with Cassie and ruined that part of their plan. Detective Fielder, do you want to add anything?"

Detective Fielder responds, "I would like to thank you and the Athena for your cooperation on this matter, but I can't say more at this time."

Sean says, "Understood. We have all suffered great losses. First, my friend Chef Bernard, then Chef Boucher. We will continue to honor their memories. We should also celebrate the hard work of the three finalists who remain and competed through difficult circumstances. Therefore, it's time to announce the results of the competition, so I'm going to ask everyone to help me make the next part of the filming a happy event. There will be plenty of time for us to remember the lost chefs and discuss the news we just shared after the results are announced."

Sean meets the eyes of each guest in turn, gaining their agreement. Then he says, "Sebastian, please restart your filming."

As the cameras record, the servers quickly reappear. This time, they're delivering a decadent chocolate creation.

Evan says, "Our dessert course tonight is a chocolate Grand Marnier crème brûlée. It's accompanied by a twenty-year-old port, which should complement the chocolate quite well."

It's hard not to discuss Sean's announcements, but I respect his request and take a bite of the dessert and follow with a sip of the port. Looking at Lowri, we share a happy moan. It's rich and creamy, and Evan is right—the port is a perfect pairing.

As we continue enjoying our dessert, Sean says, "We have kept our three finalists in suspense far too long."

Anticipation is wreaking havoc with my emotions. Butterflies are fluttering around my stomach, my heart is pounding, and my hands are shaking. We're about to find out which one of our lives is going to change dramatically.

Directing his next comments to Trenton, Kai, and me, Sean explains, "You each have a box sitting in front of you."

He's referring to the four-inch square boxes wrapped in glossy red paper and tied with gold ribbons. Apparently, these boxes hold our fate.

Sean continues, "You each selected a name for the restaurant you would run if you won the Guest Chef Competition. If your gift has that name on it, then you have won. On the count of three, unwrap your boxes. One. Two. Three. Open!"

We each reach for our box and start unwrapping. Kai opens his first and reveals a gold bracelet engraved with the name Tropic. He exclaims, "I can't believe it. I won!"

Trenton and I stop unwrapping our gifts to congratulate Kai and to try to hide our disappointment from the cameras. I knew I wouldn't win, but I'd held onto a tiny ray of hope. I can't argue with Sean's choice though. After the sabotage inflicted on Kai, I'm happy that he won.

Sean says, "Congratulations, Kai. Trenton and Cassie, please do me the favor of unwrapping your gifts as well. I hope you'll like them."

We comply, opening ours simultaneously. Trenton shows off his gold bracelet with the name NY Roasted on it. Then I look at mine. It says Pinot & Pie. That's the restaurant name I picked to honor my friend who lets me post on her website. She gave me permission to use the name if I won. We're all looking at each other confused and start peppering Sean with questions.

Sean says, "Congratulations, you have all won. It turns out that each of you won one of the cooking rounds. Therefore, we decided that you are each worthy of being a guest chef. As a guest chef, you will each plan the menus for one month and be given the opportunity to learn how we run our restaurants here at the Athena. One of you may even be chosen as the full-time chef for the restaurant at the end of your month. We'll work out the details and dates for each of you tomorrow. And in case you're wondering, you'll each receive the cash prize, so congratulations!"

Sebastian yells, "Cut!"

I jump up, pulling Lowri up with me. Hugging her, we jump up and down like schoolgirls. I'm in shock. I can't believe this is happening.

My mind is switching between thoughts faster than I can comprehend them. My dream of being a chef has come true. I don't have to look for another job yet. I'm no longer a suspect in a murder investigation. Evan and I can spend more time together. I think I love him, and I'm willing to take a chance on us. Lowri's here to share my happiness.

This is the best day of my entire life!

Sean continues, "For now, please enjoy your dessert and drinks. Afterward, Amy and the crew will be filming interviews with each of you. Also, your cell phones are being returned now, but we ask that you and all the guests wait forty-eight hours to reveal your winning status because the video of the last episode will not be released until tomorrow evening."

We all jump up and exchange hugs with each other and our friends and family who have joined us.

Lowri can't resist saying, "Now, aren't you glad you finally listened to me and applied?"

I smile and agree.

The next half hour goes by in a blur. It's like a dream. We finish dessert, and Amy interviews us between more hugs and congratulations. The judges stop by to tell me they know my month as guest chef is going to be a success based on my performance in the competition. Apparently, I actually won the dessert round!

Finally, Evan makes his way over and pulls me into his arms.

"I'm so happy for you. Your name is cleared, and your dream of a culinary career just came true. And as an added bonus, this means we can have more time together. You can come with me to Europe."

"I just can't believe that I won." I lean into him for another hug.

"Believe it," he whispers into my ear.

Detective Fielder walks up, interrupting us. "Ms. Edwards, please let me add my congratulations. I'd also like to apologize for suspecting you were part of what happened to Chef Boucher. Unfortunately, the trick with the fingerprints led us down the wrong path for a while."

"I certainly understand how it looked. I'm just glad you caught the real criminals in the end."

"Thank you for your understanding. I wish you a successful tenure as guest chef. Hopefully, I'll have the opportunity to stop by the restaurant when you're at its helm."

"Please do."

As Detective Fielder prepares to leave, he turns to Evan and with a slight bow says, "And thank you, Your Royal Highness, for all your help. It was a pleasure meeting you. Goodbye."

Huh? I turn to Evan. "Why did he call you 'Your Royal Highness'? Is it an inside joke you haven't shared with me?" I tease.

Evan looks mortified, and for the first time ever, he looks like he doesn't know what to say. I step back as shock takes over. Is that really Evan's title? Is he royalty? The look on Evan's face confirms it's true.

If Detective Fielder knows, everyone else must too. It's not an inside joke. I'm the only one in the dark. Everyone must think I'm a fool not knowing the true identity of the guy I've been dating.

My mind begins to race, and my heart pounds as the depth of his lie sets in. Before he can respond, I bolt for the door.

"Cassandra, please wait. I can explain everything."

I hear him call after me, but I don't stop. I run away from Evan as fast as I can.

48

CASSIE

I barely make it out of the Wine Cave before tears start streaming down my face. Reaching the elevator that will take me to my room, I repeatedly punch the button, urging the doors to open. I need to get to my room before Evan finds me—assuming he even tries.

Out of breath, Lowri catches me and slips through the closing doors. As the elevator rises, it occurs to me that I have my cell phone back and can use it to find out who Evan really is.

I type "royal Evan Catalinius," and photos of Evan in full royal regalia pop up. Under one photo, it says he is Garret Evan Louis Francesco, Prince of Catalinius.

Catching her breath, she asks, "What's wrong? What happened?"

I show her my phone, saying, "Evan's a prince, and I've been royally played. Literally. He invited me to his father's retirement party. He left out a *minor* detail. His father is the effing King of Catalinius. There's no retirement party. What the hell?"

I'm fuming. Lowri's speechless.

As the tears pour from my eyes, I say, "He lied to me. He made me look like a fool. I bet everyone but me knows exactly who he is. And even worse, I was falling for him. I can't believe he let me think we were a possibility when he knew all along there could be nothing real between us. I'm not royalty. I'm a commoner. He probably isn't even allowed to date me. Clearly, Mitch was telling the truth. I was just a fling so Evan would have someone to sleep with while he was in Las Vegas. And like a naïve fool, I fell for the whole lie."

"You slept with him? That's fantastic. You finally got past the second date."

"That's all you heard?"

"Of course not, but it's an important part. Don't worry about anything else. We've all been played before, and not many of us can say it was by actual royalty."

Lowri's my best friend. She's supposed to understand. How can she brush this off? My feelings for Evan aren't just about sex. I gave him my heart.

"You're not helping! I let myself fall in love with him. He said he'd find a way to make us work!"

I take another look at the Google search results for other images of Evan. The results sicken me. He always has a beautiful model or princess on his arm. I'm neither of those. He was slumming it with lowly me.

The best night of my life just turned into the worst one. Everything between Evan and me was a lie. I'm just another of his many conquests. How could I be so gullible?

49

EVAN

Fuck! Raking my hands through my hair, I'm at a loss as to how to fix this cocked-up mess.

Sean warned me. I should have told her sooner. It just felt so good to be treated like a normal, albeit rich, guy, so I kept putting off having the "talk" with her. I pace in front of the wine barrels, trying to think how to explain that I enjoyed getting to know her as Evan rather than the prince.

Sean approaches, handing me a drink. "What's wrong, Evan? Why did Cassie take off?"

I take a steadying sip.

"Detective Fielder referred to me as 'Your Royal Highness.'"

"Shit. Well, I guess that makes ending things easier. Based on the way she ran off, she'll take care of that for you."

Practically taking his head off with my glare, I admit through gritted teeth, "I don't want to end things. I invited her to my father's retirement party and my brother's wedding. I just left out the part that my father is retiring from being king, and my brother is the crown prince."

"You did what? Are you saying that you actually planned to take her home to meet the family? Are you that serious about her?" he asks.

"Yes. Now, help me fix this mess."

"I don't know if you can fix it. You could try a grand gesture to show her you're serious. That works in movies."

"Brilliant. First, I need to find a time and place where she can't run away so she'll let me explain everything."

"One option is to find her now and grovel." Sean grins as though he'd love to watch that.

"That won't be enough. I need something more impressive."

"Tomorrow afternoon, the chefs are being interviewed for a cooking show on the Food, Fun & Travel Channel. It won't be easy to run out of the interview."

"Perfect. That gives me an idea. I need to call in a few favors. We'll also need Lowri's help. Hopefully, she can comfort Cassandra and make sure she shows up to the interview. Can you talk to Lowri for me?"

"Of course. And after you win back your princess, let's sit down and finally have that chat about your future," Sean responds enthusi-astically.

"If I win her back, then I'm certain my plans will work out."

50

CASSIE

The FFT Channel is filming an interview of Kai, Trenton, and me today in one of the Athena's ballrooms. They've turned it into a temporary film studio with spotlights, cameras, a stage, and an audience of a hundred people or more. It's definitely a more intimidating environment than the more intimate setup for the cooking competition.

I'm excited but sad at the same time.

Last night, I couldn't sleep. I vacillated between crying because my time with Evan is over and wanting a chance to tell him off for lying to me. As a result, I look horrible today. My eyes are puffy, and I'm exhausted. This isn't how I want to look for the most important interview of my life on FFT's Chef News.

Lowri tried to cheer me up and insisted that the show must go on. The makeup artist also did the best she could to hide the remnants of my sleepless night. But there's a limit given what she had to work with.

We three winners—I'm still getting used to that part—drew chips once more to determine the order of our interviews. I'm thankful that mine is last. It gives me a little more time to pull myself together. I need to forget Evan for an hour or two and concentrate on the next chapter of my life, which begins with this interview and the amazing opportunity to serve as the guest chef at the Grand Athena for a whole month.

When it's my turn, Amy's assistant escorts me onto the stage, where I sit in a dark-blue swivel chair near the interviewer. After the competition interviews where we had to cook and talk at the same time, I should be ready for this one. All I have to do is sit in a chair and answer a few questions. The hard part is smiling and pretending my heart isn't broken.

The host for Chef News begins by introducing me to the live audience.

"This is Cassie Edwards. She is another one of the winners of the Guest Chef Competition at the Grand Athena. Welcome, Cassie."

"Thank you. I'm thrilled to be here."

"What can we expect when you are the guest chef?" she asks as she swivels toward me.

Hands clasped in my lap to prevent fidgeting, I explain, "Well, I believe great food and wine bring people together and help them create wonderful memories. Whether for a romantic dinner or a celebration with friends or family, we'll offer an experience that makes the evening extremely special for everyone who joins us at Pinot & Pie."

I turn my head toward the audience, acknowledging their gracious applause.

"That sounds wonderful. We understand you were the only finalist who didn't have a professional culinary background. Were you surprised to be selected as one of the competitors?"

"Absolutely, but I decided to seize the opportunity. I didn't want to look back with any regrets."

The host pauses, and I detect a hint of tension. Did I say something wrong? Then her smile returns, and she continues, "It turns out that we have another surprise for you today. Everyone, Prince Evan of Catalinius is joining us. He wants to say a few words."

Oh no. Not now. I can't handle this. My heart is racing, my vision is blurry, and my hearing is muffled. Grabbing the arms of the swivel chair, I attempt to control my emotions and stay firmly planted.

I vaguely hear the host saying, "Please welcome His Royal Highness, Prince of Catalinius. Have a seat next to Cassie. I understand that you have a surprise for her. Is that correct?"

Evan—or should I say Prince Evan—sits in a nearby chair that suddenly appeared. He swivels toward me, staring intently. My gaze drops to my lap as I continue digging my fingernails into the upholstery on the arms of the chair. I hope the mic isn't picking up my ragged breathing.

Without taking his eyes off me, Evan responds, "Yes. That's correct. I suspect that Cassandra is not particularly happy with me right now, but I would like to share a story with everyone if I may."

"Please do," the host responds as my mind swirls through the possibilities of what he's going to say.

Speaking softly, Evan explains, "Cassandra and I met during the Athena's Guest Chef Competition. We hit it off and started seeing each other, but I made a big mistake. I never told her that I'm a prince. She knew me as Evan. I must admit that it was freeing to be just Evan. I knew she liked me for me, not because I was a prince."

The audience murmurs and sighs.

I did like that version of Evan, but he was hiding who he really was.

He continues, "Initially, I didn't think my identity would ever matter, but my feelings for Cassandra grew to be more than I ever expected. I invited her to visit my home in Catalinius. I just didn't mention that my home is a palace."

The audience laughs.

He should've known that was an important detail.

"I'd planned to tell Cassandra about my family last night, but someone let my secret slip before I had the chance. As you would expect, she was hurt and upset that I'd kept my full identity from her."

Loosening my grip on the chair, I let my hands fall to my lap and look up at Evan, wondering if he really planned to tell me last night.

Gazing deep into my eyes, he reaches out to touch my arm.

"So, Cassandra, I'm here today to tell you, in front of everyone, that I have fallen in love with you. I, Prince Garret Evan Louis

Francesco, Prince of Catalinius, want you to come to Catalinius with me to meet my family. While my being a prince complicates the protocol, I'm still the same man you came to know, and I care very deeply for you."

I'm in shock. I can't believe Evan would pour out his heart in front of the world.

I fell madly, irrevocably in love with the person I spent time with, not the title. Any doubts I have fly away when I look into his eyes, seeing the look of pure happiness and hope in his as he gazes at me. The possibility of exploring my new career and being with the man of my dreams is real. I just have to take the chance, but I need to ask a question or two first.

"Evan, I mean, Prince Evan, or is it Your Royal Highness? I don't even know what to call you."

"It doesn't matter. Please say that you'll go home with me."

"Who you are changes everything. I'm a commoner. I can't imagine your family will approve."

"Oh, but, Cassandra, you're wrong. My family is looking forward to meeting you. I promise, and you know I keep my promises."

I nod. He's proven that.

Evan opens a beautiful, blue velvet box. Everyone gasps.

He turns it toward me, and I'm staring at a diamond-encrusted key dangling from a gold necklace."

"I'm presenting you with the Prince's Key. It was flown over on the royal jet last night for me to give to you. It represents a special invitation requesting your attendance at the upcoming events in Catalinius."

A collective "Ah!" rises from the audience.

"You will be my honored guest. Please say yes. Be my plus one."

Giggles erupt from the audience at the prince's use of the casual term.

I'm overwhelmed by the invitation and the willingness of Evan to go to such lengths to publicly make up for his lie of omission.

"I'd love to be your plus one."

Evan smiles and quickly places the beautiful key around my neck. Then he kisses my forehead.

The host asks, "Does this mean that you won't be returning as a guest chef at the Athena?"

"Of course I'll be returning."

Evan adds, "Why wouldn't she be? She worked hard and earned that opportunity. If she doesn't mind, I may find a way to come back with her."

It's reassuring to hear him publicly respect my work. And did he just say he wants to return with me?

The host concludes the interview and thanks us for joining her. Evan pulls me from the chair into his arms. He leans down and looks into my eyes as he says, "All along, I've been calling you my princess because you're so special to me. I was just afraid I would lose you if I told you about my family. I wasn't ready to take that chance. Please forgive me."

"You have to promise me that there won't be any more secrets."

"I promise. I love you, princess."

"Evan, I assumed the term princess was your standard term of endearment for the women you date. But I love you too."

Evan gently kisses me and whispers, "No, only you. I've never used that term for anyone else."

EPILOGUE
CASSIE

I'm sitting on the royal jet with Evan, and we're flying to meet the King and Queen of Catalinius—his parents. The changes to my life over the last few weeks are beyond dramatic.

Boarding the plane, they treated us like royalty. I had to laugh at the thought—it's not like I could forget that Evan is actual royalty. Clearly, there's going to be an adjustment period for me.

The jet is like private planes in movies with polished burled wood that shines like a mirror and plush, cream-colored leather chairs. The flight attendant handed us our favorite drinks the second we boarded and presented us with menu options for our long journey to Catalinius.

The pilot announces we need to take our seats in preparation for takeoff. Unlike commercial flights, we've barely clicked our seatbelts closed when we surge down the runway.

The corners of my lips tilt upward as I recall my time with Evan since the Final Dinner.

It's been a week, and I'm still wondering when I'll wake up from this dream. I can't believe this is my new life. After the FFT interview, Evan arranged for me to speak with his mother, the queen, to calm my nerves over meeting his family. She was kind, reassuring me that I'm welcome and that they look forward to meeting me in person.

At Evan's insistence, we spent the last week in Las Vegas selecting clothes and accessories for me to wear to the events we'll be attending. While I insisted on buying most things myself, it's interesting how the financial security from the prize money made me more comfortable accepting a few gifts from Evan. I think it's because I now have the means to reciprocate, such as with the gold cufflinks I bought him. In between shopping trips, we had outrageously great make-up sex, christening almost every surface in the Athena's Monarch Suite.

After reflecting this past week, I also accepted that my parents would be proud of me even though my career path is deviating from their plan. They wanted me to have a happy, successful career, and they thought following in their footsteps would guarantee that outcome. They were wrong. I don't have the passion for corporate law they had. It's not what makes me happy, and they loved me too much to want me to be stuck in a job that was unfulfilling. Finally at peace, I can pursue my true passion and see where it leads me without the guilt that has followed me for so long.

Evan gestures to the window, and I watch us soar into the air, catching a final glimpse of the glitz and glamour of the Las Vegas Strip. We're on our way to his home for what he keeps referring to as his father's retirement party, but I'm still curious about how a king retires. Evan said it's a long story that's part of an old Catalinius tradition. Now that he's captive for hours, I want all the details, so I fire off my question.

"It's time you tell me why your father is having a retirement party. Kings don't retire."

Evan laughs. "It is a long story, but we have time now. In years past, the reigning monarchs tended to live unexpectedly long lives, with some reigning until they were eighty-five or older. This meant that when the king or queen passed away, the crown prince or princess was typically sixty-five years old or older. The crown princes and princesses were frustrated that they were expected to assume the throne at that age. However, the only alternative would be to abdicate and let their oldest child reign."

"Why not do that if they didn't want to rule later in life?" I ask.

"In my country, abdicating is considered shameful if you are physically and mentally able to take the throne."

"That leaves them stuck then."

"It did until King Lorenzo. He assumed the throne as a teenager due to an accident that led to his father's untimely death. After reigning for more than forty years, he wanted the freedom he had been deprived of when his time as a prince was cut short. King Lorenzo had the clever idea to allow monarchs to retire, but only under specific circumstances. He wanted to ensure that the crown prince or princess was at a stable and settled point in his or her life before the reigning monarch was allowed to retire. Therefore, in Catalinius, the reigning monarch may retire at age sixty-five, but only if the crown prince or princess is married. If that condition is not met on the reigning monarch's sixty-fifth birthday, then the reigning king or queen must remain on the throne until death."

Fingering the Prince's Key around my neck, I ask, "I gather your father is turning sixty-five and wants to retire, right?"

"Exactly. My father's birthday is approaching quickly, and he wants to retire, but my brother, Alexander, the crown prince, isn't married yet. That's a problem."

"Why doesn't your father change the rules to give your brother more time to marry?"

"Unfortunately, that's not a reasonable option. In instituting the rules for retirement, King Lorenzo, clever as he was, made it almost impossible to change the conditions under which monarchs could retire. My father can only change the rules if he then immediately abdicates, which would put a substantial blemish on his reputation and admirable reign. He would never do that."

"It's perplexing that after what you describe as an admirable reign, stepping down would tarnish his accomplishments. In the US, people step down from high-ranking positions all the time to retire."

"It's our duty. Everyone born into the royal family is expected to put Catalinius's interests above any personal interests. We're taught that from birth. My older brother is in a difficult position though. He never thought this rule would come into play because my father loves being king and always said that he wanted to rule for life. He recently changed his mind after a health scare and declared he wants to step down from the throne on his sixty-fifth birthday.

Reaching out to touch Evan's arm in concern, I ask softly, "Is your father okay?"

"Fortunately, he fully recovered, but it made him rethink his plans for the future. He and my mother decided it's time to pass the throne to Xander. They want to travel and spend time together without the weight of the country on their shoulders."

"How will that happen if your brother isn't married?"

"Xander *is* getting married. We're going to attend his wedding while we're in Catalinius. Then we'll attend the king's retirement festivities, which is also his birthday party. See, it's a long, complicated story."

"You're right. It's definitely complicated. The concept of retirement for monarchs makes sense. It's unreasonable to expect someone to work until they die unless it's what they want. But the strictness of the marriage rule is ridiculous. Your brother shouldn't have to marry just so your dad can retire."

"No kidding. My brother was in shock when Dad made his announcement."

"I can only imagine. Who's your brother marrying? Do you like her?"

Evan shrugs. "I have no idea."

"What do you mean you have no idea? Do you mean you don't know if you like her yet?"

"What I mean is I have no idea who my brother is marrying. He hasn't decided yet."

Mouth agape, I ask, "When is the wedding?"

Evan responds matter-of-factly, "This month. He'll find a bride in time. He has to."

"That's absolutely ludicrous."

Evan reaches for my hand and intertwines our fingers. He laughs.

"I agree, but it should be fun to sit back and watch the fireworks. It'll also make your first foray into royal life easier. Everyone will be concentrating on my brother rather than us."

Not knowing what else to say about this bizarre scenario, I mumble, "That sounds helpful."

I'm grateful the problem is Xander's, not ours.

Wriggling his eyebrows, Evan says, "Enough about my family for now. You know there's a bedroom in the back of the jet. Would you like to take a nap?"

"I don't need a nap. I'm not tired yet."

With a mischievous sparkle in his eyes, he says, "Neither am I, but we can change that."

"Oh. I like getting tired. Lead the way."

Hands intertwined, we walk to the back room, where a sign on the door says, "The Royal Monarch Butterfly Suite." That's weird. His suite at the Grand Athena was the Monarch Suite. As I start to ask about the name, Evan pulls me into the bedroom, kissing me senseless and making me quickly decide that my question can wait until we're in Catalinius.

THANK YOU FOR READING *RIVAL SECRETS*! JOIN MY NEWSLETTER AND RECEIVE a copy of the **Free Bonus Epilogue** at

https://dl.bookfunnel.com/ihlov2noqv

CHECK OUT NEXT BOOK IN THIS SERIES, *ROYALLY DECEIVED*.

Time is running out for Evan's brother, Xander to find a bride. And he soon learns there's even more at stake. Check out *Royally Deceived* and get ready for romance and adventure. *Royally Deceived* is available at

https://geni.us/RoyallyDeceivedAMZAUD

STAY IN TOUCH

I love to hear from my readers. The easiest way to keep in touch is by following me. That way you won't miss out on the latest info on new releases, bonus material, and other updates.

Facebook: facebook.com/JDCarothersAuth
Instagram: instagram.com/jdcarothersauth/
Amazon Author Page: bit.ly/amazon_author_jdcarothers
Goodreads: bit.ly/goodreads_jdcarothers
Bookbub: bookbub.com/authors/j-d-carothers
Website: jdcarothers.com
Newsletter: jdcarothers.com/#subscribe

Also, if you enjoyed Evan & Cassie's story, please consider posting a review on your retailer's site, on Goodreads, and/or other sites where lovers of books look for their next read. Posting reviews helps other readers find new authors and titles, which is appreciated.

ALSO BY J. D. CAROTHERS

Want more contemporary billionaire romance with a guaranteed HEA?

Don't miss the other books by J.D. Carothers

Love Over Murder Series

Rival Secrets (Book 1, Standalone)

Royally Deceived (Book 2, Standalone)

Reckless Chance (Book 3, Standalone)

Royal Spies Series

Risky Match (Book 1, Standalone)

Flawless Match (Book 2, Standalone) coming soon

The Holiday Series

Christmas Assignment in Paradise (Book 1, Standalone)

ACKNOWLEDGMENTS

I am extremely grateful to everyone who has supported my efforts to bring the characters and events of *Rival Secrets* to life. Thank you to my husband for his willingness to listen to plot ideas over dinner and proofread early drafts. Thank you to Suzi for everything; you are truly amazing. And thank you to my friends and family whose encouragement motivates me to continue writing.

To my ever-growing editing team: you make me a better writer with each draft, and I thank you all for every red line and comment.

The audiobooks for this series would not be possible without East House Productions, including the talented cast, engineers, and team assembled by Shane East. They did an exceptional job. I know you'll enjoy the audiobooks.

And thank you to everyone who helped with the launch of *Rival Secrets*.

J.D.

ABOUT THE AUTHOR

When not immersed in her law career, J. D. Carothers loves to cook for her family and friends, read or listen to romance novels and murder mysteries, eat chocolate, and sip wine while watching the sunsets in the Southwest.

Late at night or early on weekend mornings, she finds a quiet place to write her next contemporary billionaire romance and trade the stress of real life for a fantasy world where twists and turns lead to happily ever afters.